THE LIES
THAT BIND

THE LIES THAT BIND

A NEIL HAMEL MYSTERY

JUDITH VAN GIESON

HarperCollins*Publishers*

HarperCollins books may be purchased for educational, business, or sales promotional use. For information, please write: Special Markets Department, HarperCollins Publishers, Inc., 10 East 53rd Street, New York, NY 10022.

FIRST EDITION

Designed by Alma Hochhauser Orenstein

Library of Congress Cataloging-in-Publication Data

Van Gieson, Judith.
    The lies that bind/Judith Van Gieson.—1st ed.
       p.   cm.
    ISBN 0-06-017705-5 (cloth)
    1. Hamel, Neil (Fictitious character)—Fiction. 2. Women lawyers—New Mexico—Albuquerque—Fiction. 3. Albuquerque (N.M.)—Fiction. I. Title.
PS3572.A42224L5 1993
813'.54—dc20   *A BK 8982*   92-53360

---

93 94 95 96 97 ❖/RRD 10 9 8 7 6 5 4 3 2 1

For Claire Zieger, my mother

Never believe anything because
probability is in its favor.

—SHAKYAMUNI BUDDHA

There is one thing that is terrible,
and that is that everyone has his reasons.

—JEAN RENOIR,
The Rules of the Game

ACKNOWLEDGMENTS

I'm grateful to Barbara Peters, Kevin Robinson, Dale Carter, Ph.D., and Dominick Abel for their help and advice. A special thanks to attorney Alan M. Uris for so generously sharing his knowledge of the law.

1

TOOK THE HIGH ROAD FROM TAOS, speeding on the straight-aways, hugging the curves, dropping down from Talpa to Nambe. The low road follows the Rio Grande. El Camino Alto, the high road, is the forest path; I was in the mood for trees and green. The cumulonimbus billowed in the big western sky; the sun reached deep into Carson National Forest and made every pine needle shimmer. A raven landed on the yellow line, flapped its wings and flew away. The tank was full of gas; the radials gripped the road. For the moment, me, my Japanese import and the highway were one. For the moment, I could almost believe that nature's laws didn't apply to me, that I'd never grow old, never get fat, never have to stop to buy gas or pee, never wake up in the night and turn on *Love Connection*, never drink Cuervo Gold, smoke Marlboros or mix up a batch of Jell-O shots ever again. I'd been in northern Rio Arriba County, the lawless county, to fight a custody battle, and I'd won. The tape that spins messages in the back of my brain spun. "You've got the power," it said.

It was the harvest season, the time of year when red chile ristras drip from the eaves, when you get rid of the old to make way for the new. I cruised through the high mountain villages of Peñasco, Las Trampas and Truchas, where time stopped a couple of hundred years ago and they still speak Cervantes Spanish, where the air is a cool clear stream, where stone houses mark one edge of the road and mountain drop-offs the other. Take a curve wide here, and you'll end up in a living room or the cumulonimbus.

I kept my hands on the wheel, my mind on the road, turned south on 84 at Nambe. In Pojoaque I passed the Indian restaurant that serves the best chalupa compuesta in Santa Fe County, but I didn't pull in; carne adovada burritos were waiting at home. Below the Santa Fe Opera, the road began to rise again. Purple asters and yellow chamisa bloomed in the ditches beside the road. In the far distance the tip of Santa Fe Baldy was covered with snow; its lower elevations were streaked with aspen gold. At seventy-five hundred feet, La Villa Real de Santa Fe de San Francisco de Assisi opened up before me like a jewel box spilling precious stones. It was late afternoon, and the lights were twinkling on, one by one. I dropped down alongside the white crosses of the National Cemetery, cut across town on St. Francis, turned south on I-25, which follows the path of El Camino Real, the royal road, which once linked old Mexico to new.

Between Santa Fe and Albuquerque I lost two thousand feet. Out here in the land that trees forgot, it's down to basics: sky, rocks, dirt, distance. There are few wildflowers on this stretch of lonesome highway and only two distinct seasons—lots of wind and none. Fall is no wind, when the dirt stays put and tumbleweeds settle down and get an address. It was twilight, the hour, some say, between the dog and the wolf. The sun lit a fire over the Jemez. The southern sky got dark enough that Sirius came out and Venus too. In fifty miles I'd be home. The Kid would be at my apartment, waiting in the living room or my bed.

I pulled a tape from the glove compartment and plugged

it in. Van Morrison singing about "The Days Before Rock N' Roll," the days before America woke up from its sexual, sensual slumber. He named the early rockers: Fats, Ray Charles, Jerry Lee Lewis, Little Richard, Elvis, the guys whose songs come out of the radio at night from places like Harlingen, Texas, and Tulsa, Oklahoma, to stab you with memories. There were women in the early days of rock 'n' roll too, but not often on the radio and not on this tape. Van Morrison's heroes were all men. I remembered a singer I saw a couple of years before in L.A., a big black woman rocking her way into middle age without missing a beat, but I couldn't remember her name. Two short words, and the first one began with an *E*. That was it.

The tape played out in Bernalillo. Night fell, and Venus and Sirius got lost in Albuquerque's ambient fluorescent glow. I turned off the interstate at Montgomery, got caught at a red light. It happened to be Halloween, El Día de los Muertos, when children dress up and pretend to be what they're not. A bunch of tricksters and clowns crossed the street, carrying their loot and their cap guns in their hands on their way to a party in the Lujan School playground. Some kids playing tag beneath the playground lights cast long shadows. A blindfolded pirate was *it* and was trying to tag someone else by the sound of a voice. "Marco," the kid yelled. "Polo," the other kids answered. It's a game that is usually played in swimming pools in the summer. Marco Polo is the background noise of summer, if you live in a complex with kids and a swimming pool. The pirate lunged at a bunch of grapes, the grapes sidestepped, the pirate fell on his face.

The light turned green, and I stepped on the gas. Three more stoplights, and I was home. The Kid, my lover and friend, had let himself in and was sitting on my bed, drinking Tecate and watching football on TV. Realizing recently that in a woman's life TV functions like romance novels, to induce sleep, I'd moved mine to the foot of the bed.

"Hi, Kid," I said, sitting down on the bed beside him.

"Hola, Chiquita." He gave me a kiss.

"You're watching football?"

"Yeah."

"Why?"

"It's Monday night." He shrugged. "Why not?"

The function of TV in a man's life is football. I'd always thought that one advantage to having a Latin American lover is that Latin Americans are not as obsessed with brute sports as American men. The Kid's game—soccer—is more delicate and subtle. The players aren't padded like gorillas, either, which makes it more fun to watch. The Kid has long, powerful soccer legs that are outstanding in shorts and were not bad stretched out in jeans on my bed. He'd been playing since he was a boy in Argentina and knew how to keep the ball in the air all afternoon if he wanted to. I watched him sometimes on the playing fields at Arroyo del Oso, bouncing the ball off his thighs and his head.

I made myself comfortable, picked up the remote and zapped off the TV.

"I was watching the game, Chiquita," the Kid said.

"I hate football," said I.

"I want to see if the Cowboys win."

"It's a replay. The score is in the paper."

"That's not the same as watching."

"*I* won," I said. So it wasn't the Supreme Court, but Ramona Chávez would get to keep her daughter and I had won. In Rio Arriba County too, where the law doesn't win that often.

"Good. I'm happy for you. Can I watch the game now?"

"No." I held tight to the remote.

The look he gave me was semi-annoyed, but he was getting my drift. Power, it has been said, is the greatest aphrodisiac, and absolute power turns on absolutely. So does only a little bit. "You want to do *that*?" the Kid asked me.

"Yup."

"Now?"

"Right now." I reached across the bed and took the phone off the hook.

"Okay," he said.

Later we got up and ate the carne adovada burritos he'd brought. As usual these days, there were two extras in the bag. "For La Bailarina?" I asked, mentioning his favorite lost cause.

"Claro," said the Kid.

While he took them outside to the parking lot, I got ready for bed.

"I think it's going to rain soon," he said when he came back in.

"Rain? In October?"

He shrugged. "I think so."

As soon as we got into bed, the thunder cracked and drops began to pelt the window. Rainy nights are one of life's great pleasures, especially when you're in your bed. We don't get many of them in the Duke City and hardly ever in October. I thought about the raindrops pounding the tin roof of the car that sheltered La Bailarina in the parking lot, but I didn't feel guilty because I knew that even if the Kid had tried to coax her inside, she wouldn't have come. The parking lot was where she chose to be—on the outside but near enough to be looking in. She'd stay dry, I thought, but the trick-or-treaters would get soaking wet. It would drive them indoors—the tamer ones anyway. The troublemakers would still be out there. The Kid's breathing got slow and regular as he drifted into sleep. I punched his shoulder before he wandered too far down that lonesome highway.

"You awake, Kid?"

"Umm," he mumbled.

"I want to ask you something."

"Dígame."

"Do you think I'd be any happier if I had a big car? If I went to work for a prestigious firm and made real money?"

"I think you're happy just the way you are."

Lightning flashed, exposing one dark peak of the Sandias, then another. A large woman rocked her way across a stage in L.A.

"Etta," I said.

"Who?"

"Etta James." It was the name that had gotten lost in the back alleys of my brain, the name of the early woman rock-and-roller.

"Who's that?"

One disadvantage of having a Latino lover, and one who is younger besides, is that you don't know the same music. You can't push a button and call up the past by naming a singer or a song.

"Nada," I said. "Forget it."

When the alarm went off at seven-thirty, my first thought was that Eddie Chávez had tested the law and I had won. My second thought was that I had the power all over again. "You awake, Kid?" I whispered. He wasn't, but I kissed his shoulder and woke him. After *that* we slept again until the sun burst through the drapes and landed on my face. The red numbers on the digital clock flashed 8:45. "Shit," I said, sitting upright. "I'll be late for my nine o'clock."

The Kid jumped out of bed, climbed into his jeans and T-shirt and shook his curls into place. I put the telephone back on the hook, staggered into and out of the shower, dressed in some boring lawyer's clothes and combed my hair. No time for breakfast sopapillas or Red Zinger tea.

He waited in the living room for me. I kissed him good-bye, opened the door, stepped into La Vista's hallway and found myself staring down at ninety pounds of disapproving mother.

The sun had crept in through an open archway and was picking out the stains on the indoor/outdoor carpet and highlighting the cracks in the peeling stucco. The woman stood in front of my door with a finger poised in preparation for pressing the bell. About five feet two, she balanced carefully on her high-heeled shoes. Her purse was suspended from a gold chain, and she clutched it to her side with a pointed elbow. Her sprayed-in-place hairdo was the color of a hard frost. She wore a powder-blue suit with gold buttons and navy-blue trim. Her eyes, a critical blue, implied that good grooming and designer clothes gave her the right to decide who was right and who wrong. I hadn't even left my apartment yet, but I was already among the wrong. While she'd been drinking her morning tea, the Kid and I had been getting laid. Our just-had-sex aura gave us away. She knew we'd been doing it. We knew that she knew, and she knew that we knew. She looked at us; we looked back. Disapproval was thick as the dust in La Vista's hallway.

"Are you Neil Hamel?" she asked.

"Yup."

"The . . . attorney?" An attorney, her tone implied, didn't have sex in the morning, or at any time of day or night with someone who is younger, darker and better-looking. Unless, of course, the attorney was a man.

"My office is on Lead," I replied. I was prepared to add, But don't bother coming because wills are not my cup of tea and neither are you, only she spoke first.

She took a deep breath, aligned her vertebrae, clutched her purse, cleared her throat. "I've been accused of killing Justine Virga," she said.

2

∧∧∧∧∧∧

SHE'D GOTTEN MY ATTENTION. The phone started ringing inside my apartment, telling me I was late for my appointment. I already knew that, so I let it ring. I don't do wills, but I do do murder cases when I can get them, and she looked like the rare suspect who could afford to pay. "Tell me about it," I said.

She looked around La Vista's hallway, at the cracks in the stucco and the closed doors that might be concealing eavesdroppers. Her eyes lingered suspiciously on the Kid as if he was a street dog who'd been trying to get into her trash. While she scrutinized him from top to bottom—his uncombed mop of hair, his T-shirt and jeans—she tightened her grip on her purse. My lover and my hallway did not please her, but if she thought I was going to invite her into my apartment and let her disapprove of that too, she was wrong.

The Kid got her message. "I go now, Chiquita," he said, his grammar clunkier and his accent thicker than it had been in recent memory.

"Bueno." I kissed him again. "See you tonight?"

"Sure. Hasta luego," he said to me. To the woman he

added with exaggerated Mexican politeness, "Buenos días. Mucho gusto." There's a fine line between politeness and insult, and Mexicans know how to walk it. Actually, the Kid's Spanish wasn't Mexican, or New Mexican either. It was South American, but the subtleties were wasted on the woman, and so was the gusto. She didn't bother to answer the Kid, and he didn't waste his time waiting. He tossed his head and walked down the hallway. I watched his long legs turn the corner and listened to the phone ringing. It had become obvious I wasn't going to answer it or ask my visitor in, but just in case she had any doubts, I inserted my key into the dead bolt and snapped it shut. The woman hesitated, and then she said, "Could you give me a ride home? We can talk there."

"Where's your car?" I asked.

"The police took it."

It had the sound of vehicular homicide, a common enough form of murder in New Mexico, where a car is a loaded weapon too.

"How did you get here?" I asked.

"Taxi."

"Why didn't you ask the driver to wait?"

"Because I wanted to talk to you."

"All right," I said, "I'll take you home, but first I need to know who you are and why you came to me."

"I am Martha Conover."

It had a familiar ring, but I couldn't place her.

"You know my daughter," she continued. "Cynthia Reid."

That was it. Cindy and I went to high school together in Ithaca, New York. Martha Conover had been widowed and was the rare single mother back then, I remembered. It gave her full responsibility for Cindy, and she took it seriously. She had Cindy late in life and was older than the other mothers—older than mine anyway—and conspicuous by her

presence in her daughter's life. She was into real estate
investment and seemed to have a need in those days that
only real estate could fill. When Cindy got knocked up by
Emilio Velásquez, a Spanish exchange student, Martha
wouldn't let her marry him. Cindy had the baby. Emilio
joined the army and went to Vietnam. A few years later
Cindy married Whitney J. Reid III, a man Martha approved
of, who was about ten years older and whose political views,
even back then, were to the right of Attila the Hun. Whit
took on Cindy's child, and people thought she was lucky to
get him. I wondered if she still thought that, if she'd *ever*
thought that. Last I'd heard, they were living in Phoenix.
She'd written me once to tell me her mother had moved to
Albuquerque and to suggest I look her up, but I didn't.
Martha hadn't approved of me when I was in high school—I
was Cindy's hippie friend—which made me wonder what
she was doing at my doorstep now. Did she think a license
to practice law had made me respectable?

I led the way across the parking lot to my yellow Nissan,
which was loaded with bumper stickers from the previous
owner, stickers I'd been meaning to scrape off but hadn't
yet. McDonald's recycled brown bags decomposed slowly in
the compost heap the floor on the passenger side had
become. The files from the Chávez case were sitting on the
seat. I put the files in the trunk, picked the litter off the
floor, took it to the Dumpster and dumped it in. I got in my
side, Martha Conover got in the other. She straightened her
back, placed her purse square in her lap and fastened her
seat belt with a metallic click.

This wasn't exactly my living room, but it was as close
as she was going to get. Here I was ready to talk, and before
we went any further there were some things I wanted to
know, like when, where, how and who. "When did this supposed homicide take place?" I asked.

"Last night around ten-fifteen, the police say." Martha

peered around her as if the other cars had ears. I continued
my line of questioning.

"Where?"

"In the road at Los Cerros, the apartment complex I own
and live in."

She was doing all right with her investments; Los Cerros
was one of the largest apartment complexes in town. "How?"

"The police say I ran her over."

"What do you say?"

"I hit a speed bump. I was going too fast, and I hit a speed
bump." Her blue eyes flashed at me. She spun a diamond
and sapphire ring around on her finger.

"Did you see anyone when you were driving up the road
or entering your apartment?"

"I don't have an apartment. I have a town house."

"Did you see anyone?"

"No."

"Did the APD indicate that they had witnesses?"

"They knocked on some doors, looking for the owner of
my car, but my neighbors were asleep and hadn't seen or
heard anything, except for the one who found the body in
the road and called the police."

"They had to have some reason to impound your car."

"There were dents in the bumper and the hood."

Was there any blood on the car, I wondered, hair or fibers
that hadn't washed off in the rain? The DA's office would
have that information sooner or later, but they were
unlikely to give it to me, not unless Martha got indicted.
There was one other question that always needs to be asked
when motor vehicles are involved. "Were you drinking?"

"I had two martinis at the Albuquerque Women's Club
meeting," she replied, folding her hands in her lap.

"Did the police take a Breathalyzer?" I asked.

"I wouldn't let them." Her eyes were defiant and proud
of it.

"They did tell you that refusing to take a Breathalyzer means an automatic suspension of your license for a year, didn't they?"

"Yes."

"You're lucky they didn't put you in jail," I said. She shrugged as if to imply she wasn't the kind of woman who got sent to jail. "Did the police read you your rights?"

"Yes."

"You should have called me last night before you said anything to them."

"I wanted to discuss it with Whit and Cynthia before I called anybody."

I had a few more questions. "Who was Justine Virga?"

"She was once my grandson Michael's girlfriend," Martha Conover said.

"You knew her?" When the accused knows the victim (and they do 86 percent of the time), it puts a different spin on things.

"Years ago."

"Virga is an unusual name. How do you spell it?" Verga, I knew, means the male organ in Spanish. Virga means precipitation that evaporates before it reaches the ground.

"V-i-r-g-a. It's not Spanish, is it?"

"No."

"I think she gave herself an English name when she came here from Argentina. Can we go now?"

I turned the key in the ignition and backed the Nissan out of its space. "Los Cerros is on—" Martha began.

"I know where Los Cerros is." In the Heights. Those who have money in Albuquerque escape to the Rio Grande Valley or the higher elevations, while the rest of us get stuck in the middle.

Martha kept her silence, and I thought about what I had to work with: a woman who'd been drinking and refused to take a Breathalyzer, a dent in a car, a dead girlfriend. It made me wish I'd kept my nine o'clock.

I found my way to Los Cerros, turned in and let Martha Conover direct me through a maze of two-story Mediterranean-style stucco buildings with tile roofs and grounds that were carefully landscaped and automatically watered. The speed bumps kept me to a boring five mph. A couple of Hispanic guys were trimming the shrubs. The lower part of the complex had ramps leading into the buildings, indicating the handicapped lived there, which could well have been a condition for getting a building permit. The middle section allowed children, and a couple of them raced their toy cars down the sidewalk, screaming. We drove past a swimming pool, a putting green and an empty tennis court. The road climbed sharply, the apartment buildings turned into town houses and the children disappeared. This was where the more desirable tenants—singles, childless couples and old ladies—lived. A couple of them were hanging around a bank of mailboxes (which also had a tile roof), because they needed their social security checks or because they liked the mailman. The older you get, the bigger role the mailman plays in your life.

"Go faster here," Martha ordered. "I want to show you what happened." I don't usually obey orders, but I was curious to see how she'd present her case and no one else was in the road, so I put the pedal to the floor. The speed bump, painted yellow, was about six inches high and hard as a wall. I'd reached only fifteen by the time we hit it, but that was fast enough. Every bone in my body rattled. The frame on the Nissan shook. A piece of muffler fell off.

"See," said Martha Conover.

"See what?" I replied.

"A body wouldn't feel hard like that," she said. "What I hit was that speed bump."

She may have convinced herself, but she hadn't convinced me. "Over five miles an hour, anything you hit feels hard," I replied.

"I was driving a Buick," she said.

"Um," said I. "Is it possible, given the darkness and the rain, that you didn't see her?"

"No. My high beams were on, and there is nothing wrong with my long-distance vision either. I only need glasses for reading."

She directed me to her place, at the very top of Los Cerros. It had a hundred-mile view, the kind of view that makes you want to think the big thoughts or earn the big bucks it takes to pay for it. We walked down the sidewalk that led from Martha's parking space to her town house. The grounds were impeccable, the walls of the town houses freshly stuccoed, and there were no cobwebs in the corners. Martha, I figured, didn't do that kind of work herself, but whoever did took pride in it. She turned the key in her lock and let me in. Her town house smelled of Lemon Pledge and was the kind of neat that made me long for La Vista. The carpet was pink pile and didn't have a hair on it. The polished furniture had spindly little legs. The sofa was upholstered in flowered chintz. Ivy in a brass pot sat on the coffee table. The drapes were drawn to keep out the long and dusty view. It was the kind of living room they do well back East where the view is limited to a lawn and the trees at the end of it, ladylike and formal, expensive but comfortable. Martha seemed to be one of those people who take the East with them wherever they go. She offered me a cup of tea.

"Do you have any Red Zinger?" I asked.

"What's that?"

"Never mind," I said. "Can I use your phone?"

"Yes."

While she made her tea, I called the office to tell my secretary, Anna, what she already knew, that I'd missed my nine o'clock.

Martha brought the teapot into the living room, sat on the sofa and poured the tea into a china cup translucent enough to see her fingers through. She took one spoon of sugar, one slice of lemon.

I took out my yellow legal pad and put it in my lap. "All right," I said. "Tell me exactly what happened."

"When I left the AWC meeting on Siringo at ten, it was pouring rain. It was ten-fifteen when I got home. After I hit the speed bump, I parked, came inside and went to bed. I fell asleep and woke up when the police rang the doorbell."

"What time was that?"

"I don't know. I'd been asleep, but I don't know for how long. It seemed like a bad dream. Men in uniform were standing at my door, telling me that girl was dead and it was my fault. They made me go outside in the rain and look at the body. I hadn't seen Justine for years, but I recognized her."

"Did you identify her for the police?"

"No. They already knew who she was; they found her identification inside her car."

"Why did they ask you to look at the body?"

"I think they were trying to frighten me into making a confession." Martha took a sip of her tea. "They also showed me my car, with the dents in the bumper and the hood."

"Can you describe Justine for me?"

"Yes. Her body was crushed, and she was lying flat on her back. Her eyes . . . her eyes were open."

"Was there much blood?"

"No; the rain had washed it away." She put her cup down. "After they finished examining the body and the scene, the police asked me if they could come inside and look around."

"You let them?"

"Yes." Another mistake that could have been avoided if she'd called me sooner. An attorney would have made the police get a search warrant. "I had nothing to hide," Martha said.

"What did they look at?"

"My typewriter. The police found a note in Justine's pocket inside a sealed envelope. They put it in a plastic bag, showed it to me and accused me of typing it on my typewriter. It was obvious that the type didn't match, but they took a sample from my Selectric anyway."

"What did the note say?"

"'I knew this was going to happen, but I couldn't prevent it.'"

That was the kind of message that sent the desert lizard racing down my spine. "Do you have any idea who would have given Justine a note like that?"

Her eyes met mine without a flicker. "No. After the police left, I called Whit and Cindy and they came over."

"They came over here?" Phoenix was almost five hundred miles away, the last time I'd checked.

"They're living here now, in a house I own at Los Verdes Meadows, the golf course development on—"

"I know where it is. When did they move to Albuquerque?"

"About a month ago. Whit is in real estate, and business has not been good in Arizona. They'd been out to dinner, and they were in bed when I called. They got up anyway and came over. It was suggested that I call you, but it was the middle of the night by then. In the morning no one answered at your office and your line was busy at home, so I looked up your address, got a cab and went to your apartment."

"Why didn't Cindy come with you?"

"I didn't ask her to."

"How is she?" I asked.

"All right. It's been difficult since Michael died, but—"

"Michael died?"

"Three years ago. He was her only son, my only grandson."

"Oh, God. How did that happen?"

"In a car accident. Cynthia and Whit want to get together with you, and I suggested you all come here for dinner Saturday. Well, are you going to represent me?"

Was I? She was my old friend's mother, but we hadn't liked each other back then and it looked as though we weren't going to like each other much now. On the other hand, homicide is more interesting than real estate and divorce, and she obviously could afford to pay. "I'll require a retainer," I said.

"I'll pay it."

"All right," I said. "I'll talk to the DA's office, and I'll be in touch."

"Dinner will be here Saturday night at six," she replied. "You will have spoken to the DA's office by then, so come at five and we'll have a chance to talk before Whit and Cindy arrive."

"I'll check my calendar," I said.

I drove out of Los Cerros in slow motion, taking the speed bumps at a pace the Nissan's aging shock absorbers could absorb. I wondered who the DA would assign to this case and why Cindy Reid hadn't called me when she moved to town. I saw a man putting on the putting green. It was a warm enough day to swim, and kids were playing Marco Polo in the pool. "Marco," one kid yelled. "Polo," another one answered. A dark-haired, heavyset guy in a wheelchair was rolling across the tennis court. He stopped and stared at me as I drove by.

3

N BERNALILLO COUNTY there's always some controversy surrounding law enforcement. The police catch the blue flu and call in sick because they didn't get the pay raise they wanted. The sheriff promotes his wife to chief deputy with a fifty-thousand-dollar-a-year salary. That could happen anyplace, but what makes Bernalillo County unique is that the sheriff holds a news conference to announce it. The latest episode had to do with a guy named Jimmie Solano, who, in the midst of an attempted suicide, lunged at police officers with a three-inch pocket knife. The officers shot and killed him and kept him from killing himself. It was only one of a number of fatal shootings recently that have given the APD one of the worst records in the West. In the past few years the Duke City police have killed more people than the police in Tucson, Austin, El Paso, Tulsa and Colorado Springs combined. Often domestic violence is involved. Usually the victims are distraught or intoxicated. The APD are trained to "shoot to stop" when they believe they or another person is being threatened, as opposed to shooting to wound. Stopping means aiming at the largest part of the body, where the vital organs are located. A police officer from Tucson was quoted in the *Journal* recently as saying that perhaps the Albuquerque police had more victims because they were better shots. "It could be when they 'shoot to stop,' they're connecting more," he said.

Deputy District Attorney Anthony Saia, who had been assigned the Justine Virga case, was an old friend and my favorite deputy DA. He had a creased, rumpled, unmade-bed kind of face. He always looked comfortable—even in his suit—as if he were sitting around on Sunday morning in his bathrobe, reading the paper, eating sugar doughnuts, drinking black coffee and smoking cigarettes. That was one reason I liked him—he had bad habits to equal my own. There aren't many people left to smoke with anymore. His office made me feel right at home too; his desk was a city dump, his ashtray overflowed with ashes and butts. I also appreciated his world-weary, jaundiced attitude. You could call it cynical, you could call it common sense: depends on your point of view.

When I went to his office on Friday morning to talk to him, he was standing in front of a mirror, brushing his hair. It was black with gray highlights, thick and wiry, the kind of hair that reacts to every change in moisture, electricity or wind. Saia didn't pay much attention to his clothes, but he was vain about his hair.

"Hat head," he said, finishing up and putting the brush in his drawer.

"Pleasure to see you too," said I.

"Hey, Neil, you know you're my favorite defense lawyer."

"That's not saying much."

He laughed and sat down at his desk. I sat in front of him. He lit a Camel with his Bic lighter. I lit a Marlboro and blew out the match.

"So the APD has the best shots in the West," I said. Just

because I liked the guy didn't mean I couldn't give him some shit.

He winced. "Don't believe everything you read in the papers. A man charging police officers with a weapon is asking for trouble."

"When the weapon is a three-inch penknife?"

He shrugged, flicked an ash at his ashtray, missed.

"If the APD shot him to keep him from killing himself, what do you call that—murder or suicide?"

"Self-defense. You know, sometimes it's just a matter of luck whether a suspect dies or not."

"Then the APD is lucky?"

"I'd say unlucky." He laughed. "I don't think *your* luck's going to be so good on this one."

"Tell me what I'm going to be reading in the papers." So far Justine's death had gotten only a brief notice in the *Journal* and the *Tribune,* but sooner or later they'd find out she'd been the girlfriend of Martha's grandson, and that was likely to move the story up to page one.

"That a witness saw Martha Conover's car entering the Los Cerros complex at an excessive rate of speed around tenfifteen. That a neighbor called the APD at eleven to say she'd found the body in the road."

He could give me the names of the witness and the neighbor if he chose to. But he wouldn't choose to unless we were talking plea bargain, and he wouldn't have to unless Martha Conover was indicted. It's tough to get any information out of the DA's office while a case is under investigation. "The body wasn't found until eleven?" I asked.

"Yeah. There's not much traffic on that road at night. Nobody lives up there but old ladies, and they don't go out." Saia picked up a rubber band from his desk, stretched it between his fingers and began moving the fingers back and forth like a sideways seesaw. "There were no brake marks on the pavement. Your client didn't even slow down."

"Have you gotten the results of the autopsy back yet?"

"Yeah. Death on impact due to massive injuries to the vital organs."

At least he wouldn't be able to depict Martha Conover as a heartless woman who'd left the victim lying alone in the road to bleed to death. "Did the OMI find any drugs and/or alcohol in Justine's blood?"

"Some antihistamines. That's all. She was Michael Velásquez's girlfriend. Did you know that?"

"Yeah."

"And three years ago, also on Halloween, she was driving the car he died in. Did you know that?"

By the time I thought of faking it, it was too late. My expression had given me away. "No," I said.

"You're slipping, Neil. I thought you'd know your clients better than that."

"Me, too."

"One of the investigators thought Virga looked familiar, and he traced her to the previous accident. She was a beautiful girl; someone you'd remember."

"Was Justine charged with any crime for that accident?"

"Nothing to charge her with. The Porsche came over López Hill, a semi was jackknifed across the road. No way to avoid it."

"Justine was driving a Porsche?"

"Yeah. It was Michael Velásquez's car."

"Where did he get a Porsche?" I was thinking out loud, which is a mistake when Saia is listening.

"Maybe his grandmother gave it to him."

"Maybe." But it didn't sound like the purse-clutching Martha I knew. "Was Justine speeding or under the influence?"

"She was going close to seventy-five." He shrugged, implying that was no big deal in New Mexico. "She took a Breathalyzer and came out clean. There *were* brake marks on that one."

"Martha didn't consult me before she refused to take your Breathalyzer, you know," I said.

"She was advised of her rights," said Saia, "and told she had the right to call a lawyer. She declined."

"Nice of the police not to put her in jail."

"Hey, she was an old lady in a nightgown, full of Halcion and booze. What could they do? Put her to bed in a holding pen full of hookers? It looked like a simple hit-and-run until the investigation turned up the fact that Conover was Velásquez's grandmother and Virga was driving the car that killed Velásquez." Saia lit himself another Camel, though one still smoldered in the ashtray. You know you're smoking too much when you've got one burning in the ashtray and another one in your mouth. I squished the butt in the ashtray with my thumb and rubbed it out, but he didn't notice.

The Halcion was something Martha hadn't told me about either, but I kept that lack of information to myself. Not only had Martha had the means, motive and opportunity to kill Justine Virga; she'd apparently had a couple of uninhibiting substances in her system as well.

"Your client told the investigating officer about the Halcion," Saia continued. "Since she refused to take the Breathalyzer, we have to assume she'd been drinking too."

It was my turn to shrug. Presumably the APD would interview (or already had interviewed) the bartender at the AWC meeting. As that bartender could be held liable for serving an intoxicated person, there was a good chance he or she wouldn't admit to serving Martha Conover two martinis. There might, however, have been witnesses.

"Do I get a copy of the note?" I asked.

"What note?" Saia replied.

"The one the police found in Justine's pocket. They went into Martha's house without a warrant, showed Martha the note and compared it to a sample they took from her typewriter."

"She gave her consent; they didn't need a warrant."

"The police woke her up and walked in on her in the middle of the night. I'd say they were taking advantage of a respectable senior citizen." Saia wouldn't give me the note if it was evidence that would convict my client. If it would exculpate her, he'd have to produce it, but not yet. The note probably wouldn't do either, but *someone* had typed it. I needed to find out who.

Saia picked up the rubber band and stretched it between his fingers. He owed me a favor from a couple of years back, and the time had come to call it in. "You owe me one, Anthony," I said. "Remember?"

"Yeah, I remember." He reached into a folder on his desk and took out a piece of white paper. "Here. I made you a copy."

I unfolded the paper and read: "I knew this was going to happen, but I couldn't prevent it." It wasn't quite as chilling as it had been when I first heard it, but it was close enough. Some letters were dark, some were light, indicating the original had been typed on a manual typewriter. The peculiarities of type were obvious; an *e* with a loop that didn't quite close, a *p* that was missing part of its tail. "Thanks," I said.

"Spooky, isn't it?"

"Very. This note wasn't typed on Martha's typewriter, you know."

"So the report says."

"Martha said it was in a sealed envelope."

"It was." Saia leaned back in his chair. "So you want to know how I call it?"

"Dígame."

"It's the anniversary of Velásquez's death, and Conover's distraught. She invites Virga over to talk and runs her down in the road. Willful, deliberate and premeditated murder in the first degree."

A smart criminal would never show premeditation; crimes committed in the heat of passion get lesser sentences. The García case had recently made it more difficult to get a first-degree conviction in New Mexico; now you had to prove deliberate intent. But Saia would have had trouble getting first degree for a case like this even before García. He knew it, and so did I. In some states juries will convict an intoxicated person of premeditation, but New Mexico is more tolerant of substance abuse than that. Here they believe a person under the influence isn't rational enough to premeditate, and Martha appeared to have been under the influence. Saia had said so himself. The only way he'd get a first-degree conviction out of a DWI fatality would be to prove depraved mind murder. He'd have a hard time convincing a jury that a woman as proper as Martha was depraved. "You don't have a chance," I told him.

"On the other hand, maybe Virga's feeling guilty," Saia continued. "Okay, Velásquez's death wasn't her fault, but she *was* driving the car, and from all accounts, she loved the guy. She's afraid of Conover, but she needs to talk to her, tell her she's sorry, ask for forgiveness, maybe, so she goes to Los Cerros. Conover sees her in the road, steps on the gas, does her, takes some pills, gets in bed and tries to pretend it didn't happen. Murder in the second degree."

"Yeah," I thought, "or Justine hates Martha. She's depressed, full of guilt and suicidal. She goes to Los Cerros, sees Martha's car, jumps in front of it, kills herself and ruins Martha's life at the same time. Vehicular suicide."

"Or else Conover's been getting into the Halcion," Saia said, "and it's making her crazy. She has a few drinks at the AWC meeting, joins the Point One O Club, gets even crazier, sees Justine in the road and runs her down in a drunken fog. Vehicular homicide."

The maximum sentence for vehicular homicide is three years, second degree will get you nine and first degree is life. If you're looking to get off easy, running someone down when you're drunk is one way to do it. Of course you'd have to be sure you'd complete drunk what you planned when sober. Most people refuse to take a Breathalyzer because they don't want to be found drunk, but a person might refuse who didn't want to appear sober. Under the influence? Sober? Martha was the only one who knew for sure. I looked at Saia. He smoothed his hair and looked at me. We were in the same business, we practiced in the same town, we'd gone to the same law school. If we were thinking the same thing, we both had our reasons not to admit it.

"Any way you look at it, there's no clear precedent for this case in New Mexico," Saia said. "So much depends on the state of those two women's minds. If you ask me, there is nothing harder than getting inside a woman's mind, and one of them is dead anyway."

I wasn't sure that getting inside my client's head would solve anything. It could be a labyrinth, with a stone wall blocking every twist and turn. Who knew whether Martha herself remembered what had happened? How much she'd planned, how much she remembered, how much she'd blacked out? It wasn't really my job to find out. My job was to present reasonable doubt and better now than later, because this was a case I did not want to take to trial. Given the evidence so far, it wouldn't be hard for Saia to get an indictment; grand juries in Bernalillo County will indict a burrito. "Martha didn't move the body or try to conceal her car, did she?"

"Nope. The body didn't appear to have been moved; the car was parked in its usual spot."

"It seems like a guilty woman would make some attempt to cover her tracks."

"A guilty woman who was sober and in her right mind would, but women who take too much Halcion aren't always in their right minds, and women who take Halcion and booze together are never in their right minds," he said. "We're seeing more of these kinds of cases now. In combination, Halcion and liquor can cause poor judgment, decreased attention span and bizarre behavior."

Amnesia too.

"The older people get, the more sensitive they are to psychoactive drugs. An automobile in the hands of an elderly person on Halcion and booze can be the equivalent of a cocked and loaded gun."

"When did the police get to the scene?"

"Eleven-fifteen."

An hour after Martha got home, an hour in which Justine's body might have been lying in the rain or might not. "What did the medical examiner give as the time of death?"

"Ten-fifteen, more or less." He knew as well as I that the Office of the Medical Investigator can't pinpoint death to the minute.

I put out my cigarette, got ready to go. "Maybe it's just bad karma that brought these two together," I said.

Saia laughed. "You and I start believing in karma, good or bad, we'll be out of a job." He looked at the clock on the wall. The minute hand had come to twelve noon exactly. "What are you doing for lunch?"

"Taking you to Arriba Tacos for a stuffed sopapilla."

"If that's a bribe, I accept." He put out his Camel and chucked the contents of the overflowing ashtray into the wastebasket. He stood up, leaned back, bent his knees to see into the too-low mirror and smoothed his hair in place.

The way I judge a man is not by how much money he makes, how many cases he wins or loses, whether he's good to his mother or his dog or even how much hair he has. My criterion is whether a guy is willing to eat with me at Arriba Tacos. They have the best stuffed sopapillas in town, but a lot of men don't appreciate that—I'd been married to one once. That kind of guy sees a drive-in shack with flames licking the red letters on the sign and thinks the food isn't good enough for him.

Saia and I sat outside, eating our sopapillas and watching the traffic go by. At high noon there was about enough shade to shelter a bug. We ate our hot food in the hot sun, the way it's meant to be eaten. An immaculate turquoise and white fifties Chevy with sparkling chrome stopped for a light.

"What do you call a Chevy on a stick?" Saia asked me.

That was easy. "Art," I said. Elevated Chevys had become an item on the New Mexico art scene. The City of Albuquerque paid an Arizona sculptor $75,000 for a sculpture of a purple tile Chevy on a green tile arch. Santa Fe got one that was balanced on a pole. Someone took a chain saw and cut that one down. You couldn't do that to our Chevy, but a lot of people would have sent it back to Arizona if they'd been able. We finished eating and lit a cigarette for the road.

"Best damned sopapillas in Albuquerque," Saia said.

"In America," said I.

4

WHEN I GOT TO HAMEL AND HARRISON, my secretary, Anna, was sitting at her desk drinking coffee, eating yogurt—the diet that kept her a size six—and talking on the phone. The receiver settled like a bird into her big hair nest. From her laugh I knew she was talking to her boyfriend, Stevie, the stereo king, proving that it is possible to do three things at once (eat, drink and talk on the phone), especially when none of them are work.

"Hold on a sec," she said to the phone, swiveling in her chair and laying the receiver down. Watching the earpiece hit the desk, I listened for the bass that accompanies Stevie wherever he goes and keeps him plugged into the source, like those heartbeat machines that mothers play for their newborn babies.

Anna handed me my mail and messages. Stevie's faint but unmistakable beat came through the telephone line.

"Where's Brink?" I asked, even though I probably already knew.

"Out to lunch."

Having done her duty by handing me my mail and messages, Anna picked up the phone and resumed her conversation. I went into my office, closed the door and opened the mail, most of which could wait until next week or next year. Baxter, Johnson, one of my least-favorite law firms, was having a cocktail party to celebrate their move to new offices in the black slab building. It would be catered, of course, with the best nouveau Mex cuisine, but I wasn't sure I wanted to be eating it with Baxter or Johnson. I put the invitation in my purse, flipped through the rest of the mail and came across a brochure for a skunk gun, a vial containing skunk juice that was small enough to fit on a key ring. "Skunk juice," the brochure said, "has been tested and proven to be the odor that repels men faster than any other." When a woman is threatened, she breaks open the vial and the skunk smell drives the assailant away. Of course the woman doesn't smell too great herself, but that's better than being attacked, and the skunk gun comes with a spray bottle of neutralizer to remove the smell. "The odorant comes from the glands of free-range, one-hundred-percent natural Northern New Mexico skunks," I read, "skunks that have been killed by ranchers because they are considered pests." I put that aside to show Anna and moved on to phone messages.

They were the usual real estate and divorce. Karen LeMond's husband had split with an eighteen-year-old and left a message on Karen's answering machine that he wanted out. What an eighteen-year-old woman would see in forty-five-year-old potbellied Tom LeMond was a mystery to me, but a man who doesn't have the guts to tell his wife he wants a divorce firsthand deserves whatever he gets. I called Karen. She wasn't home. I left my own message on her machine. "Call me back," it said.

The next pink message slip was from Sharon Amaral and incorporated both real estate and divorce. Her husband hadn't been making his child support payments, she hadn't been making her mortgage payments, the bank was threat-

ening foreclosure. In newspapers all across the country these
days the real estate sections are filled with notices of foreclosure auctions. Foreclosures are at the highest rate since
the Depression. There are bottom feeders out there who buy
up these properties cheap and wait for better days. Fortunes
get made that way out of other people's misfortunes. There
are also close to one million bankruptcy filings a year, and
the national debt has reached four trillion dollars, a number
too big to comprehend, the twenty-four-wheeler of numbers
careening out of control down the highway.

The nineties are paying for the excesses of the eighties.
You see it daily in my business. A lot of the excesses began
late one night in 1980 on the floor of the House of Represen-
tatives, when Congressman Fernand Saint Germain added a
rider to a bill deregulating the savings and loan industry and
upping the amount of federal deposit insurance from
$40,000 to $100,000. Deregulation handed savings and loan
owners and their cronies an engraved invitation to steal.
The rider raised the amount they could steal by 150 percent.
With nobody policing them, the S&Ls squandered their
deposits on bad loans, junk bonds, junk developments and
the campaign contributions that induced politicians of both
parties to look the other way. Charles Keating of Lincoln
S&L fame invested $3 million of depositors' money in polit-
ical contributions, and when asked if he thought he was
buying influence, he replied, "I hope so." An economy
pumped up by S&L steroids created an artificially induced
boom that led to a very real bust. The taxpayers are going to
have to repay the squandered deposits to the tune of fifteen
hundred dollars each, and the amount is rising daily.

Given this climate, you could probably talk a bank out of
foreclosure in most cities for a little while anyway. The real
estate market has fallen so drastically that a lot of properties
are now worth less than the mortgages that were placed on
them a few years ago. Banks are often better off making a

deal than foreclosing and trying to unload a property in a depressed market. The trouble for Sharon Amaral was that Albuquerque never went through the boom and it wasn't going through the bust either. Real estate prices had remained low but stable. Our S&L crooks hadn't had the nerve or the imagination of their neighbors in Arizona.

"How's it going?" I asked when Sharon answered the phone.

"It sucks, if you really want to know," she replied. Tommie and Joey, her twins, were screaming in the background, and Sharon sounded close to tears herself. I had a vision of dirty faces, sticky fingers, runny mascara, toys on the floor, stupid pets, an ex-husband who was in a bar somewhere having a brewski, and a run-down ranch house in a declining neighborhood, which was Sharon's and the twins' only hope of financial security.

"How much are your mortgage payments?" I asked.

"Two fifty." Not much in the big picture, and nothing at all to the top one percent of our society who controlled most of the wealth, the rich who kept on getting richer. In a lot of places, you couldn't even find a property with a $250-a-month mortgage. But a blip is a mountain when you're broke.

"Who holds the mortgage?" I asked.

"New West." It had been a local bank, locally owned, locally managed, until a few months before, when it collapsed and was taken over by a larger bank in Phoenix.

"How long have you had the house?"

"Seven years."

"Is there any chance you could just pay the interest?" I knew the answer before I asked. Even after seven years, 80 percent of the payment would still be interest.

"No."

"You could try to get social services to track Bobby down and make him pay, but they're overloaded and it'll take a while." If they ever found him at all. She could also hire a private investigator—if she had any money, but if she had any money why waste it looking for a deadbeat like Bobby Amaral? "Is there anybody—family, maybe—who can help with the payments?"

"Are you kidding?" She laughed. "They're worse off than I am."

The next question was, if she couldn't pay her mortgage interest or a private investigator, how was she ever going to pay me? I didn't ask. There was always the possibility that I could resolve this with a phone call. "I'll call the bank and see what I can do."

"Thanks," she said.

I got Joe Bench, the only person I knew at New West, on the phone. "Jeez, Neil, I don't think I can help," he said. I could picture the sincere concern on his earnest face while he was saying it and his fingers tapping a pencil against his desk, but the friendly-local-banker act doesn't fool me. Every litigator knows that the last person you ever want to put on a jury is a banker; his job is to say no, and bankers' hearts are hardened to it. "All the mortgages are being handled out of Phoenix now."

"Some states are forcing banks to cram down their mortgages and reduce the payments to fit today's poor market, you know."

"New Mexico? Are you kidding me? In the first place, we don't have a lousy market. In the second place, you've been here long enough to know cram-downs aren't gonna happen in the Land of Enchantment."

"Is there anybody I can call in Phoenix?"

"Try Eric Winston."

"Thanks."

"It's nothing," he said.

He was probably right, but I called Eric Winston anyway. He wasn't in. I left a message, and that took care of real estate and divorce for one day.

So I pulled a legal pad out of my drawer, flipped to an empty page and began drawing circles around the red line down the side. I started at the center of the circles and spiraled out. When I'd looped my way to the bottom I flipped to a new page and drew a straight line down the middle of the yellow sheet. On one side I listed the reasons why I didn't want to represent Martha Conover. On the other side I listed the reasons why I should.

On the plus side I wrote: "You shouldn't judge a woman unless you've driven a mile in her car on her substances. The most interesting thing about crime is that ordinary people will commit it under extraordinary circumstances. To meet your nemesis alone on a dark and rainy night in control of a loaded weapon when you're under the influence and have less than a second in which to act is one of the most revealing things that can happen to a person." Those are some of the platitudes that keep those of us who don't do it for prestige or money in the legal business.

On the down side of the page I wrote: "I wouldn't like Martha Conover even if she hadn't committed a crime."

On the plus side: "You need the money."

On the no side: "You don't like to represent women on medication, and you can't effectively represent clients who lie or don't tell the whole truth. One reason you went into business for yourself is so you don't have to take on clients you don't trust or like."

Yes, "But another reason you got into this business is your interest in those rainy nights when human beings reveal what they are capable of."

True, only, "There are holes in Martha Conover's story big enough to drive her Buick through."

Maybe, "But if she were lying, wouldn't she have made up a better story? Besides, you'd be up against a deputy DA you like, and how can you say no to Cindy Reid's mother?"

Back to the minus column: "You haven't seen Cindy

Reid in years. What makes you think you owe her any-thing?"

My final entry was: "It's not real estate or divorce."

I flipped the page, started drawing loops again, down one side, up the other. Martha's list was reminding me of another time, another mother, another pad, another list, a kid who was keeping score. That kid drew a line down the middle of a page and printed I HATE MOMMY on one side of it and I LOVE MOMMY on the other with a third grader's block letters. When she was mad at her mother she drew a verti-cal line in the appropriate column. When she wasn't, she made a mark under love. When she had four scores in either column she drew a line through them and moved down the page. One day she got tired of the game, ripped up the paper and threw it away. She knew which side was winning anyway. Her mother found one piece of the paper in the trash, the piece that said I HATE MOMMY. "Did you write this?" she asked, large and disapproving as only a mother can be. The kid stared her down, belligerent and bratty as only a kid can be. "Yes," she said. It was one of those moments that nobody asks for but that are a bend in the road when they happen. The kid was eight years old. She never knew what the mother's excuse was—the mother didn't stick around long enough for the kid to find out—but that was the beginning of the exit ramp for those two. Things were bad anyway, and they got worse. Maybe you have to become a parent yourself before you can really understand and forgive a mother. I don't know yet what it takes to forgive an eight-year-old kid.

I needed some comic relief after that, so I went out to the reception area to see Anna. "You're not going to believe this," I said, "but women are using skunk smell these days to protect themselves." I showed her the skunk gun brochure.

"What happened to dogs?"

"The smell of a skunk is worse than the bite of a dog. Besides, you can carry one around on your key ring. Look at how small they are."

She read the brochure. "They're only twenty-nine ninety-five. Let's get one. I don't have a gun, and you always leave yours unloaded in your drawer."

I had a Smith & Wesson LadySmith .38 myself. It had protected me, but not as well as I would have liked. The Kid complained about guns around the house, so it had been sitting unloaded and half forgotten in my desk drawer. "All right," I said. "Call and order a couple and charge them to the office account. Heard any good jokes lately?"

Anna was our office comedian. Comedians are society's psychic sponges; they absorb everybody else's pain and let us squeeze the laughter out of it. It's a tough role to play. Fortunately for Anna, her jokes were always about lawyers; they didn't go that deep or get that funny.

She had begun tapping at her keyboard. "What do you call a lawyer with an IQ of fifty?" she replied without missing a beat.

That was easy. "Congressman," I said.

5

I WAS AWAKENED SATURDAY MORNING by a ringing phone and the angry voice of Martha Conover in the receiver, not the best way to start a weekend. "Did you see the *Journal* this morning?" she snapped.

"Not yet."

"I am on the front page." Some people might like to find their name on page one, but not Martha.

I reached for a cigarette, looked around to see if the Kid was awake yet. He was. In fact he'd already gotten out of bed and left for work. Saturday was just another day at the car repair shop for him. "Your case was bound to get some attention sooner or later, considering the circumstances," I told Martha. I found a Marlboro on the bedside table and lit it.

"Did they have to interview Mina Alarid?"

"Who?"

"Justine's aunt, the one she lived with when she came here from Argentina. She told the reporter that she saw me driving up and down her street the weekend before Halloween. She said Justine was staying at her house and that I had been stalking her."

It was a good story; you couldn't blame the paper for printing it.

"Isn't there anything you can do to stop them from repeating Mina Alarid's lies?"

"Not really," I said. Lawyers aren't gods, sometimes they're not even humans, especially early on Saturday morning. "Look, I'll read the article, and we will talk about it when I get to your house tonight. All right?"

"All right," Martha said and hung up.

I tried to go back to sleep, but it was impossible after that, so I got out of bed, dressed, went to La Vista's vending machine and bought a copy of the *Journal*. As usual the machine didn't like my quarters, and it took three before the door flopped open and the paper fell out. The story was on page one, just as Martha had said. I brought the paper inside, made myself a Red Zinger tea, sat down and read the article. Either some enterprising reporter had tracked down Mina Alarid or she'd called the paper herself. The article didn't say. There wasn't much I hadn't already heard from Martha or Saia, except that Mina Alarid was specific about what she'd seen, a late-model gray American car, driving up and down her street the weekend before the accident. She'd be a good witness for the prosecution.

When I got to Martha's town house at five-twenty, Dan Rather was on the TV, trying not to look too pleased that some third-world disaster had upped his ratings. Martha had stuck pink Post-it notes all over the back of the door—her shopping lists. One of them fell to the floor when she opened the door to let me in. I picked it up and handed it to her. Vodka and peas, it said.

She already had the vodka. It was in the glass in her hand, with two olives and, maybe, a splash of vermouth. It hadn't made her any happier with her attorney. She still looked at me as though I was a delinquent teenager, although one who'd gotten old enough, at least, to drink. She asked me if I'd like one.

The answer was yes, but would I accept one? "No," I said; we had business to discuss.

Gunga Dan finished the news and signed off with a smarmy smile. Martha hit the remote and got rid of him. I sat down on the chintz sofa, took out my yellow legal pad and prepared to start my interrogatories, but Martha spoke first.

"Did you see the paper?"

"Yes."

She was still fuming. "It's outrageous that Mina Alarid is permitted to make statements like that."

"Your car is a late-model Buick?"

"Yes."

"What color is it?"

"Gray. That doesn't mean anything. There must be thousands of late-model gray cars out there."

"You didn't drive by Mina's house that weekend? Not even once?"

"Absolutely not." Martha put her drink down on a coaster, aligned her vertebrae and looked me right in the eye. Her eyes didn't wander to the left or the right, the way the eyes of a person with a guilty conscience might. Either she was telling the truth and didn't have a guilty conscience or she lied better than most. "You did talk to the DA's office, didn't you?"

"I did."

"What did they say?"

"The police are investigating. Deputy DA Anthony Saia, who is handling the case, is considering whether to file charges."

"What charges is he talking about?"

"Second-degree murder or vehicular homicide."

"What are the penalties for those?"

"A maximum of nine years and ten thousand dollars for second-degree, three years and five thousand dollars for vehicular homicide."

Martha picked up her drink and took a large sip. "And if I was driving while under the influence?"

"Most likely vehicular homicide. There's something I need to get straight with you right off," I said, "and that is I don't enjoy getting surprises from the DA's office or from the newspaper either. What I learn about you I want to learn from you, not from somebody else."

"Oh?" Martha said.

"For starters, Saia told me that your grandson was killed on Halloween three years ago and that Justine Virga was driving the car. You're the one who should have told me that."

"I was very close to my grandson. He was living with me when he died. I . . . I find it difficult to talk about him."

"Saia also told me that Justine was driving Michael's Porsche."

"That's right; she was."

"Where did Michael get a Porsche?"

"His father gave it to him." That didn't sound like the Emilio Velásquez I'd known, but I let it pass for the moment.

"About your Buick—does anyone have access to the keys?"

"No. I never give the keys to anyone, not even Cynthia."

"Where do you keep them?"

"In my purse."

Her purse stuck to her arm as if it was made of industrial-strength Velcro. "Have you had any work done on the car recently?"

"I had the oil changed at Mighty last week."

"Which one?"

"On San Mateo."

I made a note of that, moved on to drugs, something else she hadn't told me about. "Saia also told me you had taken Halcion that night. Do you take it often?"

"Only when I am under stress."

"And then how much do you take?"

"A half."

"You know there's a forty-five-minute gap between the time you got home and the time Justine's body was found, and an hour before the police got here."

"It seemed longer to me."

"What did you do in that time?"

"Slept."

Martha's monosyllabic answers weren't taking up much space, but I flipped to the next page on my legal pad anyway, just to break the rhythm. "Is there anything else you'd rather not talk about? Anything else you haven't told me?" She might find denial comforting, but it wouldn't help me defend her.

"Actually, I do have an idea about what happened to Justine," she said. "Drugs." She folded her hands in her lap as if she had just explained everything, but she hadn't explained a thing to me. I don't consider drugs the great catchall explanation for everything that goes wrong in America.

"The only drugs found in her system were antihistamines," I said.

"I didn't say she had taken drugs. I believe she was selling them."

"And why do you think that?"

"She was very secretive about her past. I asked Michael why she came here from South America, but he never would give me an answer. Virga is obviously an assumed name. At Michael's funeral I overheard her telling Mina Alarid that *they* were following her. She was driving very fast; I think she was being chased."

It wasn't all *that* fast for New Mexico, but I didn't say so. "By who?" I asked.

"Drug dealers."

There are illegal drugs and legal drugs. Pick your poison. In Martha's world the good people took the legal ones, the bad people took the others. "You think drug dealers set you up?"

"Possibly."

"Why would they do that?"

"To divert suspicion from them."

It had a certain kind of Halcion-and-vodka logic. "Just because someone happens to come here from Latin America, that doesn't make her or him a drug dealer," I said. "There are lots of other reasons to come to this country."

"Justine was carrying a revolver the night she was killed," Martha said.

The pen that was scrolling across my legal pad stopped in midstroke. "How do you know that?" I asked.

"One of the policemen, the one who was acting like the nice cop, was holding it inside one of their plastic bags, and he showed it to me. The gun had two empty chambers, he said, and he asked if Justine had fired it. Maybe he thought it had been an attempted robbery and was trying to get me to say I'd acted in self-defense. If I had killed her in self-defense, I asked him, would I have put her gun in the glove compartment?"

"That's where they found it?"

"Yes. The keys were in her pocket. They went into the car looking for her identification."

"How did they know which car was Justine's?"

"It was the worst-looking car in the parking lot."

Martha had been pretty observant for someone who was under the influence. But being accused of killing someone and asked to look at a dead body in the middle of the night might be enough to sober somebody up. It sounded to me as

if the police officers had been sloppy; they shouldn't have
entered Justine's car. They should have towed it away and
impounded it as evidence. On the other hand, they were
probably thinking of Justine's death as an ordinary hit-and-
run at that point. Sometimes police carelessness works in a
defendant's favor, sometimes not.

Justine had a revolver in her car, not that unusual in
New Mexico, where your car is considered your house in
the eyes of the law. It could have been a .38, a gun women
favor. Sensible people leave the chamber under the hammer
empty for safety reasons, which would mean that only one
bullet had been fired. I had no way of knowing who or
where. As for when, I'd say recently, or Justine would have
reloaded. The police had the investigatory resources to find
out who and when, but Saia wouldn't tell me what they discovered, not yet anyway.

Martha's hands pressed together in her lap like a closed
book. "Justine Virga was a killer. She carried a gun," she
said. "The DA let her get away with killing my grandson,
and now he wants to charge me with murder. That's his idea
of justice? What kind of a name is Saia anyway?"

"American." I stood up. "I'd like to use your bathroom."

"It's down the hall."

I walked down the hallway to Martha's bathroom, which
had the same pinky-beige carpet that covered the rest of her
floors. White hand towels with the initials *MCC* embroi-
dered in pink hung on the rack. I flushed the toilet for camouflage and opened her medicine chest. A lot of women
have their own private Idaho, a place where the grass is
greener—a little stash of marijuana, Xanax, José Cuervo or
whatever it takes, substances that work when used spar-
ingly, cause worse problems when used to excess. Martha's
little helpers were on the shelf in a brown plastic container
with a white prescription label. I picked up the container,

made a note of the doctor's name, Muldauer, and pushed down on the childproof lid, which would be a challenge for anyone not at the peak of reflexes and conditioning to twist open. It was already loose. Martha probably kept it that way so she could get at the Halcion easily in the middle of the night. The pills were smooth white ovals about the same size and shape as Xanax but without the dividing line down the middle. None had been broken in half, and there were plenty of them, more than enough to encourage abuse.

I knew something about Halcion, a drug that—along with romance novels and TV—puts ladies all over America to sleep. It had been in the news lately, and the news had not been good. A half is not supposed to hurt you, but sometimes a half stops working, and then it's a whole and then two or three, and before you know it you've got a jones on. There's a narrow margin between a safe dose of Halcion and a dangerous one, because the body metabolizes it so quickly. Alcohol exacerbates the effects of Halcion. Alcohol exacerbates everything.

I looked into the container in my hand and tried to enter that part of Martha's mind where an anger burned that drugs and drink apparently hadn't extinguished. I saw it as a smoky, smoldering dump. There were already a number of cases before the courts in which people (usually—but not always—women) had committed murders (usually—but not always—of family members) and were using the Halcion defense. It wasn't the kind of defense I'd choose, because I'm not sure that Halcion causes psychotic or violent behavior. It could be that it keeps the bad dreams away and prevents the little aggravations from being expressed daily until finally, after years of repression, they explode. Deal with it now when it's a problem child, deal with it later when it becomes an adult monster. Sooner or later you have to turn the headlights on in your life.

I looked deeper into the Halcion container. Would Martha miss three or four? I wondered. Probably not. I took three and put them in my pocket. I'd never taken Halcion, and I wanted to see what a few plus some drinks would do, but my motives were not entirely investigatory or pure, I'll admit. Every now and then I lift something just to prove to myself that I can.

On my way back to the living room I passed an open door, stopped and looked in. A typewriter sat on an antique desk along with a collection of pictures in silver frames. The doorbell rang. "Whit," I heard Martha say. "Unlike my daughter, he is *always* on time." While she went to answer the door, I stepped into the room and took a look at the typewriter. It was a Selectric, not a manual, and couldn't be the typewriter that had typed the note. Next I looked at the pictures. The majority were of a fair-haired boy, a boy any mother—or grandmother—would be proud to claim. He started out little, curly-haired and cute and grew up tall, blond and handsome. He had dark eyes, fine features and a perfect smile. He was as good-looking as his father, but he didn't look like him. Michael was his mother's boy—in appearance anyway. One of those children who look so much like one parent that the other seems almost incidental. There were pictures of him as a baby with a teddy bear, as a little boy with a soccer ball, as a middle-school boy in a soccer uniform, as a teenager running down the field. There he was in a graduation cap and gown, standing next to his mother. There were no pictures of him with his girlfriend, Justine Virga, his father, Emilio Velásquez, or even his stepfather, Whit Reid. Although there were pictures of a young Whit Reid by himself, pursuing his chosen sports, holding a hunting rifle, standing next to a horse, skiing. In the only other picture of Cindy, she stood smiling with Whit on the church steps on their wedding day, a day I never saw because by then I was long gone from Ithaca, New York. Something about the frames caught my eye, and I moved up close to examine them. They were different shapes and sizes, but all were sterling silver and every one was engraved with the initials *MCC*.

6

WHIT REID WAS STANDING in the living room when I got back. The Whit I knew in Ithaca looked like the photographs on Martha's desk—tall, skinny, athletic, with blond bangs that fell across his forehead. The Whit who entered Martha's apartment was still tall and still blond, but he was no longer skinny, and his hair didn't flop anymore—it stuck to the top of his head, where it had been slicked into place to hide a bald spot. He was wearing khaki pants, a white shirt and Top-Siders with no socks, and he'd put on a lot of weight. He looked athletic, but heavy athletic, a tackle instead of a quarterback. He reminded me of my ex-husband, Charles, who might once have been skinny athletic too, but it was long before I knew him. Sometimes I think there are only two or three types of men in the world and it's a woman's fate to keep meeting them over and over again.

Whit shook my hand. He had thick fingers and was wearing a gold ring on his little finger. "Nelly," he said using my high school nickname. "Good to see you."

"Hello, Whit. My name is Neil."

"We're so glad to have you on Martha's team." He moved on to Martha and kissed her cheek.

His nose was flatter and broader than I remembered, as if it had gotten broken somewhere along the way, and he wheezed when he breathed. It was the kind of thing a less secure man might have gone to the trouble to fix.

"Would you like a drink?" asked Martha.

"Stay put," he replied. "I can get it myself." He made an end run around Martha's spindly furniture and went to the kitchen, where he helped himself to a large Jim Beam, no ice. "Neil?"

"No, thanks," I said.

Whit brought the drink back to the living room, put it on the coffee table and sat down heavily on the sofa with his legs apart and his hands resting on his knees. In one way he looked as though he belonged on the sofa, and in another way he didn't, like a large and sloppy dog who has climbed up on the forbidden furniture so often he's made himself at home. His glass made a wet ring on the table.

"Whit, use a coaster," said Martha, handing him one.

"Oh, sorry," Whit replied, picking up his glass and putting it on the coaster. The routine had the smooth feel of a performance they repeated often.

Whit looked at his watch. "Cyn's late," he said.

"You know our Cynthia," Martha replied.

"So you have your own law practice, Neil?" Whit said to me, drumming his fingers against his thighs.

"Me and my partner."

"Where's your office?"

"On Lead."

"Who's your partner?"

"Brinkley Harrison."

"Don't know him."

"How long have you been in Albuquerque?" I asked.

"About a month."

It was a little soon to know *all* the lawyers, but I didn't say that. "What brought you here?" I asked. Most Arizonans consider Albuquerque the place the wind blows through on the way to Texas.

"The recession," he said, taking a big sip of his drink. "Albuquerque hasn't been hit nearly as bad as Arizona. Rental units have a ninety-eight-percent occupancy rate here." He turned to Martha. "That reminds me. I've been thinking about Property Management, and I don't think they've been doing that brilliant a job with Los Cerros. I'd like to try someone else."

"Would you?" asked Martha.

The doorbell chimed. "Now *that* has to be Cyn," Whit said, looking at his watch again. He put his drink down on the coaster, pulled himself up off the sofa, dodged the coffee table and a floor lamp, went to the door and let her in.

You have to expect changes in someone you haven't seen for a long time, but it's startling anyway. The Cindy I saw smiling in the doorway had been hit hard by the past twenty years. She still looked younger than her husband, but not by much. Marriage has a way of evening out the age differences. In high school Cindy had had a blond and boring prettiness that might well have turned into her mother's china-doll perfection but hadn't. There were crinkle lines under her eyes. She was carrying some extra weight, which softened her chin and filled out her breasts, making her seem fragile and maternal at the same time. She didn't wear any makeup. Her fine, pale hair had been tied back at some point, but now it was falling down around her face. She wore a lavender T-shirt, baggy jeans and worn running shoes.

"It's great to see you, Neil," she said, but she was looking off over my shoulder even before she finished saying it. She gave me a hug, stepped back, smiled and said, "Hello, Whit. Mother," but she didn't exactly look at them either. Her blue eyes were evasive, and she had the guilty manner of a woman who has been sleeping with her best friend's lover.

"Your shoes are wet," Whit said.

Cindy looked down at her feet. "You're right. Of course." She took the shoes off and left them beside the door. "I think it's time to turn the sprinklers off for the season, Mother."

"I'll talk to Rafael about it," her mother said.

"I can do it for you," said Whit.

"I can manage," replied Martha.

"I'm *so* glad you're going to be representing Mother, Neil," Cindy said. "Can you imagine? Who would have thought that *you*, my old hippie friend, would become a lawyer? And that you'd end up representing Mother. Or that *she'd* ever be charged with murder. Life is too weird sometimes."

"Are you considering the Halcion defense?" asked Whit, the self-appointed legal expert. Every family has at least one.

"I only took a half," Martha replied.

"No charges have been filed yet," I said.

"How's dinner coming?" Cindy moved into the kitchen, opened the refrigerator door and looked in. One thing you can count on is that getting together for dinner will either defuse family tensions or exacerbate them. "Can I get anybody a drink?" Cindy asked, taking a tray of ice from the freezer and putting it down on the counter.

"All right," I said, since we seemed to have moved from the business part to the social part of this meeting. I got up and joined Cindy in the kitchen. Martha followed us.

"I don't need anything," Martha said. She sipped her vodka more slowly than anybody I'd ever seen.

"What'll you have, Neil?"

"A tequila. Up." With some salt and lime juice to squeeze on the back of my hand was the way I liked to drink it, but I didn't ask.

Cindy pulled the handle on the metal ice tray and cracked loose the ice. "I don't think Mother has any tequila in the house."

"I don't," Mother agreed.

"How 'bout a vodka? There's plenty of that."

"All right," I said. Cindy opened the freezer and pulled out a bottle of Stolichnaya, which was smoking with cold. She took a glass from a shelf and began to pour my drink.

"Don't use that one," Martha ordered. "You put those glasses in the dishwasher the last time you were here, and they came out spotty."

"I was trying to help, Mother."

"Use the ones on the second shelf."

"What's for dinner?" Whit entered the kitchen and took up more than his share of the limited space.

"Smells like roast beef," offered Cindy.

"Leg of lamb," said Martha. "Baked potatoes and peas."

"Of course," said Cindy.

"Of course what?" asked Martha.

"Peas. We always have peas with lamb, and actually, we always have them with roast beef too. Here, Neil." Cindy handed me my vodka and not a second too soon.

"What's wrong with peas?" asked Martha. "I thought you liked peas."

"I do, Mother. Everybody *likes* peas. How can you not like peas? But we *always* have peas. With everything. You're supposed to serve mint jelly with lamb."

"If you want mint jelly, there's some in the cupboard."

Cindy looked through the shelves and found the jar. "Mint jelly should be *cold*."

"And just *what* is wrong with you tonight?" snapped Martha in her best disapproving-mother voice. In this family every sentence had at least one underlined word in it. "You've done *nothing* but criticize me ever since you walked in the door."

"Nothing is wrong with me, Mother. *Nothing*. Everything is peachy keen."

"It wasn't easy raising a child on my own, you know, and I certainly didn't get any help," Martha said. Every paragraph in this family had at least one cliché in it too. "I always tried to do my best. I gave you a good home surrounded by beautiful things. I took Michael in when he was having trouble. It's not my fault he met Justine."

"I know. I know you have beautiful things. I know you took Michael in, Mother. You don't have to tell me. I *know*." Cindy picked up the ice tray, intending to put it back in the freezer, but it fell out of her hands and smashed into the sink. The metal tray hit the stainless steel hard, and the ice clattered as it fell out. Cindy gripped the counter and stared at the ice. A silence followed that was more than welcome to me, but Whit filled it up.

"Welcome to the Conover family," he said.

The hard-core members of this family, Cindy and Martha, the ones that were in it for life, looked at each other over the sink full of broken ice. "It wasn't Justine's fault, Mother. You'll never understand that. Justine didn't kill Michael. It was an accident. It's terrible that Michael's dead. It's worse that Justine's dead too. Sometimes, if you want to know, I don't think I can stand it."

"It's not my fault."

Cindy sighed. "Of course not. Sorry you have to listen to this, Neil."

I shrugged. Domestic disagreements were one way I earned my living. Everybody hates them, everybody has them. Most people would rather argue about peas and mint jelly than life and death.

Martha took the leg of lamb out of the oven and placed it on a platter. "You carve," she said to Whit.

"Be glad to," he replied.

"Do you want another drink?"

"A splash." He handed her his glass, carried the platter to the table and started hacking off pieces of gray meat that appeared to have had every ounce of juice cooked out of it. As a butcher he lacked finesse. A child with a dull knife could have done it better, but the man's right and obligation to carve the meat were a tradition that remained intact in some families.

Dinner was served on white linen place mats. The china was white with a gold border. The flatware was engraved with the initials *MCC*. The candles in the silver candlesticks never got lit. The peas were soggy, the lamb overcooked. The mint jelly quivered in its crystal dish, but nobody broke through the surface tension to take a bite. The conversation concerned real estate and was dominated by Whit. I discerned a once-familiar pattern. The woman of the house was the boss when it came to domestic matters, but when the family sat down to dinner, everybody shut up and let the male dominate, especially when he talked about business—and Whit's business was real estate. So was Martha's and so was mine, but I've never considered it a fit subject for dinner conversation.

"Interest rates are down to eight percent," Whit said to nobody in particular, "the lowest point in twenty years. What are you paying on the mortgage here?" he asked Martha.

"Nine and three-quarters," she said.

"It's a little soon to think about refinancing. You ought to wait until there's a full two-point spread."

"Really?"

"I'd give it to next spring. The administration will want to keep the economy pumped, and the Federal Reserve'll be cutting the prime rate. It ought to get down below eight percent by April."

"Did you know that Katie Pollock is living in Scottsdale, Neil?" Cindy asked me.

"No," I said.

"She's opening a day care center, and she wanted me to go into business with her, only we came here." Her attempt to grab the conversational ball didn't work; she got blocked by tight end Whit.

"A day care center. Now there's a great way to lose your shirt," said Whit. He changed the subject to one that was more to his liking—big money. "Has anybody been watching the Keating trial?" he asked. "CNN has been televising it. Everyone's out to get Charlie now, but they forget what a boon he was to Arizona. The economy was pumped when he had control of Lincoln."

Boondoggle would be more like it. A ton of office buildings, apartments and resorts were built that nobody needed or wanted. Federally insured deposits were used to pay for them and pad the pockets of Keating and his friends to the tune of a couple billion dollars. Now the empty buildings were rotting in the desert, and Charlie Cheating's boon was going to cost every American taxpayer dearly.

"What did he do that was so bad anyway?" asked Whit.

"How about he invested people's retirement income in junk bonds?" said I.

"High-yield investments are high risk. You pay your money, you take your chances."

"Only he never told people what the risks were."

"Caveat emptor." Let the buyer beware, which more often than not means let the buyer get fucked.

"I saw a Cheating cartoon the other day," I said. "He's in jail, reaching his hand out through the bars, and a guard walks by, mumbling under his breath, 'That goddamn Keating's asking for the Grey Poupon again.'"

Cindy laughed. Martha helped herself to a slice of cooked-to-death lamb. Whit said, "I don't get it."

Either you have a sense of humor or you don't. You can't

explain jokes to people like that. Whit didn't give me a chance anyway. He went right on talking.

"I was playing tennis today with Ed George from First Western Bank. Do you know him, Neil?"

"No."

"It went three sets. He had me down four love in the third, but I rallied and took him. Ed's not a bad tennis player, but he has a weak backhand. It's his grip, I think. I've been working on mine with Jim, the pro at the country club. He teaches skiing at Sandia in the winter. Have you ever skied there, Nel . . . Neil?"

"No," I said again.

"It's not every city that has its own ski area. It's funny that the economy in Albuquerque never took off. I was asking Ed about it when we had dinner with him on Halloween, and he doesn't understand it either. What was the name of that place we went to, Cyn?"

"Chez Henri."

"That's right. Great desserts, but the crepes were soggy and the service was terrible. Now Taos is an interesting area. Remember when we skied there, Cyn? Great runs, super powder, but there is absolutely nothing to do at night. It's dead as Tucson in the summer. Give me Europe or Aspen any day. I don't understand why Ernie Blake didn't do more to develop Taos. First Western would have backed him, I know."

Whit talked, Cindy and Martha ate, I yawned. Who needed Halcion when you could spend the evening with Whit, the kind of guy who warms up his vocal cords in the morning by looking in the mirror and singing "Me, me, me"? He reminded me of the joke about the man who talks about himself all evening and then says, "Enough about me. Tell me about yourself. What do you think of me?" One of nature's laws is that the more successful men are, the more they talk and the less they listen. It's never been my idea of bliss to sit around and listen to men talk about themselves.

"It's amazing how Santa Fe got through the eighties without experiencing any dip in property values at all. In fact the valuation of property in Santa Fe County increased six times. Did you know that?" Whit asked the table, but it did not answer. "The price of an average home there now is a hundred eighty thousand. It's incredible. Most of the influx comes from second-home buyers, flex households with flex jobs. They're the force that's driving that economy. Here I think it'll be high-tech. The salaries and cost of living are so much lower here than California. That's got to make Albuquerque attractive to venture capital." It also made us the equivalent of a third-world country. One of our fifty states was missing again.

After the vanilla ice cream, Whit paused from his mono-logue to light a cigar, which was all the excuse I needed to get myself out of there. "Thanks for the dinner," I said.

"Let's get together for lunch next week, Neil," said Cindy. "How about Wednesday?"

"Okay."

She gave me her number and made me promise to call.

"You'll be calling me as soon as you hear anything from Saia?" asked Martha.

"Yes."

"You ought to get to know Ed George, Neil," said Whit. "I'll be glad to get the two of you together sometime."

"Right," I said.

Cindy let me out. Her wet shoes were still sitting beside the door. As I walked down the sidewalk toward the parking lot and my car, a color TV flickered and signaled like a campfire from the window of a town house across the lawn. An older woman was sitting in front of it, stoking the fire alone. That's how it happens these days. The children (if you ever get around to having any) move away, the men split or die off, the women end up alone eating frozen dinners, watching TV, taking little helpers at bedtime. The sidewalk I was walking on was dry as a diversion channel in winter, not a wet spot or a puddle on it. The sprinklers that kept this part of Los Cerros grass green were not running.

7

∧∧∧∧∧∧

IT DOESN'T MAKE ANY SENSE to leave a car at Mighty to get the oil changed when Jiffy Lube will do it while you wait and you know a mechanic who will do it for nothing, but I called them on Monday anyway. "Mighty," the guy who answered said. "Ramón Ortiz speaking."

"Neil Hamel," I replied. "I'd like to bring my car in for an oil change."

"When?"

"How about noon on Wednesday?"

"No problem. Do you want to use our courtesy van?" He had a slight Hispanic accent, but it wasn't native New Mexican, I knew; it didn't have the right rhythm.

"Yes." It beat sitting around the waiting room on a plastic seat reading *People* magazine. Besides, I was due at Cindy Reid's for lunch at twelve-thirty.

"No problem," he said again.

I called Cindy and got directions to her place. It was in the Heights and not far from Mighty. "Eleven Juniper Road in Los Verdes Meadows," she said. "It's a house that Mother built, and she's renting it to us. You won't have any trouble finding the place; it has Mother written all over it."

"I'm getting my oil changed at Mighty, and I'll have the courtesy van drop me off," I said.

"Okay," she replied.

When I got to Mighty, Ramón Ortiz was standing behind the counter talking on the phone and wearing a pin that had his name on it. He was tall and good-looking, and he knew it. He had a bullfighter's arrogant expression, a hawk's steely eyes and an aloof manner, a man more comfortable in spurs and a cape than a white Mighty shirt. He sized me up while he conducted his phone conversation, as if he were deciding whether I was worth waiting on or not. "Loosen up, dude," I wanted to say. "I'm only asking for an oil change."

"'Ta luego," he said to the phone and hung up.

"I'm Neil Hamel."

His eyes moved across the checklist on the counter. "An oil change?"

"Right. It's the yellow Nissan." I handed him my keys. He wrote Hamel on a tag, attached it to the keys and hung them on the keyboard near the phone.

"You want to use the courtesy van?"

"Yes," I said.

I happened to be standing next to the door to the shop and could hear men joking in Spanish while they elevated a car on the hydraulic lift. "Chico." Ramón raised his voice slightly, and one of the guys came around the corner. Ramón's aristocratic manner gave him some kind of pedigree; Chico's appearance wouldn't get him a bone. Chico was a street dog, scruffy and scrawny. He wore jeans, a T-shirt, shabby running shoes. He had a broken front tooth that would cost more than someone who worked at Mighty could afford to fix. Unlike the guys in the shop, he wasn't wearing a mechanic suit, and his hands weren't stained with grease either. He was the driver, not a mechanic; a lightweight or the newest illegal alien.

"Dónde están las llaves?" asked Chico.

"Yo las tengo," replied Ramón, taking a set of keys from the keyboard and handing them to Chico. They had the same way of pronouncing y and ll, like the s in measure, the way they do in Argentina. I knew that because it was the kind of Spanish the Kid spoke. Before I heard that sound I would have thought Ramón spoke Castilian, except that you usually don't find people who speak Castilian Spanish working in auto repair centers or even owning them. You didn't use to find Argentines doing that kind of work either, until their country fell apart.

"Argentinos?" I said.

"Claro," said Ramón, using an expression Argentines like, meaning "right." "How did you know that?" One elegant eyebrow went up, the other remained wearily in place, a mix of passing interest and permanent disdain.

"I have a friend from Argentina."

"Where are you going?" Chico asked me, squinting his eyes and studying my face while I replied. His English was several years behind Ramón's, but the accent was similar.

"Los Verdes Meadows. You know where that is?"

"Sure," Chico replied. "No problem."

Ramón looked at his watch and then at me without changing his superior expression. "Your car will be ready in one hour. Call when you want Chico to pick you up." It wasn't exactly service with a smile, but I kind of preferred his indifference to the aggressive politeness you often get these days. At least he didn't have to know how I was or wish me a nice day.

I followed Chico outside to the Mighty van. Los Verdes Meadows was only about a mile away. I thought I'd have to direct him, but as he said, he knew the route. He drove as if we were in a grand prix event and the Mighty minivan was a formula one racer. It took a certain amount of optimism or inexperience to try to turn an elephant into a greyhound. The minivan resisted, jerking forward when Chico braked, hesitating when he accelerated, swinging wide when he cut a corner.

Los Verdes Meadows is a name that is known in the trade as real estate Spanglish, a combination of English and Spanish or a word that looks like Spanish but really isn't. It was a destination development, the kind of place that has a golf course, swimming pool, sauna and workout room. The only reason you'd need to leave it would be to go to work or get food. If you clipped coupons and had your food delivered, you wouldn't even have to do that. A lot of Duke City developments have sentry boxes at the entrance, but mostly they're empty, just there for the looks. Los Verdes Meadows's box happened to be inhabited by a guard, whose role was to keep the riffraff and solicitors out. He recognized the Mighty van and/or Chico and waved us in. It could be that a lot of people from Los Verdes Meadows had their cars serviced at Mighty, I thought. I'd never live in a place with a guard myself, even if I could afford it. But in Latin America they were commonplace. There they finish off the tops of their walls with shards of broken glass and rolls of razor wire, and their guards carry automatic weapons.

Chico waved back to the guard. "Nice place," he said to me.

"I'm going to Juniper Road," I said. "Do you know where that is?"

"Sure," he replied.

The houses in Los Verdes Meadows were built around a gully that was an extension of the golf course. The grass in the gully was sparse and sun-dried brown; the ticking sprinklers hadn't been able to keep the course green. They should have dyed it grass color, the way they do in California. The

houses were big and came right up to the edge of their lots
and the edge of the gully. One bold and ugly architectural
statement clashed with the next, but the strangest one of all
was number 11, the house Whit and Cindy Reid lived in. It
was a large white two-story clapboard Colonial with columns
next to the front door and black shutters on the windows. It
would have blended right in in New England. It stuck out like
a maple tree in the desert here, one that spread pollen and
soaked up valuable water. Martha had tried to leave home
and had ended up taking home with her. You had to wonder
why she hadn't stayed put.

Cindy came jogging down the road as the van let me off
in front of the house. "Muchas gracias," I said to Chico.

"De nada," he replied, backing slowly out of the driveway.

Cindy wore a gray warm-up suit, and her tied-back hair
was falling down. She ran the way girls used to run—awk-
ward as the Tin Man. Her elbows were pressed to her sides,
her hands flopped loose and her heels swung out. She was
sweating, so I knew the exercise had gotten the heart pumping and the blood flowing, but her movements lacked grace
and power. She jogged like a woman who was going through
the motions but deep inside was ambivalent about being
strong. She stopped when she got to me, put her head down
and caught her breath. "Whew," she said. "Find us okay?"

"As soon as I saw the white clapboards, I knew this was
the house that Martha built."

She laughed. "Mother knows what she likes. C'mon in."

I followed her through the front door into a large central
hallway, which was guarded by a great white-hunter trophy,
a stuffed bear standing upright with one paw extended as
though he wanted to shake your hand. His claws could have
used a trim, his eyes were glassy and his fur needed a good
beating to get the dust out. It wasn't something you'd want
to stumble across unexpectedly or in the dark.

"Where did *that* come from?" I asked.

"Whit's grandfather shot it in Montana. It's been in the family for ages."

There was a gun rack along the wall, filled with ancient and dusty-looking rifles that had probably been in the family forever too. Hunting is the kind of skill that gets passed along from father to son. The rifles rattled as I walked by. The Oriental rug on the floor was so worn in places the hardwood floors showed through. I tripped on a loose edge and caught myself against the banister. A large mirror with a gilt frame balanced over a spindly-legged table. A stairway led up to the second floor. Someone had been here before us and left his trail: scuffed and muddy riding boots flopped at the foot of the stairs; a sweatshirt hugged the banister; a few stairs up, a navy-blue T-shirt had collapsed in a heap. Cindy began climbing the stairs, picking up the clothes one by one. I followed. When we got to the second-floor landing we found white riding pants stained with dirt. What came next? I wondered. Jockeys? Boxers?

Boxers. Cotton, pale blue and lying beside the shower stall in the bathroom at the top of the stairs. Cindy picked them up too, opened the closet and dumped the load in a laundry basket.

"Whit," she said. "He grew up with maids and never learned to pick up after himself. One summer when he was a kid, the maid quit. The family had a dinner party their last night in the summer house, and they just got up and left the table the way it was, full of dishes, and the kitchen full of dirty pots and pans. The next summer, when they remembered what a mess it was, they hired a new maid to go in and clean it up."

I'm not the neatest person in the world, but I do pick up my own clothes, and sooner or later I do the dishes when I use dishes. The towels on the bathroom racks were navy blue with the white monogram *W&CR*, I noticed. Their edges were frayed, and the nap had worn off long ago. Wedding presents? I wondered. I tried to remember how long ago it had been. Twenty years? Old money hadn't wasted any money on new linens.

I followed Cindy back down the stairs and through the living room. The sofa was big, beige and ugly. The cotton stuffing was oozing out of the upholstered arm of a wing chair. A large portrait of somebody's mother in an evening dress hung over the fireplace. "Mom?" I asked.

"Whit's," said Cindy. "The furniture is hers too. She left it to him when she died."

It was the old-money-pretending-to-be-no-money look, what was good enough for mother and father is good enough for me, and we care more about the dogs and the horses than we do about the house anyway. There's a fine line between antiques and junk; I've never been able to see it.

Considering the size of the house, there had to be several more rooms downstairs: a kitchen, a dining room, a library maybe, a den. We went to the kitchen next. The freezer door hung open, and water dripped onto the floor. An ice tray sat on the butcher-block counter, floating on a puddle of water. "Damn," Cindy said. "He got himself some ice and left the freezer door open." She took a sponge, soaked the water up and squeezed the sponge into the sink. Then she opened the refrigerator and took out a bowl of chicken salad, cucumber sandwiches and a pitcher of tea. There was no ice for the tea; it had all melted. We sat down at the kitchen table. Cindy poured the tea, served the sandwiches and the salad, brushed the hair away from her face and took a look back into another decade, another man. "Do you remember Emilio, Neil, how good-looking he was?" She sighed.

I remembered. Emilio's appearance in those days went beyond good looks into the danger zone of perfection. He was David who had just stepped out of Michelangelo's marble, Elvis Presley before the army got him. He had warm brown eyes that could convince you to leave home and school and never come back. His kind of looks were bound to piss somebody off: gods, parents, the people who wore uniforms and suits. He wasn't spoiled by it—not then anyway. Who knows what came later? He wasn't arrogant either, which made him even more appealing. "Had me creaming in my jeans," I said.

"I never knew how many friends I had until Emiliano started hanging around. Even you, Neil—you came over a lot more."

"Me?"

"Yeah. That's the trouble with having a good-looking guy. Your friends are always coming on to him, and half the time they don't even know they're doing it. One thing I can say about Whit: nobody's trying to get into his pants."

"I know where they are, if anybody's interested." She laughed and brushed the hair out of her eyes. "Some women might be trying to get into his checkbook," I said.

"Not anymore they're not. Arizona is in a deep recession. That's why we came here. I meant to call you once we got settled." They looked settled to me. They looked, in fact, as though they'd been in this house forever. "We were only here a few weeks, and then this business with Mother and Justine . . ." She looked at her plate, poked at a piece of chicken with a fork.

"What do you think happened?" I asked her. One classic investigatory technique is to find disgruntled current or former employees who know the suspect and get them to bitch. I didn't have an employee, so I turned to a family member. Even criminals need to confide in someone, and who else did Martha have to talk to?

"I don't know," Cindy said. "Mother hated Justine, and she is not a forgiving person." She speared the chicken with the fork, picked it up, ate it automatically. "If you find out, let me know—or maybe I don't want to know. I don't know."

Some defense lawyers' mantra is: It's better not to know, but I've let curiosity get in the way of business before. "Do you have any idea how much Halcion she takes?" I asked.

"Mother's little helper?" Cindy smiled. "She got started on that after Michael died. She was crazy about Michael and was devastated by his death. He was the son, the husband, all the men she'd never had. She probably takes more Halcion than she should, but who knows how much? Probably she doesn't even know herself. Her doctor hands them out like candy. I snitch a couple now and then when I need them, but she never notices."

"Actually, I took a few myself," I admitted.

She was startled. "You?"

"I wanted to see what kind of effect they would have combined with a couple of drinks."

She laughed. "I guess I'd better lay off for a while. She might notice double dipping." She touched my hand, brushed her hair out of her face and looked into my eyes. "I'm glad you're here, Neil. As far as I'm concerned, you're the best thing about Albuquerque, maybe the only good thing. When this mess gets straightened out and El Dorado sells, Whit wants to go right back to Arizona. You must like New Mexico—you've been here so long—but to me it seems poor and empty."

"That's what I like about it. What's El Dorado?"

"I'll show you." She went into another room and came back with a watercolor of an enormous adobe-colored building that appeared to be floating above the desert, suspended on clouds of illusory money. "It's a planned development and destination resort that Whit was building outside Phoenix. This is the hotel. There was also going to be an eighteen-hole golf course with home sites around it." It looked to me like the kind of development they call Las Tramponus in Santa Fe, a place that uses up all the natives' water and tax dollars but won't let them in. "He lost it to the bank," Cindy continued. "We lost just about everything when the real estate market collapsed. They let us keep our house, but by then the mortgage was worth more than the house was. Whit lost his polo ponies, his cabin cruiser, his collection of antique cars. El Dorado is being sold at auction, and we're hoping to get enough out of it to go back and start again. In the meantime Whit's been working for Mother."

"Who'd buy a property like that at auction these days?"

"Foreign investors."

"Um," said I. Maybe they'd like to buy some oceanfront property in Gallup too, I thought. It's okay to share secrets with an old friend but not necessarily to tell the truth. El Dorado means "the golden place," but in this case I'd say it was fool's gold. The truth was that if El Dorado was being sold at auction, the Reids were far more likely to end up owing than receiving. It was a truth Cindy could have found out for herself easily enough if she wanted to. Foreclosures rarely sell for the amount of the mortgage. By the time the banks get them, the properties have often been trashed, and in the eighties real estate was often overvalued by appraisers and overmortgaged. If the bank didn't recoup the amount of the mortgage, the Reids could remain liable for the difference.

Cindy sipped her tea and moved the conversation back to a more entertaining subject. "I hear you've got a, um, young hunk, Neil."

"The Kid? He's too skinny to be a hunk. Who told you that?"

"My mother."

"Your *mother* said the Kid is a hunk?"

"Not exactly. She said he was tall, thin, had lots of black hair and was . . . Spanish."

"Is that anything like being a spic?"

Cindy threw up her hands. "You know my mother."

"Actually, he lives in Albuquerque, was born in Argentina, grew up in Mexico. His father is of Spanish descent, his mother Italian. He speaks English, Italian, Spanish and Portuguese. He has a business here. He has a green card. I'd say that makes him an American."

"Hey, you don't have to defend him to me."

"Okay."

"Are you getting in deep?"

"Not that deep."

"So is he good-looking or not?"

"He's all right. The Kid doesn't care what he looks like."

"Don't bet on it. The older Michael got, the more he looked like Emiliano, and that was a problem for Whit. Here, I want to show you something." She took a small box out of her purse and opened it. Inside was a silver heart-shaped locket on a bed of cotton. The locket was engraved on the back with the initials *VF*. Cindy opened it and showed me the picture inside, a handsome young couple smiling like newlyweds for the camera, a fair-haired boy, a dark-haired girl. "Michael and Justine," she said.

"People still wear lockets?" I asked. "It seems kind of old-fashioned."

"This one had been in Justine's family for ages. Mina Alarid gave it to me at the funeral Sunday. She said Justine would want me to have it."

"What does *VF* stand for?"

"Verónica Falcón. It was Justine's grandmother's name."

I examined the picture. I still thought Michael looked a lot more like Cindy than Emilio, and I said so.

"Really?" she asked, surprised. "Michael and Whit never got along very well, and it got worse as Michael got older. That's why he came here to live with Mother. I had Michael for such a short time, Neil, and I loved him so much. He was a wonderful kid. I wish you could have known him. You would have loved him too. Losing him was like cutting my heart out with a pair of pinking shears and flushing it down the john. Sometimes I've almost wished I'd had an abortion. I wouldn't have had Michael, but I wouldn't have lost him either. You know I would have had an abortion, but Mother found out I was pregnant and wouldn't let me. Besides, I didn't have the nerve."

"It takes courage to raise a child too," I said. And to have an illegitimate child back then took a lot.

"But an abortion? They performed them on the kitchen table with a paring knife and no anesthesia. Remember?"

"Yeah."

"Emilio enlisted and went to Vietnam when Mother wouldn't let us get married. You knew that, didn't you?"

"Yes." That's what the sixties were like. The women had illegal abortions, and the men fought an illegal war. Both of them confronted their darkest fears, found out exactly what they were capable of, and nobody was ever the same again.

The phone on the kitchen counter rang. Cindy stared as if it were a coiled snake and let it go on ringing. It takes a lot of patience or a lot of denial to sit beside a ringing phone. I don't have that much of either. I was close to picking it up myself, when Cindy sighed and reached for the receiver. "Hello," she said in a tentative voice and then: "This is Mrs. Reid."

She kept a message pad beside the phone, and she drew birds in flight on it while she listened. "You'll get it next week," she said. She hung up and went back to our talk. "I've envied you sometimes, Neil."

"Why?" Because I wasn't married? Because I was a lawyer? Because I had a lover who was younger and darker and fixed cars for a living?

"Because you've had so many men. I've only had two, Emiliano and Whit."

She'd hit the high end and the low; maybe what was in between was filler. "It only takes one good one," I said.

"Guys always liked you. Why, do you think?"

Because even back then I had the husky voice of a woman who smoked? "They didn't like me *that* much."

"Yeah, they did. Come on, what was it?"

"Tits."

"That's it?"

"Basically. Do you ever wonder what it will be like to walk into a bar or anywhere else and not have every guy in the place staring at them? It's like going through life holding an armful of squirming puppies. I kind of look forward to being a gray, sagging old lady that nobody notices."

"There's got to be more to it than your body."

"Men are easy; you like them, they like you. My mother always liked men; maybe it's genetic."

Cindy probably remembered that my mother was a lonesome highway that I didn't often travel on, but she took a tentative step. "They say the best thing you can do for your daughter is give her a happy mother. Was your mother happy, Neil?"

"Why not?" I asked. "She always did exactly what she wanted to do." That was about as far as I was willing to go. "What about yours?"

"Are you kidding? She knows duty, she knows doing the right thing, she knows survival, but happy? That's one word she'll never know the meaning of."

The phone rang again. Cindy picked it up on the third ring. She listened for a while, said okay and hung up. "Whit broke his glasses," she told me. "He's downtown at the Small Business Association. He works there as a volunteer, helping minority businesses get started, and he wants me to bring him his extra pair."

Working as a volunteer for anything sounded out of character for the self-centered Whit. I let that one go by, but I had my say about the rest of it. "Whit wants you to go all the way downtown to bring him another pair of glasses?"

"It's not that far, and I can drop you off at Mighty on the way."

"The Mighty van will pick me up here. Whit's a grown man. Why can't he just tape his glasses back together?"

"That's the way grown men are, Neil. Spoiled. The ones who grew up rich anyway. They're told from childhood that they're wonderful, and they believe every word of it." She stood up and grabbed her purse. "I think we should get going. He'll complain if I'm late."

"Let him."

"It's not worth the aggravation. Believe me."

It was her house and her husband, and she was determined, so I followed her out to her car, a beat-up blue station wagon with Arizona plates and a country club sticker on the rear window.

On our way to Mighty we passed the Arroyo del Oso soccer field, where a girls' game was in progress. The girls wore short plaid uniforms and knee socks. One of them scored a goal, and while her teammates cheered, she ran down the field strong and graceful as an antelope. When she reached the end, she did a cartwheel and a flip that were victory in motion. Some progress had been made in the last twenty years, I thought. Girls had learned how to run.

8

WHEN CINDY DROPPED ME OFF AT MIGHTY, Ramón Ortiz was standing at the counter, surrounded by admirers, two miniskirted young women with big blond hair and one older woman with tight blue curls.

"Is my car ready?" I asked, pushing through to the counter.

"Neil Hamel, right?" He studied me with eyes that seemed considerably less cavalier than they had in the morning.

"Right."

He pulled out my bill, and I paid with plastic. He searched through the keyboard and found my keys among a bunch that had probably been sitting on their hooks as long as or longer than mine. There were only two keys on my ring—one to the Nissan's door, one to its trunk—but some people kept all their keys on one ring, I noticed: keys to their cars, their houses, their mailboxes, maybe even their hearts. They left them here all day on Ramón Ortiz's keyboard, disobeying one of nature's more important laws: never trust a man who knows he's good-looking. A guy wearing a grease-monkey suit came in from the shop and took a set of keys from the rack.

"You guys aren't very careful with your keys," I said to Ramón.

He handed me mine with a look that said: So? His words, however, were "What is it you do?"

"I'm a lawyer," I replied, expecting to be either asked for advice or dismissed as a scumbag.

"Verdad?" he replied.

"Yeah," I said. True.

On my way back to the office I took a detour by the Albuquerque Women's Club on Siringo, where Martha had attended her two-martini meeting. It was a sprawling one-story stucco building landscaped with the kind of non-native plants that take water greedily from the environment and give back generously in pollen. The garden club met here, I knew, as well as the AWC. I drove down the driveway, which ended in a parking lot. The parking spaces started behind the building, circled the lot and were filled with large American cars. Nobody makes them larger. Anyone who parked on the far side of the lot facing away from the building wouldn't see the front of the car before getting into it. If you parked the same way when you got home, you wouldn't see it then either. If you were under the influence, you might not notice if your car wobbled or handled funny. It was a long shot, but it was one way Martha Conover and her car might have been set up. Another was in the unaccounted-for hour between the time she left here and the time Justine Virga's body was found in the road.

A meeting had just ended, and women were coming out of the building, saying good-bye to each other and walking toward their cars. They were gray- and white-haired ladies, well dressed and prosperous-looking. There wasn't much physically to distinguish one from another. No one was enormously fat, exceptionally tall, strikingly beautiful. No one was emitting any more pheromones than anyone else. I wondered what it's like when looks and capacity to attract men are no longer a factor and you're judged not on what you've been given and worked to preserve but on what you've done, what you've raised, what you own. The path I was taking, that wouldn't be much.

The ladies finished their long good-byes and drove away. I got out of the Nissan and took a look around. The only outside lights were attached to the building, I noticed, and wouldn't do much to light the far side of the lot. I examined the paved area, looking for evidence like broken glass or metal on the ground, but I didn't find any.

I got back in the Nissan and drove north on Siringo, the route Martha would have taken on her way home. About ten minutes from the Women's Club and five from Los Cerros, there's an empty fifteen-acre parcel of land called the Atalaya lot, which is well known in the legal and real estate professions for the amount of litigation it has produced. There aren't many large empty lots left in the Heights, and developers had developed a yen for this one. Fifteen dry and barren acres had generated reams of paper and hundreds of thousands of dollars in legal fees simply because of their location, location and location, the big three in the real estate world. The developers figured the highest and best use would be as a shopping mall, but the neighbors disagreed. The local residents happened to be people with money and influence. They'd fought the developers and—so far anyway—had won. But the developers hadn't given up, and every time they came back they had a more grandiose plan, and each hearing became more acrimonious than the last. A yellow sign attached to a stick in the ground told me another hearing was coming up soon.

I wanted to take a closer look at this place, so I parked the Nissan behind the branch library on Siringo and walked across the lot, following pink scars, the paths dirt bikes had scraped, peeling the skin from the near-naked landscape. This particular piece of town had been imprinted by the tires of boys, not the watering cans of women. Some limp weeds had taken root, had their brief moment in the sun and turned to straw, but most of the ground cover was just passing through. Lizards rustled in the tumbleweeds. A rabbit crossed the path, stopped, wiggled its ears, kept on going. Plastic bags blew into the tumbleweeds and got hung up there. The neighborhood dogs had found their own best use for the property, so I kept my eyes on the ground while I walked it.

When I reached the concrete diversion channel that bisects the lot, I stopped at the edge and looked around. A hawk's black silhouette rode the air waves. A triangular kite got a lift, took a dive. A jet trail disintegrated in a sky that used to be bluer. The Sandias wandered south till they became the Manzanos. I was in the middle of the city and surrounded by space, standing on wasteland; just a few acres away, a condo development sat in a green oasis. A sprinkler system had made the difference.

The diversion channel, which carried runoff from the Sandias to the Rio Grande, was ten feet deep and dry as bone. I followed it east across the lot to Calle San Sebastián. When the street is major, the diversion channels go underneath it. San Sebastián is not that heavily trafficked, and the channel had cut it in two. There's a church on the north side, a school on the south, and you can't get from one to the other unless you go through the ditch, which is marked by yellow wooden barricades to keep people out. Diversion channels present a powerful temptation to the more reckless members of our society, especially when the channels are full of water and the reckless are full of alcohol. The school parking lot was full now, but it wouldn't be later. The church was hidden from view by a high stucco wall that ran along San Sebastián. I was five minutes away from

Los Cerros, but this was as lonely a spot as you'd find in the city, and at night it would be even lonelier.

There was an opening in the concrete wall of the diversion channel, where a pipe drained in. "Darlene Bador's hole" some adolescent had painted in large orange letters. I hoped Darlene would forget about it and grow up to find some kind of personal power, but I hadn't come here to worry about Darlene Bador. It was Justine Virga and Martha Conover that I was thinking about. There were places on either side of the channel where cars had driven onto the lot and parked. The kinds of places where, in the old days, you used to find condoms in the morning and maybe you still did. The dirt was crisscrossed with tire tracks, too many and too mingled to distinguish any one. On the school side, where I was standing, I saw a large dark spot where someone had changed his oil. I inched my way down the steep side wall of the channel and up the other side, where I found a patch of broken glass. Some shards were clear, and some were tinted sunglass brown. Headlights? I wondered. A windshield? I picked up a couple of pieces and put them in my pocket.

Someone could have hot-wired Martha's car, I thought, and driven it here while she was at the AWC meeting or after she went to bed. Someone with keys could have done it faster and been less conspicuous. Justine could have been run over on this lot and the body moved to Los Cerros. Who would be around on a rainy, dark night to notice? A criminal who really wanted privacy could have moved the barricades farther down the road and prevented access altogether. It was also possible that Justine was killed somewhere else, hit by another car, that Martha's car was dented and evidence planted on it here. I saw oil on the ground, but I didn't see anything that looked like blood. Blood washes away; oil lingers forever. It had rained hard on Halloween, and the diversion channel would have been as full and churning as the Rio Grande in snowmelt. Any evidence that fell or got thrown in would have washed to Belen by now.

I felt exposed suddenly and vulnerable as a rabbit when the shadow of a hawk passes overhead, as if something dark and hungry were watching me. A big gray American car with tinted glass drove down San Sebastián on the other side of the ditch. Whoever was in it could see me clearly, but all I saw was dark glass. The car stopped when it got to the barricades, stared at me with a blank black windshield, then backed down the road, making it impossible for me to get the license number.

When I got back to the office I called Saia and told him what I'd observed. "The Atalaya lot," he said. "People park there all the time. They walk their dogs, change their oil. At night kids get drunk or get laid. They fight, headlights are broken. What's unusual about that? We'll have less trouble when it's turned into a mall, gets paved over and lit."

"Maybe it will never get turned into a mall."

"Right. I know a bridge in Massachusetts you might like to buy too."

"It's not far from the Women's Club and Los Cerros," I said. "Someone could have hot-wired Martha's car, driven it over there while she was at the AWC meeting or after she got home, hit Justine and driven the car back. There was time. The APD has Martha's car. You could check out the glass on the lot and see if it matches."

"Come on, Neil, your client hit her. Admit it. She ran Justine Virga down in a Halcion mad-on. And now she's got a Halcion forget-on and doesn't want to remember she did it. Who would hot-wire a car in the Women's Club parking lot anyway? It's too busy."

"Los Cerros isn't that busy. You're the ones who said no one passed through there in the forty-five minutes between the time Martha got home and the time the body was found."

"Martha Conover's car can't be hot-wired."

"Why not?"

"It has a kill switch."

"What's that?"

"An antitheft device that disconnects the battery. You push it in when you park the car, unlock it when you're ready to go."

"Suppose someone had a key?"

"Like who?"

"She left her car at Mighty the week before Halloween," I said. "The key was sitting around on a keyboard all morning just waiting to be copied."

"All right," Saia said. "I'll send someone out to Atalaya to take a look."

While I was talking to Saia, my partner, Brink, wandered into my office, acting like a bored teenager waiting for someone to tell him what to do and how to do it. "Stop drumming your fingers on my desk and get a life" was the assignment I wanted to give him. He humped his eyebrows as I hung up, which meant a question was on the way.

"Are you going to represent Martha Conover?" he asked.

"Looks like it," I said.

"Did she do it?"

"She says she didn't."

His frown created a diversion channel that led from his receding hairline to the bridge of his nose. His eyebrows met across the furrow and squished together in a fuzzy caterpillar kiss. "You think we ought to roll the dice with a wobbler?" he asked.

"A wobbler? What the hell is a wobbler?"

"An unwinnable case."

"It's not *that* unwinnable," I said.

"You gotta hear your horoscope for today," Anna called

from her desk, where she was busy opening a package and reading the newspaper at the same time.

"Why?" I replied.

"It says, 'In your life you are both the marble and the sculptor, and your greatest pleasure is doing what other people say you cannot.'"

"Um," I said.

"Hey, look at this," Anna said, pulling two small black tubes from their padded envelope. "Our skunk guns are here."

"Let me see." I went out to her desk to take a look. I held mine in the palm of my hand. It was, just as the ads said, small enough to carry on a key ring. Anna pulled a larger, white spray bottle from the box. "What's that?" I asked.

"Neutralizer. You spray it around to get rid of the skunk smell."

Brink didn't buy it. "You can never get rid of the smell of a skunk," he said.

"These are all natural, free-range, native New Mexico skunks," I said.

"It beats getting beaten up or murdered," said Anna.

The Kid came for dinner, and we had our personal big three—tacos, tequila and Tecate—at my coffee table. He had already stopped in the parking lot and left a couple of extra tacos with no hot sauce for his buddy, La Bailarina. "How's la viejita?" he asked over dinner, meaning the little old lady Martha Conover.

"Difficult."

He squeezed some lime juice on the top of his Tecate can, took a sip. "She's an old lady, Chiquita."

"She's not that old, and even if she was, that wouldn't give her an excuse to be a narrow-minded bigot." You could say that what we become when we are old is the sum of all the things we do when we are young. Martha Conover had been bigoted when she was younger too. "You feel like going out for dessert, Kid?" I asked when dinner was finished and I'd cleaned up by throwing the paper wrappers away.

"Dessert? Why you want to go out for dessert?"

"I feel like it."

"If you want dessert I'll make you dulce de leche."

Dulce de leche was an Argentine favorite made by sticking a can of evaporated milk in a pan of water and boiling it until it caramelized. It's about as unappetizing as the maté they sip from straws for tea, but in a different way. One is too sweet, one is too bitter. "There's a French place on Academy," I said. "Let's go there."

"Why?"

"I feel like having a French pastry."

The Kid didn't feel like having a French pastry, but he was so startled by my request that he agreed to come. Chez Henri, the French place on Academy, was in a faceless strip mall identical to a hundred thousand strip malls across the West, with a dry cleaner, a semi-ethnic restaurant, a stationery store, a Furrs Cafeteria and an exercise studio that had gone belly-up. The mall made up in parking space for what it lacked in distinction. The interior of Chez Henri aimed for Provençal charm, with rough plaster walls, dark beams in the ceiling, red and white checkered tablecloths and candles in wine bottles. It missed, but it wasn't entirely off the mark. The Kid ordered a Napoleon and an espresso that was dark and thick enough to dissolve a quarter in. I ordered fresh raspberries with cream in spite of my stated desire for a pastry. I had no idea where the raspberries came from at this time of year, but they were plump and delicious. I had a dog, a malamute, when I was a kid, who used to walk up to raspberry bushes and—very carefully—bite the berries off. He thought they were worth the trouble. Me, too.

Chez Henri was small enough to have only one waiter,

who moved at the pace of a somnolent snail. His movements had the deliberate slowness of someone who didn't much like his job, or the people he was waiting on. As Whit had said, the service here wasn't great.

"Some people I know recommended this place," I said when the waiter finally showed up with the desserts. "She's in her late thirties, he's fiftyish. They both have kind of blondish hair. He's big, looks like a football player, in fact, but his hair is getting thin on top. They were here on Halloween."

"Oh, yeah," he said. "Them. They were with another guy, who talked on his cellular phone all night. I don't know who *he* was trying to impress." That would be Ed George, the banker. "They stayed until eleven-thirty. I couldn't go home until they left, and I thought they'd never stop talking."

"Once Whit Reid gets talking, it is hard to stop him," I agreed.

"They didn't leave any kind of tip either." He served the Kid his Napoleon, slouched over to the next table.

"How you like your dessert?" asked the Kid.

"Delicious," said I.

"Who are those people you were talking about?"

"Cindy and Whit Reid. Cindy is Martha Conover's daughter and my old high school friend. Whit is her husband. I was checking on where Whit said they were the night Justine Virga died."

"Why you do that?"

"Just curious."

I shifted to another lane. "I had my oil changed at Mighty today."

"Why? I change your oil for you."

"I know. Martha had her oil changed there the week before Halloween, and I wanted to see what the place was like—if anybody could have taken her keys and copied them. The guys there speak Argentine Spanish. You don't know them, do you?" One of the first things recent immigrants do is find other immigrants from the same place and pool their resources. It's the time-honored way to make it—legally or illegally—in America.

The Kid stirred a couple of teaspoons of sugar into his espresso. "No. I was only ten years old when we left Argentina. I don't know many people from there. Argentinos don't think I am a countryman anyway. Because I lived in Mexico, to them I am a Chicano."

I've never been able to figure out what to call Spanish-speakers myself. A Chicano to me is someone with close ties to Mexico, maybe an illegal alien, maybe not. When one of them is accused of a crime, he or she becomes a Mexican national to the police and the newspapers. I know native New Mexicans whose families have been here for hundreds of years who call themselves Chicanos. It means la raza, the race, and has a certain kind of "this is who I am, roots and all" militancy. Besides, New Mexico was once part of old Mexico, and if you go back far enough, New Mexicans are Mexicans too. If you go back even further, they are descendants of the original Spanish settlers, and I also know native New Mexicans with roots who call themselves Spanish, and sometimes they're related to the ones who call themselves Chicanos. On the other hand, when Martha Conover says Spanish, it sounds like an insult. As for me, I'm an Anglo but never an Angla: nobody uses that word, although a female Chicano can be a Chicana. I'm a WASP too, but people in New Mexico also don't use that word.

"The Argentinos are muy arrogantes, the Mexicans say. Because they don't have Indian blood, they think they are more European and better than the other Latinos," the Kid continued.

"They don't have Indian blood because they killed all the Indians off."

The Kid shrugged. "They did that in this country too, Chiquita. The Argentinos think they are better educated and have more culture than the other Latin Americans, the Mexicans say. Who knows? Maybe they do."

The waiter showed up with the check, a subtle hint that it was time to leave. I ignored it and ordered a cappuccino. The Kid asked for another espresso. A candle flickered in the middle of the table. We leaned over it and whispered like conspirators, even though there were only a few other people in Chez Henri and none of them were in hearing distance. It was the kind of place that made you want to whisper and linger. Some zippy accordion music in the background wasn't all that different from the kind of music the Kid played. We were only a few blocks from La Vista, but the setting was so far removed from any we'd ever been in together that it put a different spin on things. I asked the Kid a question that I'd asked him before but he'd never completely answered. "Why did your family leave Argentina?"

Maybe because he was out of his element, or an espresso buzz had put him in a talkative mood, he answered me this time. "It was the time of the dirty war, and it was crazy there. The left, the right; the comunistas, the fascistas; the guerrillas, the military; the Perónists, the anti-Perónists; the Montoneros, the anticomunistas—everybody was fighting everybody else. The military leaders owned their zones. They could put in prison and torture anybody they wanted, and nobody could stop them. They had a torture machine they called Susan. They poured water on people, tied them to the machine and shocked them or killed them with electricity, but they did it so there were no marks on the body. Twenty-five thousand people died or disappeared in the dirty war—Los Desaparecidos, they called them. The military took them from their homes, put them on the floor of a car and put a blanket over them so no one knew where they were going. Sometimes they buried Los Desaparecidos in big holes, sometimes they threw them in the river, sometimes they put cement on their feet and they dropped them in the ocean. You could see them on the bottom, moving like *that*." His hand made a motion like grass swaying in water. "The military took Los Desaparecidos children and raised them themselves or sold them. They hated the parents enough to kill them, but they wanted their children. Crazy, no? They have a saying there, God is an Argentino, but when something bad happens, they say God was busy in another place. My father taught at the university. The military took away his job, and we went to Mexico before they took away him." It was a long speech for the Kid, and he finished with a gulp of espresso.

"What did your father teach?"

"Filosofía."

It seemed pretty harmless to me. "Why did the military eliminate his job?"

The Kid shrugged. "Maybe he gave somebody's son a bad grade. Maybe they think filosofía is revolutionary. Who knows? They could do what they wanted."

"The woman that supposedly got killed by Martha Conover's car is from Argentina too."

"Where?"

"I don't know."

"Why did she come here?"

"Maybe for the same reasons you did. Would you ever go back?" I asked. There he was the son of a professor. Here, in some circles anyway, he was a wetback and a spic.

"No, I am a norteamericano now. The Argentinos are funny people. They are inteligentes and sensitivos but they can also be stupid and cruel. Here people are impulsivos; they kill when they feel like it. There they think about it first. They are . . . how you say it?"

"Calculating."

"And cruel. They tortured people and made them suffer.

Politics were an excuse for the criminals to steal and kill. Here nobody needs an excuse. That's freedom, no?" He smiled, but then he turned serious again. "I think about what happened to my father, and I will never go back. They took away his work and his life. I have my own business in America. No general can take that from me."

"Things have gotten better in Argentina, haven't they?"

"Sure, but you never know when they are going to get bad again. I like it here; it is the land of opportunity."

That's how it looked to him, but to me we seemed to be becoming more third world every day. The rich got richer, the poor poorer, the national debt multiplied like bacteria, even the air seemed grayer than it used to be. "Did your mother die after you got to Mexico?" I asked.

"Claro. Something inside her broke when she left Argentina."

The Kid and I came from different backgrounds, different countries. He was younger and better looking, and we didn't listen to the same music. You could say that trying to reconcile the opposites generated the heat, but when it's not broke, I don't analyze it. We did have one thing in common—both of us had lost our mothers. In her own way, my mother was a desaparecido too.

The waiter yawned as he made another pass by our table. "Vamos," I said to the Kid.

"Bueno," he replied.

Coming here had been my idea; I paid for the coffee and dessert, leaving the waiter a large tip, more than he deserved, but he'd told me what I wanted to know and I wouldn't want anybody to think I had cheapness in common with Whit Reid.

We had taken the Nissan, and when we got back to La Vista I parked it in its numbered space. La Bailarina's van was parked in the visitor's space next to the Dumpster. She was there every night when I went to bed and gone when I got up in the morning. Either she had someplace to go or she didn't want to be seen here in daylight. She had one of those sun screens that had a pair of dark glasses on one side and said NEED HELP. CALL POLICE on the other. The dark glasses were facing out. The curtains over the other windows were pulled tight.

The Kid and I went inside, turned out the lights, got into bed and made love in the dark. Afterwards he went right to sleep—he always does, even after three cups of espresso. I stayed awake and watched the wind sway the curtains and shift the patterns of light on the floor. Winter was in the wind. It caught a dry leaf and rattled it against the window. A train cried as it passed through the city, a siren circled from somewhere near Tramway, car waves crested and broke with the lights on Montgomery—the sounds of a night that's in motion. The woman climbed into her convertible, put the top down, started the engine, backed out of the driveway and left a garden behind for her husband to water. She was going to meet a man, and she was laughing. She was at the peak of her power, and she thought she could stay there forever. Her brown hair lifted behind her and floated. I made a sound that woke up the Kid. He rolled over, put his arm around my waist, his cheek against the back of my neck.

"You have that dream again, Chiquita?"

"Yeah," I said.

9

NEEDED TO TELL MARTHA CONOVER what I had seen at the Atalaya lot, so I stopped by her place the next day on my way home from work. I didn't call first; I wanted to see what she was like on the afternoons when she wasn't expecting visitors, how quickly the vodka went down then. I got gas at the Texaco on Wyoming, one of those stations where you didn't have to pay in advance—in the daytime anyway. As I pulled the nozzle from the regular unleaded pump, the gas gushed out, down the side of the pump, around my feet, across the ground. "Son of a bitch," I said. A smarter woman than I ran out of the convenience store, took the nozzle from my hand, flicked off the switch in the handle that keeps the gas flowing automatically and hung it back on the pump.

"Why would somebody put the nozzle back with the switch still on?" I asked. "*How* could somebody put it back with the switch on?"

"Got me," the attendant said. "Be glad you weren't smoking."

My shoes smelled of gasoline, but I didn't feel like going all the way home to change them. I went on to Los Cerros, hoping Martha wouldn't notice. It looked promising when she came to the door with a half-empty glass in her hand.

"You doing anything this afternoon?" I asked.

"No," she replied. She was home all alone, but she was dressed in a suit and heels, as if she was going to tea.

"I need to talk to you," I said.

"Come in."

The ice rattled in her glass; background music tinkled on the CD. "I've been listening to a Mozart sympathy," she told me. The phone rang. She excused herself and walked into the bedroom to take the call, marking time with the ice cubes in her glass.

I sat on her chintz sofa and waited while she talked. Waiting isn't my forte, but I can do it when I have to. I found myself listening to the music, which at the moment was just a piano. There wasn't much else to do; Martha was too far away for me to eavesdrop on her call. I'd heard Mozart before—who hasn't?—but I'd never listened. The sun came in through the open drapes and settled in my lap like a cat. The pianist's fingers moved over the keyboard with exquisite precision, lingering on every note. I imagined fingers roaming slowly over that part of my body where the vital organs are located. It was deeply sensual music, music that knew all about loss and desire, and it had a familiar kind of tension to it. I wanted it to last forever at the same time I longed for the end. When I felt like I couldn't stand it another minute, the orchestra rolled in with a crash and broke the spell.

I got up, pouring the sun out of my lap, crossed the room, picked up the CD container Martha had left on top of the machine and read the program notes. She had been wrong; it wasn't a sympathy, or a symphony either, I'd been listening to. It was Mozart's ninth piano concerto. The pianist was Alicia de Larrocha, a woman approaching her seventies, who lived in Barcelona. It was a wonderful gift to play so sensually at that age, at any age. Mozart fathered six children, and four of them died in infancy, according to the program notes. He was only thirty-five when he died, half of his allotted span, but thirty-five years wasn't so bad for him, because he lived twice as fast as anyone else. He was the supreme genius of music, the notes read. "If only the whole world could feel the power of harmony!" Mozart was quoted as saying, and "The function of harmony is to proceed toward a resolution." It's also the function of litigation.

I heard the disharmonious tinkling of ice that said Martha Conover was coming back into the room.

"You like Mozart?" she asked when she saw the CD notes in my hand.

"It's very sensual music," I said.

"Mozart? Mozart is not sensual. Mozart is orderly. These days, people your age think about nothing but sex. Sex has caused more misery than all the wars put together. I've never understood what all the fuss was about, and if you ask me, it is the most overrated activity in America."

"I don't know. There's football."

"I hope you're using one of those things men wear."

I didn't answer, just watched her sipping at her drink. It might not have been the right time for some business, but for the business I had—to discover what Martha Conover was like when she'd been seriously drinking—it was perfect. She turned the music off, walked over to the sofa, sat down, put her glass precisely in the middle of the coaster, scoring a bull's-eye. Except for the slip about the symphony, it appeared so far that Martha Conover when she'd been drinking wasn't all that different from Martha Conover when she was sober. "What did you want to talk to me about?" she asked.

"Do you remember where you parked your car at the AWC meeting?"

"Of course I remember."

"Was it facing toward the building or away from it?"

"Why are you talking so loud? You don't have to shout at me."

"Who's shouting?" I asked. I repeated my question in a deliberate voice with long spaces between the words, as if I were talking to a pet or a three-year-old. "Where did you park your car at the AWC meeting?"

"At the far end of the lot, away from the building."

"Did you notice anything wrong with it when you drove it home?" I asked. "Did it handle poorly?"

"No."

"It is possible that your car was stolen from the AWC parking lot or from this lot, that Justine was hit somewhere else, the car returned and Justine's body moved to Los Cerros. The Atalaya lot is dark and lonely at night, and it's not far from here," I said. "Did you have the kill switch on?"

She looked right at me with her blue eyes, but she hesitated before she spoke. Maybe she was looking for the best answer. Maybe she was trying to remember. "I think so," she eventually said.

"Do you always have your car serviced at Mighty?"

"No. That was the first time."

"Did you know the man who runs the place is from Argentina?"

"No."

"Why did you go there?"

"Whit recommended it."

"Is there anyone *you* know who had a motive to kill Justine and set you up for the murder?"

"Her aunt, Mina Alarid, dislikes me. You saw those lies she gave to the newspaper."

"Why would she dislike you?"

"Because I didn't think her niece was the right kind of girl for my grandson."

"Why not?"

"Too Spanish."

"Your grandson was half Spanish, wasn't he?"

"He wasn't raised Spanish."

What she didn't say—she didn't need to—was that he didn't look Spanish either. I had crossed the room and was sitting next to her on the sofa. She wrinkled her nose and sniffed, either at me or at the too-Spanish Justine. "What's that god-awful smell?" she asked.

"Gasoline," I said.

When I left Martha's and drove down Los Cerros hill, it was getting dark, and the lights in the apartments were coming on one by one. Martha's computerized system had the jump on the tenants. The outside lights had already been lit automatically. She may not have done that well with her personal life, but she knew how to manage a building. The bare arm of an aspen scratched at the sky. Here and there, a gold leaf was suspended from a branch like an ornament left hanging when Christmas is over. The full moon lit the backside of the Sandias in preparation for a show-stopping debut. The speed bumps kept me to a creeping five miles an hour, and I looked idly at the rear ends of the parked cars as I drove by. I read the bumper stickers first. VISUALIZE WHIRLED PEAS—that one had to be from Santa Fe. VISUALIZE OPERATING TURN SIGNALS—that could be anywhere in the Land of Enchantment, where they don't bother with car inspection. Next I studied the license plates, taking my own private survey of the state of the national economy. When times get tough, the unemployed get going, and their first stop is often an apartment complex in the Sunbelt. I saw Massachusetts, of course, and California, New Hampshire's Live Cheap or Die, North Carolina's First in Flight, the red and white of Arizona, the S&L fraud state, which caused me to slow down to two and a half, as those plates happened to be on a big blue station wagon with a country club sticker on the window. It was parked at the bottom of the hill in the handicapped section, and I had to wonder what Cindy and/or Whit was doing there. Martha hadn't been expecting either of them, I knew.

I parked the Nissan and got out. If it was Cindy, I'd say hello. If it was Whit, I'd leave. It was dinnertime, and the sprinklers on the lawn here were running. The wind blew the spray across the sidewalk, and my feet were getting wet. The condition my shoes were in, a wash couldn't do them any harm. As I walked down the sidewalk to a building marked 53, a roadrunner ran from a piñon and hid behind a juniper. My running shoes squished on the pavement, the sprinklers tickety-ticked. There were four apartments in this building, and I had no idea which bell to ring, so I looked at the windows. Two were dark, one had drawn curtains. The drapes in the fourth apartment were partially open, and the light was on. I walked across the soggy green lawn, past the tree-and-pebble landscaping, and peeked in. Dusk was on my side. I could see into the light, but the occupants couldn't see out into the evening. Cindy was sitting on a bed, holding hands with and talking intensely to a man in a wheelchair, whose back was to me. Whatever she had been acting so guilty about at her mother's the other night, it looked as though it hadn't been sex. It also looked like a private moment, one that even I was embarrassed to be spying on, so I got into the Nissan and went home.

On the way, I thought about what was for dinner. It was the Kid's night to play the accordion at El Lobo, so he wouldn't be showing up with a bag of tacos under his arm. My mind took a walk through the shelves of my refrigerator and encountered four half-full bottles of Pace picante sauce, with blue fuzz forming on top of the red salsa, and an open bag of Ortega tortillas, crisp and curling at the edges. I moved on to the refrigerator door, where I discovered a bottle of raspberry-vinegar salad dressing, a jar of mayonnaise, another of mustard. Was that Grey Poupon or Gulden's? I couldn't be sure. Next I entered the vegetable bin and exited quickly—a couple of limp carrots, a calcified lime, a slimy jícama. When I opened the freezer and found only ice, I decided to stop at Brown's and pick up a couple of Lean Cuisines. Brown's is my favorite supermarket; the checkout clerks are downright surly, and a surly clerk is hard to find in Albuquerque, the city of aggressive politeness. I paid for my Lean Cuisines. The checkout guy took my money, gave me my change and never once looked at my face. He didn't ask about my personal life, wish me a nice day or get someone with whiskey breath to help me put my bags in the car. I felt right at home.

When I got to La Vista I remembered that the Kid wouldn't be showing up with tacos for La Bailarina, and I didn't have anything to give her. I didn't feel like going out again. The van's curtains were closed, the sun screen was in place, and she seemed to be asleep anyway. The invitation to Baxter, Johnson's party was still in my purse. I pulled it out and slid it under her windshield wiper. When I turned around I saw Truman, the night watchman, standing beside the Dumpster with his hand out, just to let me know he hadn't been ignoring La Bailarina's presence in the parking lot for nothing.

"Evening," he said

"Evening," I replied. He was waiting for me to fill his palm with liquor or silver. I slipped him a twenty.

"Why, thank you, ma'am," he said.

"It's nothing," I replied.

As I crossed the lot to my apartment, I noticed a parked truck, a shiny black one, with the lights on. *Passion* was scrolled in purple neon across the back end, and purple lights lit the pavement underneath the truck like the landing gear of a UFO. It was somebody's idea of macho cool, but the engine wasn't running and nobody was sitting in the cab. The owner had probably come home before dark and forgotten his lights were on. I thought about knocking on doors to find him, but I went inside and unbagged my groceries instead.

There are people who cook and people who heat. Those of us who heat know how fast water boils in the high New Mexico air. I cooked the Lean Cuisines in their plastic pouches, and when they were done to perfection I scooped them out and ate them. Before I got into bed I made my offering to the sleep god—a shot of tequila—but José Cuervo was having an off night and it wasn't enough. I kicked the sheets and squeezed the pillow until I was good and bored, and then I grabbed the remote and zapped the TV on. When it comes to flipping channels, I have one of the fastest trigger fingers in the West. It was the hour when the secure, the steady, the regular and the married are fast asleep, when the guy in dark glasses plugs God, the fat boy dances in the street, when the couples on *Love Connection* do their dance of approach and avoidance, the Juice Man sells juice, when what looks like a real program is a hard-sell pitch, when Suzanne Somers squeezes her Thighmaster and powers a lot of bad jokes, and Vicki LaMotta sells rejuvenating face cream, the time of night when men get older but women don't. In thirty years on TV, Johnny Carson went from smug to mature, from dark hair to white, from rich to richer to richer still. Through the wonders of modern science, Vicki LaMotta might look the same when she's a hundred and ten. But the function of life is to move toward a resolution. It's programmed in the cells to be young, older, old. Not to live out the cycle is to get stuck. The one thing worse than a clock that ticks too loud is a clock that doesn't tick at all. When I finally fell asleep, I dreamed about the woman who'd stayed thirty-five for thirty years. When I woke up, the TV screen was blank, the numbers on the digital clock flashed 2:25. I looked out the window. The truck was still there, but its purple passion had burned out. I got up, went to the bathroom and took one of Martha Conover's Halcions. Like the manufacturer says, it acted quick. If I had any more dreams—good or bad—I didn't remember. Mother's little helper didn't leave me drowsy the next day, and if it caused any bizarre behavior or loss of inhibitions, I didn't notice. I *was* late for work, but it doesn't take drugs to do that.

By the time I left La Vista, the parking lot was empty (the passion truck had gotten its batteries recharged, and La Bailarina had gone wherever it is she went in the daytime) but the streets were full. It was one of those days when everybody out there seems crazy or drugged. They were going somewhere and just as fast as the traffic would allow. We all travel the same highways, but we'd like to do it at our own speed. The boy behind me in a blue Honda wore a baseball hat turned backward. He was pissed that I had stopped at a yellow light and disobeyed the three-left-turns-on-yellow rule. I could tell because I could see him glaring at me in my rearview mirror. "Lighten up, dude," I said, but he wasn't listening. The boy passed me as soon as he could and was replaced by a couple who stared straight ahead in stiff and icy silence as if they were balancing between them a hostility balloon inflated by years of bad marriage. Driving in city traffic requires full attention, but not many were giving it their best shot. My fast-acting Halcion had already passed through my system and wasn't interfering with my driving skills, I hoped, but I had to wonder what everybody else out there on the highway had done: who was hung over, who had smoked grass last night, snorted coke, swallowed Xanax; who was angry, who was depressed, who was getting divorced, who was getting senile; who hadn't had any breakfast, who had had too much coffee; who had taken antihistamines, who was sneezing her head off. Everybody was driving high-powered machines, but how many of us were up to the job?

My first stop was Los Cerros, the handicapped section, building number 53 to be exact. I wanted to know who had been giving Cindy wet feet and why she'd acted so guilty about it. There were no cars parked in front of the building. Everybody seemed to have gone to work, just as I'd hoped. The sprinklers were off, the sidewalk was dry. I parked and walked into the middle of the building, where the front doors and mailboxes are. The apartment I was interested in, right front, had a D on the door. I looked at the metal mailboxes, but there was no name on the box, only the number, 53D. I already knew that. A TV blared from behind the door of the apartment across the hall; someone else hadn't gone to work. I heard the sound of a metal walker scrape the floor. The door opened, and I recognized the theme song of a daytime soap. An old woman stood in the doorway, supporting herself on the metal walker and staring at me. I'd forgotten that the elderly don't go to work. Her face was lined and cracked like the floor of Death Valley in summer. White whiskers sprouted from her chin. Her curls had a bluish tint. Her back humped as she hunched over her walker. Her skin color went beyond unhealthy. It was the color of the ashes long after the life force has gone up in smoke. But her eyes were bright and shrewd, a couple of gemstones that had survived the fire.

"He's not home," she said, an indication she'd been watching me through the peephole in her door.

"Who?" It was my subtle attempt to get the name of the occupant of 53D without revealing who I was or why I wanted to know.

It didn't work. "Him." She nodded toward the door. "He went to the Last Chance Thrift Shop. Took his typewriter and some old clothes with him. He asked me if I had anything to give away, but I don't."

"Actually, I'm looking for Paul Rodríguez." It was a name that came to me from out of nowhere.

"You coulda got the wrong building," she said without conviction. "*Maybe* you want fifty-five D."

"Maybe I do."

"You watch the soaps?" she asked. I might have been the first woman she'd talked to all day, maybe even all week, and now that she had me in her web she didn't want to let me go.

"No. I work," I said. I consider watching the soaps about the most unproductive daytime activity a person can engage in, but I didn't say so. She wouldn't have listened anyway.

"Sallie and Jesse are getting a divorce. And Lucy is pregnant with Teddy's twins, but Teddy is in jail for killing Joe, who was sleeping with Lucy, but the twins are really Teddy's, even though he thinks they are Joe's."

So this was what women who stayed home did when they got together during the day—talked about all the inexplicable things people do, like screw and kill each other, the same things I talked about at work. I looked at the place on my wrist where a watch ought to be. "Nice meeting you, but I have to get going. I need to track down Paul."

"I'll be ninety years old next month," the woman said, hunching lower over her walker and fixing her stony eyes on me. Once the very old get you in their orbit, they don't like to let you go. "Do you know what that feels like?"

I smelled the overcooked broccoli smell drifting out of her apartment, listened to the blaring soap, watched the hair quiver on her chin. "Well . . . ," I said.

"It's no fun. I can tell you that. Here he comes now."

"Who?"

"The man you're looking for." Her gemstone eyes said I hadn't put anything over on *her* and had been a fool to try.

A man in a wheelchair was rolling down the walk. He wore a white T-shirt and black leather gloves with no fingers, which protected his palms from the wheels. His legs were limp and useless, strapped into the chair, but he had a hefty upper body. He was a wheelchair athlete—the one, in fact, who had stared at me from the tennis court the previous week. His wheelchair was a streamlined, racing model, but the exercise hadn't exactly gotten him in shape. His skin had a marbled look, as if layers of fat had slipped between the muscle. His face was full, and his features seemed obscured by the flesh.

"How's it going, Dorothy?" He spoke to his neighbor but his eyes were on me.

"She's looking for you." The woman nodded in my direction. I tried to find some excuse for standing in front of his door, but what? That I had cookies or magazines or God to sell?

He rolled up close and looked at me. His eyes were the color of Jack Daniel's. His grin was quick and sharp as a bite. "Hello, Nellie," he said.

There aren't many people around who know my old high school nickname. Hardly any are Hispanic, and only one of them knows Cindy Reid. "Emiliano?" I asked. "You can't be Emiliano Velásquez."

"Yeah," he said. "I can and I am."

The Emiliano I'd known had gotten fat and crippled. David had sunk back into the marble. The boy god had become an imperfect man, which had to be about the worst thing that could happen to a god. Before I could stop them, two words slipped out. "Oh, no," I said.

"Don't worry, Nellie," Emilio said. "Everybody does it."

But I wasn't everybody. I had been a friend in another, better time. "I'm sorry," I said.

"Shit happens, or as Dorothy likes to say, life sucks and then you don't die. Right, Dorothy?"

"Right," Dorothy agreed.

"This is a lot worse than shit," I said.

"Don't worry about it. I'm a survivor."

"Well, I see you two have a lot to talk about," Dorothy said. When nobody denied it, she turned around laboriously in her walker, went back into her apartment, shut the door and scraped across the floor.

The fact that I was standing and Emilio wasn't didn't make this any easier. "Vietnam?" I asked.

"Yeah. The last step I ever took was on top of a land mine."

"Why didn't Cindy tell me?"

"She had her reasons. I'll tell you all about 'em, but first let's go inside."

"Okay," I said.

10

EMILIANO'S APARTMENT WAS SMALLER than the Reids' kitchen. It had about as much furniture as mine but a lot less mess. It was, in fact, as neat as a motel room ready for the next traveler. There were no unread magazines and newspapers on the coffee table, no overflowing ashtrays, and no clothes on the floor. Emilio picked up after himself.

"You keep a tight ship," I said.

"That's what Cindy says." He smiled. "I'm too poor to be a pig. I don't do so bad for a cripple or an otherly abled. That's what they're calling us now: otherly ableds."

"Is that anything like calling a divorce lawyer a marriage counselor?"

"Something like that," he said. "Hell, I'm a paraplegic. I live in a fucking wheelchair. I'll never use my legs again. No matter what you call it, it sucks, but I've had plenty of time to get used to it by now. How'd you know I live here, Nellie? It's not something Cindy or I have been advertising."

"I didn't know. I just happened to see her car parked here yesterday on my way home from Martha's. I thought I'd stop and say hello. I saw her talking to you through the window, and—I'll admit it—I wanted to find out who you were.

Cindy gave me the feeling the other day that she was hiding something; you were it."

"Cindy thought that now that her mother can't drive anymore, it would be all right to leave her own car out front. We didn't think about you. You're pretty observant."

"I try to be."

"Can I get you a drink?"

"How 'bout a glass of water," I said.

"You got it."

The only decorations in Emilio's living room were two photographs in brass frames, standing on a table. While he went to get the glass of water, I picked up the pictures. In the first one Justine Virga was leaning against a wall, wearing a black beret and a black leotard with a scooped-out neckline. I'd seen her before, but this was the first time she really came into focus. The blackness of her hair and the leotard gave her pale skin the look of moonlight floating on dark water. She had a long, graceful neck, and she held her head high, making a deep shadow under her chin. A black curl that had fallen loose was a question mark on her forehead. She had the pouty lips and high cheekbones of a model but the eyes of a desperado. They had the sad, passionate recklessness of a gaucho, a tango dancer, a gypsy, and there were dark smudges under them that hadn't been caused by smeared makeup. Martha had said those eyes were open as she lay on the ground at Los Cerros. What was she looking at when she faced the final mystery? I wondered. Headlights?

The other photograph was of the fair-haired Michael Velásquez. He was leaning against the silver Porsche, wearing jeans, a T-shirt and running shoes and smiling dreamily. It was easy to see how these two had fallen in love: one was gentle, one was wild, both were beautiful—and now both were dead.

Emilio came back into the room. "They were two good-looking people," I said.

"They were beautiful on the inside too."

"Justine looks older than Michael."

"She was by a couple of years, which Martha didn't approve of. Justine had more experience too; Martha didn't like that either."

"Did it bother you to have a son who looks so much like his mother?"

"Not when the mother is Cindy," Emilio said. "Miguel looked Anglo and was raised Anglo, but Justine brought out the Latino in him—another thing that didn't make the old lady happy."

"What was Michael doing with a Porsche?" I asked him.

"You won't believe this, Nellie." If he had been anyone else I would have told him not to call me that, but he was my old friend Emiliano. "It was the weirdest thing. Miguel found this ad in the newspaper for a Porsche for five hundred dollars. I said it was a mistake, there had to be some zeroes missing, but he said what the heck, he'd give the guy a call. There was a divorce going on that the husband didn't want. He'd agreed to sell all the couple's possessions and give the wife half as a settlement, so he sold them all dirt cheap. It was his way of getting even."

He was right. I didn't believe it. I also didn't believe I was going to win the lottery or get married and live happily ever after. I knew for sure I was never going to own a Porsche. It sounded like one of those apocryphal stories you hear all over America that everybody swears happened to somebody that somebody else knew. Like the one where a pet python gets loose and ends up in the pipes of an apartment building. Someone is going to the toilet, looks down and sees the python staring at her. "It reminds me of the story of the python in the punch bowl," I said.

"What?"

"Nothing," I replied. "Justine looks like a gypsy."

"She mighta been," he said. "She was from Argentina, you know."

"When did she come here?"

"Several years ago. She lived with her aunt, Mina Alarid, for a few years before she met Miguel. After he died she moved to Colorado, but she came back every year on the anniversary of his death."

"When did she get here this year?"

"The Saturday before Halloween. After Miguel died I had a hole in my heart big enough to put your fist through. Justy and I helped each other, and she got to be close as a daughter to me." He shook his head. "Now she's gone too. When death gets into a family, sometimes it won't let go. Miguel and Justy are like waves. I can forget about them for a while, and then the wave comes along and pushes me under. Bad as Justy's dying is, Miguel's was worse. That was a wave that came out of nowhere and flattened me. Of all the rotten things that can happen in life, you never think your son is going to die before you do. Justy didn't surprise me so much; I kind of knew we'd lose her someday."

"Why?"

"She didn't care whether she lived or not after Miguel died. She had that faraway look in her eye. It's a look I've seen too much of."

"Vietnam?"

"Yeah. I got my green card out of it, but I hated that war. You know what was even worse?" He gripped the wheels of his chair and stared at me until I thought the brown would bleed through his irises and stain the white. "I loved it too, and I hated it that I loved it. I went through some bad, bad times when I got back."

"Drugs?" I asked.

"Drugs, alcohol, you name it. I was trying to kill myself

without taking the responsibility. But I got my act together eventually and was a good father to Miguel. I learned that the only way you get over something is to go through it. At least we had the time we did. Except for the year with Cindy, it was the best part of my life."

"How long have you been living here?" I asked.

"I got here not long after Miguel did. Whit Reid wasn't being any kind of a father, and Miguel asked Cindy to find me. When I found out where he was, I moved here. With my disability pay I can live anywhere."

"Cindy tracked you down?"

"Yeah. She's learning how to stand up to the old lady."

"Doesn't Martha know you're here?"

He laughed. "Are you kidding? I could roll right by her and she wouldn't know the difference. People in wheelchairs are invisible to her. She only put this section for the handicapped in because she had to to get her permit. Believe me, it wasn't out of the kindness of her heart. To her we're just government checks. Besides, even people I used to know well can look right in my eyes and not recognize me these days."

"I'm sorry," I said again.

"Don't worry about it. You look good, Nellie."

"Not that good. I go by Neil now."

"That's right. You're a lawyer, aren't you? Cindy tells me you're representing Martha."

"I am."

"That's why Cindy couldn't tell you I was here, you know. She didn't want to put you in the position of having to hide something from the old lady. Will you have to tell her?"

"I don't know yet. I won't if I don't have to."

"She's a hard-hearted woman, but she's gonna need your help, because in one way or another she killed Justy."

"How?"

"She never stopped blaming her for Miguel's death, and she wouldn't let Justy forgive herself."

"You know a note typed on a manual typewriter was found in Justine's pocket that said—"

"'I knew this was going to happen, but I couldn't prevent it.' Right?"

"How did you know that?"

"The old lady told Cindy, and Cindy told me."

"Who wrote it? Do you have any idea?"

"A psychic, I think." I looked into his whiskey-colored eyes. The typewriter that his neighbor Dorothy had seen on its way to Last Chance was floating down my mind's river, through a channel, out to sea. If he was lying, I wasn't ready to confront him with it yet.

"A psychic?"

"Yeah. There's a New Age fair going on at the Pyramid, and Justy went there the day before she died."

"Did she tell you who she saw?"

"Some woman from Santa Fe named Sky."

"You don't mean Cielo?"

"Yeah, that's it. You know her?"

"Yeah. What did she say?"

"Justy wouldn't tell me, but it wasn't good. I could tell that much from her expression when she got back."

I felt I'd seen and heard enough about bad news and death for one morning. I put my hand on Emilio's shoulder; he put his hand on top of mine and gave it a squeeze. "I'll be in touch," I said.

"I hope so, Nellie," he replied.

I called Cindy the minute I reached Hamel and Harrison, but Emilio had gotten to her first. "You could have told me the truth about Emilio," I said.

"I didn't lie. I didn't tell you everything, but I didn't lie. It's not the same." Cindy and her mother had more in common than she thought.

"It's pretty damn close."

"I knew you before you became a lawyer, Neil," she said.

And I knew her before she became a liar. At least I thought I did. "You should have told me. It's not my idea of fun to come across Emilio in a wheelchair and have him watch the expression on my face when I find out he's a paraplegic."

"You didn't have to follow me."

"I wasn't. I happened to be leaving your mother's, and I saw your car."

"I couldn't tell you, Neil. You're working for Mother, and we don't want Mother to know. She'd be furious."

"You think Emilio has been living at Los Cerros for years and your mother doesn't know? She may be a . . . She may be difficult, but she's not stupid."

"You didn't recognize him. Why would she? Besides I hardly ever go there; only when I know Mother won't be driving by. Usually when we get together we meet somewhere else."

"Um," I said.

"Promise me you won't tell her, Neil."

"I can't," I said. "If I don't want my clients to lie to me, I can't very well lie to them. There are a couple of things I need to ask you."

"Go ahead."

"Does your mother usually use her kill switch?"

"Always. She's paranoid that someone will steal her Buick."

"Did Whit recommend she have the car serviced at Mighty?"

"Yeah. He'd been there and he liked the place."

"Emilio told me a crazy story about Michael buying his Porsche for five hundred dollars from a guy who was getting a divorce. Do you believe that?"

It was one thing to accuse Cindy or even her mother of

being a liar, quite another to accuse her son. Her voice had the cold smoke of her mother's vodka bottle. "Michael was a very sweet boy, Neil," she said, in a voice that came from the back of the freezer. "He never lied to me or anyone else."

"And he didn't take drugs either."

"That's right. He didn't."

"What about Justine? Your mother thinks she was involved with drug dealers."

"You know my mother. She likes to believe the worst of people."

"Emilio said Justine didn't care if she lived or died anymore. You don't think she might have thrown herself in front of Martha's car, do you?"

"It's possible," Cindy said. "Justine wouldn't forgive herself until Mother forgave her, and Mother never would do that. People Mother's age went through some hard times with the Depression and the war. That's what the sixties were all about, weren't they? Trying to escape from our parents' difficult lives?"

"Maybe."

"Hard times make hard hearts."

"Not always," I said.

"Just so you don't think I am hiding anything else, there is something I should tell you, Neil. Nobody likes to think their Mother is capable of murder, but mine *has* killed."

"Your mother?"

"Her best friend, Kay Hooper, was dying of cancer. Mother got a prescription for painkillers from her own doctor and gave Kay an overdose. 'It was something I had to do,' Mother said."

"That's different. The woman was dying anyway. She was probably in terrible pain."

"So was Justine," Cindy said.

And so was Cindy Reid.

11

I WENT OUT TO THE RECEPTION AREA, to find Anna reading the *Journal* and drinking coffee. Brink stood behind her, reading over her shoulder. It was Friday, when the paper lists the weekend's coming events. "Do me a favor, will you?" I asked Anna. "Check and see if the New Age fair is still on."

Brink's eyebrows scrunched way up in an exaggerated gesture, like that of an actor trying to reach the last row. "*You're* going to a New Age fair?"

"You don't even listen when I read your horoscope," Anna said.

"It's business," said I.

Anna flipped through the pages. "On again this week-end."

"Good," I said. "Remember the psy-chic from Santa Fe, the one who knew Lonnie Darmer?"

"The one who washes her hair in Perrier?"

"Evian."

"Does that make her a bubblehead?" asked Brink.

"It makes her a babblehead," said Anna. "She psychic-babbles."

"She babbles for bucks," I said. "And makes more money

at it than we do." If Brink or I could ever afford a big house in Santa Fe, it wouldn't be in this lifetime.

"What about her?" asked Anna.

"Justine Virga went to see her the day before she died. A sealed note was found in Justine's pocket that said: 'I knew this was going to happen, but I couldn't prevent it.' Maybe Cielo wrote it."

"You mean she gave Justine a note saying she was going to die, then told her not to open it?" Anna asked. Her eyebrows went up too.

"It's possible."

"Way weird," said Anna.

"Have you ever been to a New Age fair?" I asked Anna.

"Once. I had my cards read."

"What did they say?" That she would meet a man with a nonstop stereo?

"That my boyfriend was smart in some ways, stupid in others, and that made him mean," she said.

"I knew a psychic once who breathed into the mouth of a chicken," Brink said. "You know what happened? The chicken died."

Anna and Brink went back to the newspaper. I went into my office, where I debated asking Saia to send an investigator out to the Pyramid to question Cielo. But I knew what he'd say. "C'mon, Neil, those psychic dames are always one taco short of a combo plate. I'd like to put all of them on their crystal balls and roll them back up north where they came from. Questioning a psychic would be a waste of an investigator's time and the taxpayer's money." Besides, telling him about Cielo would be disobeying one of a defense lawyer's primary laws—never give up a witness, especially when you don't know where that witness will lead.

I called him and asked if anyone had been out to the Atalaya lot yet.

"Yeah," he said.

"What did you find?"

"Not much. Some broken glass."

"Did it come from Martha's car?"

"We're checking on it," he said.

The taxpayers weren't paying my salary—Martha Conover was. On Saturday I had nothing better to do, so I went on my own personal truth quest at the Pyramid. The New Agers had set up their tables in the main ballroom. I walked up one aisle and down the next, getting asked to remember the goddess, choose my own reality, reverse the aging process, journey into the body, quit smoking, turn pain into joy and create a more fun, vibrant and conscious me. There were tables advertising colorpuncture, vibrasound, psychic surgery, brain machine relaxation sessions and Native American tarot enlisting the assistance of power animals. That was one I might get interested in.

At the end of the third aisle I found a table with the sign *Forward Life Progressions by Cielo* inscribed in silver ink on a black background. She stood beside the table, surrounded by adoring groupies, women who were shorter, older and less striking-looking than she was. Most people are less striking than Cielo, a.k.a. Ci, especially when she's dressed in her psychic costume, and I'd never seen her any other way. She wore her trademark silver, a broomstick-pleated skirt and a matching shirt with a concho belt over it. It's a look they call wearable art in Santa Fe, rip-off anywhere else. Around her neck was a crystal suspended on a silver chain. Her Evian-washed hair hung full and loose to her shoulders. Silver streaks framed her face. Dangling turquoise earrings matched the color of her eyes exactly. It's a color you often see in turquoise, never in eyes, and it made me wonder if she didn't put the eyes in every morning right before she put on the earrings.

Most of her admirers were women who had the time and money to indulge in the fantasy that they'd have another life, which would be better than this one, and there had been enough of them to buy Ci a big house in Santa Fe. New Mexico is the one place in America where psychics make more money than lawyers.

"Pluto is the creator and the destroyer, the Hindu god Shiva," she trilled to her admirers in her silvery voice. "It is not a very subtle influence. When Pluto transits your chart, the message is to regenerate or die. Only very evolved people can regenerate without suffering. Our life's work is to suffer. We are both the marble and the sculptor in our own lives." Maybe she'd been reading the same horoscopes Anna had. Her audience hung on every word, which made me wonder if she hadn't started charging by the syllable. She finished her talk by spinning her arm in a circle around her head. I heard a tinkling sound—money changing hands or something shaking inside the silver ball she held. Her groupies moved up close to question her. They were so wrapped up that I was able to push my way to the front of the pack. "Well, Neil Hamel," Ci said when she saw me. "The woman warrior."

"I need to talk to you."

"What about?"

"Could we go somewhere a little more private?"

"Where?"

"The lobby?"

"All right."

She followed me to the lobby, where she chose the spot— two cushy pink velvet armchairs in front of an artificial waterfall with an artificially soothing sound, the Muzak of the hotel lobby world. The water babbled down the front of a rock, got pumped up, babbled down again. I began to sit, but Ci put a hand out to stop me. "Wait," she said. "I'm clearing the vibrations." Like a dog, she had to circle several times before she got down.

"I like muddy vibrations," I said, but she waved her hand all around the pink chairs, up the front and down the back, tinkling her little silver ball.

"There," she said when she was finished. She sat and arranged her pleats around her legs and her streaks around her face. I happened to notice there was an ashtray on the end table and no No Smoking sign in sight. I lit up. Ci waved her hand in front of her nose. "Smoking is the modern person's suicide," she said. "If you went deeply into your purpose in life and found your true mission, you wouldn't need to smoke anymore. You should start doing some soul work, because you are going to have to come back again and again until you get it right."

If you smoke in this lifetime, does that mean you'll come back as an ashtray in the next? I wondered. But what I said was: "Did you know that there are over five billion people alive on earth, more people than have lived and died in all of recorded history?"

"So?"

"How can there be more reincarnated people than there were people to begin with?"

"New souls and souls that have split," she answered without missing a beat. I might have known that Ci would find some way to multiply the fishes to feed the masses. "Besides, you're only talking about recorded history."

A family was checking in at the front desk. The little boy's attention was focused on the palm of his hand, where he saw his future in an eighty-dollar Game Boy. The little girl had blond ringlets, wore pink overalls and carried a teddy bear. She wandered our way and was standing beside my chair, staring at Ci. "Ruthie," her mother called, "come back here right now."

Ruthie slowly wandered back. "Mommy," she said in a loud voice, "why is that lady wearing tinfoil?"

"She's from Santa Fe," her mother said.

Ci rattled her silver ball. "Did you come here to talk to me about reincarnation?" she asked.

"No. About Justine Virga."

"Justine Virga. Why do you want to talk about her?"

"I'm representing the woman who is suspected of running her over."

"Well, well, well," said Ci. "Karma has brought us together again, just like karma brought Justine and your client together." That was one possibility I didn't want to consider. As Saia said, if I ever started believing in karma, I'd be out of a job. "Your client will reap more karmic justice in the next lifetime than in any court of law. Trials have nothing to do with justice anyway. They are merely a performance, and the best performer wins." She ought to know; she wasn't such a bad performer herself.

"Did you see Justine?" I asked.

"I saw her, but I can't tell you what was said. I have to protect the confidentiality of whatever a client tells me. You must have some similar arrangement in the law." She leaned forward. Her crystal pendant picked up a light beam from somewhere and shot back rays of fire. "I can tell you that Justine had the red energy. Her aura was extremely agitated when she came to see me. An agitated aura is like light moving across a rock, the reflection of sunlit water. If you move your hand through the water you stir up the reflection. Your client was stirring the waters of Justine's aura. If someone wants you to die, it's hard not to let that seep into your consciousness. Martha Conover wanted Justine dead."

"If you thought Justine was going to die, why didn't you do something to stop it?"

"I have the gift of true sight. What I see has already been written; it can't be stopped. Postponed, maybe, with a very high level of consciousness and concentration, but never stopped. It was Justine's time to move into the light."

She had also been blessed with the gift of true ego—that couldn't be stopped either. "Did you give her a note in a sealed envelope?"

"I can't tell you that, but I can tell you that if you don't come to terms with the mother within, you'll keep meeting her without. We choose our parents and our families when we incarnate, for the lessons we need to learn in this lifetime. The mother you carry within is the positive expression of motherhood; the one you project without is the negative. You have to build your own Saturn, your own internal mother structure inside, especially if you are a woman. Remember there is a 'her' in mother."

"In father too."

"Exactly," said Ci. "Justine left her mother too young, before she had had time to build the edifice. Martha Conover is the mother without, and their collision was foreordained. She was the instrument of Justine's destiny." Ci leaned back, smiled and rearranged her pleats around her legs. Life and death were just a living to her.

"Why did Justine leave her mother so young? Did she tell you?"

"She didn't have to tell me; I knew. But that is confidential. I can tell you about your mother too, if you want to know."

"I don't," I said.

Ci went back to her table. I stayed in the lobby and had another cigarette. Why do people consult psychics, study the stars and get their cards read anyway? I wondered. To find out about the two areas of life where no rational rules apply: love and death. There's no explaining love. As for death, you can eat right, stay fit, quit smoking and still drop dead tomorrow. Most people would rather talk about love than death. Justine was still young, Michael had been dead for three years; maybe she was looking for a new love. And if she was, she probably wouldn't have told Emilio about it. Ci might have talked to Justine about her death and her mother. She might also have told her that love was just around the corner and happiness was on the horizon, that she was both the marble and the sculptor in her life, that her life's work was to suffer and what better way to open yourself to suffering than to fall in love? Any successful psychic has to have the gift of true romance, and Ci was as successful as any. I hadn't gotten an answer from her about the note, but I hadn't really expected one. I had gotten a feeling. The feeling was that Ci was an opportunist capitalizing on people's need to believe and I ought to go looking for Emilio Velásquez's typewriter.

12

I PUT OUT THE CIGARETTE, left the Pyramid, got on the interstate and headed south. The Big I was as clogged as a Southern Baptist's arteries. The diesels were pumping out nimbuses of black smoke. The clearer the air, the darker the exhaust looks. I hit the Seek button—top forty, country, golden oldies, classical love songs, Big O Tires, Garth Brooks. Albuquerque has too many stations and was having a radio war to eliminate a few, but I found nothing I wanted to listen to. I turned the radio off, abandoned the interstate near Central. Instead of going west on Lead toward my office, I turned south on Broadway, which was having a bad case of the orange-barrel blues. I negotiated my way through the barrels and the black arrows of road construction into a neighborhood that is only a few blocks away from Hamel and Harrison but way deeper into seediness, the kind of neighborhood where you find faith temples, thrift shops, soup kitchens, lawyers' offices and a new café that believed in economic miracles, but the only miracle you can expect in a neighborhood like this is the roses that bloom in summertime. There's always one house in the grayer parts of town with a porch or a trellis that drips roses in June and says that someone lived here once who loved this place. The windows in the lawyer's office were covered with bars. The walls of the faith temple were covered with murals of gods and conquistadors. The pumps at Getty Gas had run dry, La Esperanza market had closed for the day or forever, the Dead End Motel was offering videos and a room for twelve bucks. A guy and his dog sat on the corner behind a sign that said KOREA, VIETNAM, WILL WORK FOR FOOD, RENT. I've seen people in Santa Fe begging for money for Parvo shots for their dog, but these two were begging for survival. The dog lay in a patch of shadow between its master's legs. It lifted its head when I stopped at the light, dropped it again when I stepped on the gas.

The sign for the Last Chance Thrift Shop was large enough to read from a block away. An arrow pointed in the direction of the railroad tracks. The smaller print on the sign said VERY LAST CHANCE DISPOSAL BIN, but I'd turned in before I saw it. The building was a warehouse, long and low, with no windows. I followed where the arrow pointed, across the parking lot, behind the building, next to the place where the bridge started to climb across the railroad tracks. Back here they gave away what no one wanted. When I turned the corner I saw a row of plastic bags and bedrolls that told me someone had either taken refuge or set up house. A skinny woman dressed in a long plaid dress looked at me with depleted eyes sunk in an angular face. Her child sucked her finger and stared. A man leaned against the building with his head down, ignoring me and everything else. They looked like a colorized Dorothea Lange photo, like refugees from the thirties. I'm used to seeing sixties time warps in New Mexico, but this was the first time I'd found myself in the Depression. I was invading a sanctuary. I knew it, and so did they. I turned the wheel and spun gravel getting out of there, wondering as I did what makes the homeless and hopeless keep on going when the young and beautiful kill each other and themselves.

When I reached the front of the warehouse, I saw that the thrift shop was on the street. I parked the Nissan and went in. The shop was handicapped-friendly and had a wheelchair ramp marked for the otherly abled. NO SHIRT, NO SHOES, NO SERVICE. NO OFFER REFUSED, a sign said. A TV was playing, and a panel of women were talking about empowerment and standing up to their men. A guy with a fat belly sat behind the counter, bending his elbows, resting his bald head in his hands and reading a paperback. A bell rang as I came through the door, but he didn't look up. I walked past him through the racks of clothes: men's, women's, children's; pants, dresses, shirts, and a T-shirt that said I HATE NEW YORK WINTERS. In a back room I found the velvet art (a bullfighter and a flamenco dancer in orange on black), the dishes and appliances. There weren't any microwaves, CD players, computers, Cuisinarts or Nintendo games here. Last Chance sold the old, fat eight-track tapes, records, record players, black-and-white TVs, toaster ovens, Waring blenders, the detritus of a world in high-tech forward motion. The furniture was yesterday's discarded styles: a canvas butterfly chair, a Naugahyde sofa, a lamp with a campfire painted on the shade, which flickered as the bulb heated up. There were stacks of drapes, pots and pans, wineglasses, salt and pepper shakers, dish towels, a full set of china for one hundred bucks. This is the place where your belongings end up when you have no kids, where everything you'd loved and saved to buy would go—out of style, out of date, marked with a white tag, sold for a pittance. "You came here to look for a typewriter," I reminded myself. There weren't any.

I walked back through the clothes racks to the front counter. "Got any typewriters?" I asked the guy, who had sunk a little lower on his elbows, gotten a few pages further into his book.

"No," he said without looking up. The light from the

window behind me reflected on his bald spot. I peered into it as if it had something to reveal, but all I saw was that I was about to tell a lie.

"I had an old manual that I liked a lot," I said. "It wasn't worth much, but it had been my father's, and I had a sentimental attachment to it. My boyfriend and I had a fight, and he brought it down here yesterday morning. A Hispanic guy in a wheelchair?"

He dog-eared a corner to mark his place in the book and looked up. "All the typewriters I get go to Santo. He collects them. Made me an offer I couldn't refuse."

"Why does he collect them?"

"He's a writer."

"What does he write?"

"Fiction," the guy said.

"Do you have any idea where I could find him? I'd like to get that typewriter back."

"He lives in Coldwater Arroyo."

"Does he have a phone?"

"Lady, he don't even have a light bulb. You want to find him and his typewriter, you're gonna have to hike in."

"Okay, so I'll hike," I said. "What was the offer you couldn't refuse?"

"Nada," he said.

The places I don't go to alone are the places where you're all alone until you confront your nemesis. The mantra of a single woman is that it's safer to be alone in a crowd than alone in the alone, on the dubious theory that one's fellow citizens are witnesses who will keep each other in check. Coldwater Arroyo is city-owned property, but that doesn't make it safe. It just gives you someone with deep pockets to sue if you get hurt, or for your relatives to sue if you get killed. It's at the base of the Sandias, close enough to town to attract troublemakers, far enough away for no one else to hear you or them. One deterrent is to make yourself repulsive, and it has been proved that skunk odorant repels men faster than any other. The best a skunk gun can do, however, is buy time, although not enough time to get out of Coldwater Arroyo, unless you're in better shape than I am. Someone who would venture up there in search of trouble might not care what he smelled like, might not smell that good to begin with. Santo could have some unfriendly dogs. Santo could be unfriendly himself and crazy besides. On Sunday I asked the Kid if he'd go with me.

"Okay," he said.

We found the path to Santo's easily enough; it was marked by hiking boot footprints and dog shit. It followed a sandy arroyo bed where boulders had been dumped by the mountain runoff in its persistent rush to the lowest level. Water is the ultimate bottom-seeker. Higher up the walls of the arroyo were pink rocks that had a hard-earned, exposed-to-the-elements character, like the faces of craggy old men. Lizards scooted across the sand. A jumping cholla jumped some spines in my direction. The brown leaves of scrub oaks hung at the edges of their limbs and gave a death rattle when they fell off. There were places where we had to climb over the boulders to follow the arroyo. Few things in life are more satisfying than climbing rocks, but I wouldn't want to do it every time I went out for a pack of cigarettes. After we'd gone about a mile up the wash, dogs heard us coming and started a loud and cacophonous barking, a once-familiar sound, the background music of every Mexican town and some in New Mexico as well. Either Santo wasn't home or he liked the sound of yapping dogs.

"I don't know about this, Kid," I said. "They sound mean."

"Don't worry, Chiquita."

"In a setup like this they could be dogs who haven't had

their shots." That was also endemic to every Mexican town. You got bit down there, and it was ten days of shots and pain or the risk of losing your life, which to a Mexican is no big deal.

We kept on walking. Eventually a footpath led out of the arroyo. We followed it around a boulder and over a rise and came upon the dogs. There were about ten of them, and they weren't chained up. They ran to within a few feet of us and stopped, snarling, barking and flashing their fangs. Some were gray, some were brown. Some were small, some were medium-sized. They had ears that stood up or flopped over, long curled tails or no tails at all. They all had the concave stomachs and protruding ribs of street dogs. They were looking for love, food or trouble, depending upon your perspective.

"Cálmate, perrito," the Kid said. He knelt down, extended his hand and spoke softly to the dogs. In a few minutes they had shut up and clustered around him, sharing their fleas, getting scratched behind the ears. If he'd had any food, they would have been eating it out of his hand.

The quieting of the dogs gave me a chance to look around. Santo's yard had been scraped raw by his pets and the elements, except that here and there plastic flowers and pinwheels were in bloom, stuck into the ground on wooden stems. A yellow pinwheel caught the wind, whirred and shivered. A red flower danced on its stick.

Santo's home was tucked into the boulders. It was made out of wood, stone, plastic, old road signs and cardboard held together with hope and spit. It reminded me of the cardboard hovels in Mexico, except that this close to a Mexican city you'd never find just one. The entire hillside would have sprouted shacks and dogs and children. Santo's hovel was surrounded by a bunch of tumbleweeds stuck together by their prickers, nature's own barbed wire fence. "Anybody home?" I called.

His wind chimes tinkled back.

"Santo?" No answer, so I made my way through an opening in the tumbleweed fence and went inside. I saw a pile of dirty rags in the corner that resembled a bed. Santo had one chair and several rickety tables made out of planks balanced on rocks or cinder blocks. The tables supported his collection of manual typewriters and candles. He had Olivettis, Royals, Underwoods and candles in all colors, shapes and sizes. Like the guy at Last Chance said, there wasn't a light bulb in sight. Apparently Santo did his writing at night by candlelight. He probably spent his days scrounging for food for himself and the dogs. The typewriters all had white paper sticking out of their platens, the empty canvas, every creative person's challenge. In one sense, Santo had met the challenge—the canvases were not empty, I noticed, as I walked around and inspected the typewriters. Each piece of paper had at least a few lines typed on it. The Olivetti:

> Fire in the drainage ditch
> The setting sun
> Drips water
> From its mouth blood red

The Underwood:

> Home is where
> You bury your dreams
> For the politicians
> To bulldoze

If *he'd* ever won a National Endowment grant, we'd be hearing from Jesse Helms. I stopped reading for content and began looking at what I came here for—type: a *p* that was missing part of its tail, an *e* that didn't close. I found them in the Royal sitting on an orange crate, an ancient, elegant machine with the brass keys all lined up in a curved row. I took out my copy of the note that had been found on Justine and compared the two to be sure, the same *e*, the same *p*, the same faded ribbon. I removed the resident poem, put in a blank piece of paper, typed "I knew this was going to happen, but I couldn't prevent it," took it out, returned the poem. The Xerox I had and this copy were identical, except that the Xerox was on paper that had been in my pocket and gotten creased and folded like a road map. I couldn't prove in court that this was the same typewriter that Emilio Velásquez had taken to Last Chance (unless I could persuade Saia to get a search warrant and dust it for fingerprints), but I believed it. So the note had been typed on Emilio's typewriter. Why did he do it, if he did do it?

The Kid came inside. "Did you find it, Chiquita?"

"I think so. Look."

"That's it," he said.

The dogs started barking again but with hope instead of fear, as if their master had come home with the kibble. Not wanting to be caught breaking and entering, the Kid and I left the hovel. We'd gotten as far as the tumbleweed fence when Santo came over the top of the rise and stood there for a minute looking ten feet tall, leaning on a crooked stick, king of his own private mountain. He had on a white cotton dress that came down to his ankles and was tied around the waist with rope. His hiking boots were clunky and caked with dirt. His bulging backpack gave him the rounded shape of Kokopelli, the Anasazi flute player. He carried a bunch of plastic bags stuffed to the max. His hair was arranged in long, dirty-blond dreadlocks with bits of paper and fuzz sticking out. The dogs ran to greet him, and he knelt down and patted every one. "Giz," he said, "and Beau and Jason and Tommie and Polonius." He reached into a plastic bag and fed them each a snack, crackers and crusts he'd picked up on his rounds. His eyes were an intense pale blue and appeared to be registering the passage of events like tightly wound clocks.

"You from *60 Minutes*?" he asked.

It took me by surprise, I'll admit it. "No. Are you Santo?"

He stood up, shook out his dress and his dreadlocks in a display that made him seem even more voluminous. "You don't recognize me?" he asked.

He did have a seen-once, remembered-forever look, but I hadn't seen it, and I didn't remember. "No," I said.

"I was in the *Journal* three times and the *Tribune* four. I've been on CBS and NBC. I was interviewed by Tom Rollins. Look." He went to the place in the yard where the plastic pinwheel was stuck in the ground, still spinning, and he picked up a rock, exposing a hole, an underground safe where he kept his valuables. He pulled out one of those tubes that zap your deposit from the drive-in window to the teller inside the bank, and he opened it up. It was stuffed full of newspaper clippings about the lengths the city had gone to to evict him. I took a look through them. He *had* gotten more than his share of publicity.

"If you're not from *60 Minutes*, where are you from?" he asked, narrowing his ticking eyes.

"Downtown," I said. "I'm a lawyer." The Kid said nothing; Santo didn't give him time.

"A lawyer?" Santo recoiled. His skirt swirled, his dreadlocks swung wide, his walking stick vibrated like a dowsing rod on a roll as he pointed it at me. It was the snake-in-the-grass reaction many have to my profession but most try to suppress. Trust a psychotic to reveal a true emotion. The dogs picked up on the vibe and began to growl at me.

"Calm down," I said. "I didn't come here to sue or evict you. I'm looking for a typewriter that figures in a case I'm working on. The man at Last Chance told me you collect them."

"My typewriters are poets. They write poems, not laws. See? The poems are in the typewriters, my fingers find the right keys, and we coax them out." He spun around like a dervish and waved his long fingers in front of my face, trying maybe to coax some poetry out of me. "You won't find *your* laws in *my* typewriters."

"You could be right. Well, thanks anyway," I said. What did I care? The type sample I needed was already deep in my pocket.

"How do you like my place?" Santo asked, waving his arms around him in an expansive gesture.

I took a good look. Up close I saw boulders, lizards and high desert cacti. In the far distance I saw Mount Taylor in the west and the Manzanos in the south and beyond that the purple haze. It was too far and too wide to take in without opening the mind's wide-angle lens, the kind of high desert where people have historically come to seek wisdom and/or God. It doesn't hurt to remind yourself now and then that we exist on the edge of a vast desert, but I wouldn't want to live there. Home ought to be a sheltered space. I limited my vision to what I knew to be Albuquerque, starting at the bottom, the green valley where the runoff ends up and turns south. The Rio Grande curled like a silver ribbon thrown to the ground by a cavalier goddess. I saw the white slabs of the downtown office buildings, which looked like tombstones in a not-so-distant cemetery or monuments of a once-meaningful religion. Next came the red-tile roofs of the subdivisions. Farther up, the irregular roofs of the Heights architectural statements. Albuquerque is full of zones: life zones, pollen zones, wealth zones. I remembered when the sky used to be bluer. I also remembered when there was no pollution haze, when the Duke City didn't have auto emission standards, or a 98 percent occupancy rate, or the homeless either. Santo had a rich person's view, but he didn't have a rich person's sensibility. He couldn't turn on the VCR and turn off the view. His eyes had been looking too far for too long, and they had started to tick.

"You do have a great view," I said.

"It's choice," he replied. "And that's why my choice is to live here, and why my poems are buried all over this arroyo. It's a holy place. This place belongs to me and to God. The city can never evict me, because God's law is in effect up here."

But man's laws were in effect down there, and they'd send their minions up if they chose to. "I wouldn't count on it," I said.

His eyes turned crafty. He spread his fingers and twisted them as if he were pulling a trump card out of the air. He smiled and exposed some brownish stumps of broken teeth. "I can play by their laws too. I have lived on this land long enough to make it mine by their law of adverse possession."

Maybe. But the law of adverse possession applies only to private property, not to property owned by the city. I handed him my card. Real estate, after all, was my profession. "Let me know if you have any problems. Maybe I can help."

He put the card in the tube with the newspaper articles, stuck it back in the ground, replaced the rock cover, righted the pinwheel, which began to whir and spin.

"Can we go now, Chiquita?" asked the Kid. He'd been more than patient.

"Yeah," I said.

"Mucho gusto," said the Kid to Santo, and "Ándale" to me.

"Come back again," replied Santo.

The Kid and I walked down the arroyo, past the pink-faced boulders, through the sandy place where water flows in summer. One of Santo's dogs followed us, and when Santo called him he sat down, threw his head back and began a long, lonesome howl.

The Kid shook his head. "People in this country are crazy," he said.

13

I'D FOUND EMILIO'S TYPEWRITER. The next step was to find Emilio and tell him. He was on Los Cerros tennis court, where he had challenged the ball machine to a game and the machine had met the challenge. When I got there on Monday afternoon, the match was on. Emilio's concentration was intense, and I leaned against the fence and watched for several minutes before he noticed me. The balls hit the ground and bounced one after another in the exact same spot. Emilio didn't have to move around much, but even so he'd probably had to set the machine to its slowest setting. The machine hiccuped, exhaled a ball. The strings thunked when the sweet spot of Emilio's racket connected. He brought his racket back, narrowed his eyes and swung hard. His intensity made me wonder if he wasn't seeing someone's face on the ball. Martha's, maybe, or Whit's. He noticed me out of the corner of his eye, dropped the racket in midstroke, rolled around to the other side of the court and turned the ball machine off.

"See that?" he asked. "I'm taking the dis out of disability."

"Go ahead and finish the set," I answered. "Don't mind me."

"It's okay. I've had enough." He wheeled up close so I was looking down at him again. If the purpose of exercise is to break a sweat, he'd achieved it. His shirt clung to his body, his dark hair formed Greek-god tendrils on his forehead. "Tennis is okay, but I'd rather be talking to you."

"You haven't heard what I have to say yet."

"That's right." His smile was a quick, hard flash. "Here or my place?"

"Your place."

"See you there." He went to his car; I went to mine. It took him longer, and I arrived at his apartment first. I waited for him at the door, wondering how I was going to explain that I had tracked down his typewriter, hoping that Dorothy wouldn't come to *her* door. All was quiet behind the facade of 53C, no sound of metal scraping or death walking. Maybe Dorothy had fallen asleep, or she hadn't gotten up yet, but that seemed unlikely, since there appears to be an inverse relationship between the amount of sleep you get and your age. By the time you reach ninety you're lucky to sleep at all. Thinking about Dorothy kept me from thinking about Emilio, and when he showed up and let me into his apartment I hadn't a clue how I was going to say what I'd come here to say.

"Want a beer?" he asked, heading for the kitchen. "I have some Tecate."

"Got anything else?"

"Lemonade?"

"I'll have one of those."

There was a John Callahan cartoon lying on the coffee table, and I picked it up. It was a picture of a dog lying on his back with a pane of glass sticking out of his chest. "How much is that window in the doggy?" the caption read. Emilio heard me laugh.

"I've got a joke for you, Nellie," he said. "There was a guy with no arms and legs who had to give up his effort to swim the English Channel. You know why?"

"Dígame."

"His ears got tired." I heard him open the refrigerator door. "Not drinking these days?"

"Not when I'm working." I sat down on his sofa, picked up the picture of Justine with the gypsy eyes and put it down.

He came back with the drinks and handed me mine. "Seeing me is work?"

"Yeah," I said. "It is." I took a big sip of lemonade. "I found your typewriter, Emilio."

He looked at me over the top of his Tecate can. "My typewriter?"

"A man named Santo took it from Last Chance. He wears a dress and lives in a hovel in Coldwater Arroyo. He thought I'd come there to interview him for *60 Minutes*."

"Glad to know someone is using it," he said.

"He is. In fact there was a poem in the typewriter that he says he coaxed out."

Emilio shook his head. His curls remained stuck to his sweaty forehead. "You're a good investigator, Nellie. How did you even know I had a typewriter or where to look for it?" Not being such a bad investigator himself, he quickly came up with the answer. "Dorothy?"

"Yeah."

"Híjole. It's worse than living at home with your mother. She's got nothing to do all day but watch me go in and out."

"When I came here the other day she told me you'd gone to Last Chance with the typewriter. I have to ask why you got rid of it, Emilio. That typewriter typed Justine's note." The next question was, Did *you* type it? But I didn't ask.

"I was afraid of that," he said.

"If you give me a sample of something you've typed, I can prove it."

"You don't need to prove it; I believe you."

"Who typed it, Emilio? I have to know."

He put his Tecate down on the table, leaving a wet ring, but it didn't matter because the veneer that masqueraded as wood was grade A plastic. "Justy, I think," he said. "She was here all alone that morning."

"Was her English that good? Wouldn't someone who didn't have very good English have said 'stop' rather than 'prevent'?"

"Her English was fine. Better than mine."

"Why would she write herself a note like that?"

"As sort of an apology to me."

"I don't get it."

"It's a long story, Nellie."

What did I have waiting for me at the office anyway? Real estate and divorce, Anna and Brink. "Dígame," I said.

"Justy and I got real close after Miguel died. She was like a daughter to me. She came here every year on the anniversary of the accident, and we spent it together. Justy was a marked woman. She might of taken steps to protect herself, and for a while she did. But after Miguel died she didn't care whether she lived or not. I think the note was telling me she knew she was going to die and that she didn't care enough to prevent it." He took a long sip of his beer.

"Who wanted to kill her?"

"A lot of people. When she was sixteen years old she fell in with a group of Argentine revolutionaries or terroristas, whatever you want to call them. It was the time of the dirty war, and Argentina was a mess then, run by a bunch of assassins. Justy's real name was Verónica Falcón, but she was known as Niki."

"She was named after her grandmother?"

"Yeah. She came from an upper-class family. Jaime Córdova, her best friend's father, was a general in Buenos Aires and a notorious pig and torturer. She went to visit her friend and took a book with her. She excused herself to go to the bathroom and planted the book under the old man's bed. It was a bomb, and it blew him up."

"Oh, God."

"Her boyfriend, who made the bomb, got caught. They probably hooked him up to the torture machine and fried his balls, but Justy escaped and she came here and lived with her mother's sister, Mina Alarid. Alarid is not the family name. He was someone Mina was married to years ago. Mina's been in this country for thirty years. She teaches Latin American literature at UNM. I guess Justy hoped the assassins wouldn't trace her here or would forget about her, or maybe she knew they would find her someday and she stopped caring."

"If it was Argentine hit men, why not just run her over themselves? Why set up Martha Conover?"

"They have a sense of humor? I don't know, Nellie. The other possibility, which I hate to even consider, is that Justy stepped in front of the car herself. Justy knew that the old lady was going to the meeting that night and would probably be coming home loaded and driving like the Terminator. The note doesn't make much sense, does it, if you think Martha Conover murdered Justy in cold blood?"

"No."

"And it wasn't given to her by the psychic if it was typed on my typewriter."

"Did you really believe it was?"

"Let's say I *hoped* it was."

"Tell me what happened the day Justine died."

"She got here about eleven-thirty. I went out to get some tacos for lunch. I'm not much of a cook. When I got back, Mina Alarid and Cindy were here. Mina picked Cindy up because Cindy doesn't like to leave her car parked outside when Martha is around. We had lunch and talked and cried about Miguel. Around four, I took Cindy home. Whit was downtown, doing his charity work. Justy and Mina stayed here for a while, and then Justy left to go to the cemetery. She liked to go alone. I never saw her again." He picked up Justine's picture and stared at her. "You would have liked her, Nellie. She reminded me of you when you were sixteen. You might of been a terrorista too, if you'd grown up in Argentina. Remember how you hated the war?"

"I still do." And looking at the limp legs in his wheelchair, I hated it even more.

"The guy she killed was a pig and a brutal assassin, who deserved to die."

He was also her best friend's father.

"She did the world a favor by getting rid of him. El muerto al pozo y el vivo al retozo."

The dead to his hole and let the good times roll.

"It took a lot of courage to do what Niki Falcón did—and she was just a kid—but it ruined her life. Loving Miguel helped, but you never really recover from something like that. I know because I've killed too. Justy and I had that in common. Only her victim was an assassin and mine was a VC who wanted me to get the fuck out of his country. She paid with her life. I lost my legs, which in a way made it easier for me to deal with it." He looked down at his lap. "The old lady's got nothing to worry about now. As the doc in rehab said, sex will always be a distant memory for me. It's hard to get into it when you can't feel a thing and you've got a catheter in your dick."

"Sex isn't everything," I said, echoing Martha Conover, but her voice had had more conviction than mine did.

"It's a luxury," Emilio said, "for people who've got something left to lose." He finished the Tecate, squeezed the can together and threw it at the trash container visible through the open kitchen door. The can hit the edge, bounced off, landed on the floor and gave a death rattle while it rolled to a stop.

"When Miguel died too, Justy felt like she was the kiss of death and there was no reason for her to go on living. But she was wrong, Nellie, there were reasons. There's me, there's Cindy."

It's easy enough to see why people believe in reincarnation. Who likes to think you'll only get one shot when the hand you're dealt is stacked with cards like that? "Did Justine usually carry a gun?"

"Wouldn't you if you were her?"

"Probably."

"I have a gun. Don't you?"

"Yeah," I said. "I do."

"Why do you ask?"

"The night Justine died, the police found a revolver with two empty chambers in the glove compartment of her car."

"Where did the bullets go?"

"I don't know. You'd think someone in Justine's situation would have reloaded the gun soon after she fired it, wouldn't you?"

"You'd think so. Something you should understand about Justy is that killing Jaime Córdova didn't make her inhuman, but anyone who does something like that is going to be living by different rules afterwards." Emiliano had killed too. What rules was he living by? I wondered.

"I'm going to have to tell the DA's office about the Argentine connection," I said. "Martha's my client. This is evidence that could keep her from being indicted."

"I was afraid of that," Emilio said.

"Why do you care?" I asked.

"She's a heartless woman. She's ruined a couple of lives, and I'd like to see her pay. If they put the old lady in jail, it's all right with me."

"Don't you care about finding out the truth?"

"Not anymore," he said.

▽   ▽   ▽

But it was important to me—more than that: it was of the essence. Although a couple of years practicing law could easily make you care more about billable hours than the truth, it was the raft I tried to navigate through the shallow rapids of the legal river. Without it I'd be scraping the bottom with my butt. Practicing law could also make a person suspicious of everyone, even old friends. Emilio Velásquez hadn't acted as though he was lying, and I didn't want to think he'd lie to me. But the black velvet bog of suspicion is seductive, and I could feel myself getting pulled by the suction. Justine Virga could have been Niki Falcón, Niki Falcón could have murdered Jaime Córdova. On the other hand, Justine Virga could have lied to Emilio Velásquez and he could have lied to me. Justine and Miguel might have been involved with drugs. It would explain the Porsche and the revolver and the deaths of two young people, except that drug dealers are more likely to carry semiautomatics than revolvers. Maybe Cindy had been kidding herself about Michael's drug use. Maybe he'd been fooling her. Emilio Velásquez could also have been involved with drugs, and in fact by his own admission he had been. Drugs might have been the bond that held Justine, Michael and Emilio together. Emilio had as much reason as anyone to want Martha to appear guilty. Just because I liked him better than Martha Conover didn't make her wrong . . . or guilty.

The Kid came over for dinner that night, and I asked him if he had heard of Niki Falcón. He did, after all, have an Argentine connection.

"Sure," he said. "She was famous all over Argentina. She was a hero to the students because Jaime Córdova, the man she killed, was an asesino." The way he pronounced asesino, it sounded like a snake hiss. "For a while her face was on walls everywhere. The military put the pictures up, the students took them down."

"What did she look like?" I asked.

"I don't know, Chiquita. I never saw her. I was in Mexico when that happened. People say she was very beautiful."

"Would anybody still care about Niki Falcón now?"

"Jaime Córdova was very powerful. He had friends and family, and those people don't forget. If she got out of Argentina alive it is a miracle, but if she is alive they will find her. There are asesinos on the right there called Las Manos."

"The hands."

"Claro. They cut off people's hands and leave them alone. There is nothing the people can do to help themselves, and they bleed to the death. The asesinos save the hands, put them in a jar and bring them out to show their friends. That's the kind of people who were looking for Niki Falcón. You think that she is the girl la viejita hit?"

"I've been told she was."

"It doesn't sound like Las Manos to put her in front of an old lady's car," the Kid said. "Why would they do that?"

"Maybe they are afraid of getting caught in America and didn't want to leave their imprint." Or maybe they were drug dealers who didn't want to leave their imprint.

The Kid shrugged. "Maybe," he said.

14

I WASN'T OBLIGATED TO TELL SAIA what I discovered in my investigations. He wasn't obligated—at this point—to tell me what he discovered in his. The DA–defense attorney relationship is a poker game, and it doesn't often work to your advantage to show what you're holding.

I got out my yellow pad and made a list of all I'd discovered since Saia and I had last talked: what was fact and what was speculation, what would be advantageous to reveal, what wouldn't. Justine and Michael might have been involved with drugs. Speculation. Ci did not give Justine the note, and the note was typed on Emilio's typewriter. Facts. Emilio believed Justine wrote the note. Speculation. Justine went to Michael's grave alone. A probable fact that the APD should investigate for themselves. They could also find out whose typewriter typed the note. It wasn't my job to do their work. Justine Virga was Niki Falcón, or so Emilio had said. Niki Falcón was an assassin who blew up Jaime Córdova. A fact that had been confirmed by both Emilio and the Kid. Hit men were after Niki Falcón. Speculation.

I decided to keep the rest to myself and pass the Niki Falcón story on to Saia. I didn't see how that information could hurt Martha, and his investigations might uncover something that mine couldn't.

"Hey, Neil, how's it going?" he asked when I called. I visualized him leaning back in his chair, putting his feet up on his desk, lighting a cigarette, flipping the match at his ashtray and missing.

"Pretty good. What's happening over there? Have you decided whether you're going to file charges?"

"Not yet. Like I said, this is a case without precedent in the Land of Enchantment."

"I've discovered something you ought to look into," I said.

"Shoot."

"I found out that Justine Virga was Niki Falcón, an assassin who planted a bomb under a general named Jaime Córdova in Buenos Aires. She changed her name when she came here."

"Yeah? Says who?"

"Michael Velásquez's father."

"He's a reliable source?"

"The Kid, who comes from Argentina and has nothing to prove one way or the other, confirmed that Niki Falcón assassinated Córdova."

"You still seeing that guy?" His voice had that edge men get when they think a rival has entered the playing field, even when they aren't interested in playing the game.

"Still seeing him," I said. "Jaime Córdova came from a powerful family. My sources think they'd send hit men after Justine."

"How long has it been since this supposed assassination took place?"

"Several years."

"I don't know, Neil. Sounds like a long shot to me."

▽   ▽   ▽

My next call was from Eric Winston at New West in Phoenix. "You called me about the Sharon Amaral mortgage?" he asked.

"Yes."

"Let's see." I imagined Eric Winston, whom I'd never met, sitting at his desk shuffling papers. He'd be clean-shaven, chubby, have short hair of indeterminate color and rosy cheeks. Would he be smiling? Probably not. "That mortgage is in default."

"I know," I said. "I called to see if you would be willing to reduce the payments to get Sharon through a bad time."

"We might be able to let her pay the interest alone until she gets back on her feet."

"What will that save her? Twenty dollars a month?"

"Fifteen," he said.

"That's not going to help any."

"It's the best we can do."

"You want to foreclose on a run-down house in a declining neighborhood in another state?"

"Her credit rating will be damaged if she doesn't get her payments current."

"Her children will be damaged if she doesn't feed and clothe them."

He paused while he went through some motions. What? I wondered. Rubbed his nose, pulled his ear, scratched his belly? "Let me run it by the committee and see what I can do. How much could she afford to pay?"

"Seventy-five dollars," I said, leaving some negotiating room but not much.

"That's it?"

"Times are tough." And the difference between $75 and $250 was food money.

"And it's a tough time to be a banker," he said. "By the way, we're interviewing law firms to represent us in New Mexico. Would you be interested?"

"Well . . . " It would be a steady source of income, which we needed. It would also mean handling foreclosures, which I hate, and real estate closings, which I don't like much better. The work would be boring at best, if not downright unpleasant. Not my brand of beer, but I did have a partner who had a lot of free time.

"We'll be conducting interviews next week. We'll fly you over to Phoenix if you'd like to talk to us."

"Let me think about it," I said.

"I'll get back to you about the Amaral matter," he replied.

My partner was hanging around the reception area, talking to Anna, who was wearing a pink sweater with matching pink ornaments in her hair and exuding a pheromone buzz. He was drawn to her wantonly and incessantly, like a bee to a flower. She wore the bright colors that attracted a mate and had the sweet smell of youth and of idleness. She knew the punch line to every bad joke. But she liked the Georges and the Stevies, good looks and loud music. Brink knew it. That was what made *her* safe and kept *him* hanging around.

"I just had an interesting offer," I said, interrupting their ritualized dance. I was the heavy in this office, which says something about me, more about the office.

"Another murder?" he asked.

"No, it was from New West Bank in Phoenix. They're looking for someone to represent them here."

"But you hate that kind of work."

"You're right, and that's why you should do it."

"Me?"

Instead of a snide but predictable "Got anything better to do?" I said, "You're so good at it." It was the old female flattery routine, and it didn't work. Brink knew me too well.

"I'm not that good at it, and I don't like that kind of work either," he said.

"We could use the money."

"I'll think about it." That meant he'd do what he usually did—nothing. The reason I had a partner who did nothing was that I didn't have the energy to do something about it.

A stereo on wheels was negotiating Lead Avenue. Even with the windows closed for autumn, I could clearly hear its progression. It stopped for a traffic signal at Fourth Street, resumed forward motion when the light turned green, cruised slowly and inevitably as fate in our direction. One of nature's laws is that the louder the speakers, the worse the music. Nobody plays Mozart or even Garth Brooks at full volume. The sound of heavy bass and heavy metal came to a stop right outside the Hamel and Harrison window, rattling the bars of our cage. Anna was already combing her hair and redoing her lipstick.

"Quitting time," she said.

"Are you going to Baxter, Johnson's party?" Brink asked me.

"Is it tonight?"

"Yeah."

I thought about what was and what was not in my refrigerator. "All right," I said.

There was the usual collection of suits and skirts at Baxter, Johnson's. The male lawyers wore their prosperity in one of two ways. Either they were tanned, fit and athletic-looking, indicating they had the time and money to take care of their bodies, or they were pale, fat and unathletic-looking, indicating they worked too hard to take care of their bodies. I looked around the room to see if there was anybody I didn't already know in person or by reputation.

A woman was loading up her plate at the hors d'oeuvres table: artichokes on top of prosciutto on top of deviled eggs and pâté, and green chile on top of that. If she ate like that normally, how did she remain so thin? I wondered. Then I realized I'd seen her before, but only at a distance or behind a sun screen. Her hair was mostly light brown, with a few strands of gray around the face. She had attempted to put it into a bun with hairpins, but the hairpins and the hair were falling out. Her skin was full of crinkles, but underneath she had a thoroughbred's fine bones. She held her head high, had a superior posture and the defined and graceful movements of a dancer, a tiny dancer. She was only about five feet tall. Her dance at the moment seemed to be the filling of her plate, and she was giving it her best shot.

Her makeup had been carefully applied, but her basic-black dress was wrinkled and her shoes had a hole in the toe. She wasn't uptight enough to be a lawyer, disgruntled enough to be support staff, well dressed enough to be a lawyer's wife, young enough to be a girlfriend, wealthy enough to be a Baxter, Johnson client. She was not the kind of person who had any reason to be at this party at all, unless, of course, someone had invited her.

I walked up to the table, put my margarita down, helped myself to a stuffed mushroom. "I'm Neil Hamel," I said.

She looked up from her plate. She had outlined her lids with black pencil and wore a lot of eye shadow. She didn't say anything, just looked at me with a deer-in-the-open-meadow expression.

"I live in La Vista, and I was the one who left the invitation to this party on your windshield." It was a bad mistake, and I knew it the minute I spoke. At least I hadn't been so dumb as to remind her the Kid had been leaving her food. Looking into her frightened eyes, I felt I had yanked form from the shadows, deer from the woods, pain from oblivion, and all of them would have preferred to stay exactly where they were. She didn't want to know who I was, and she didn't want me to know her.

"I beg your pardon," she said, straightening her back and lifting her head. She *had* been a dancer and would always have that. She had probably, in fact, been a swan when I was still a duck. She put her overloaded plate down on the table, pretending she didn't need the food, although I knew she needed every vitamin and mineral and calorie that she could get. Damn it, I thought. Why didn't you keep your mouth shut?

Her voice was precise and elegant. Her words were "There's been some mistake. You and I have never met." She turned and walked away with a proud, toes-out ballerina's step. I wanted to stop her and ask her something, only I didn't know what.

15

THE BALLERINA COULD BE A PERSON who'd been more harmed than helped by the women's movement, I thought. One of those who didn't have the skills or a man to get her across the Sahara desert of middle age to the trickle of social security that waited on the other side, someone who'd ended up with no place to live but a van in La Vista's parking lot. The gulf that separates us from them isn't a whole lot wider than that parking lot. Sometimes all it takes to get off the street is a month's deposit on an apartment. In the old days, a woman like La Bailarina would have married and stayed married, and the man would have been expected to stick around and support her, but nowadays the man might not have a job either.

I had lunch the next day with a woman who'd also had to make her own way but who had been ahead of her time in her ability to do it. Martha Conover had prepared herself well for middle age and beyond, financially anyway. I wondered if, given a choice, she would have preferred to have a man do it for her. You wouldn't think so to look at her, but by now she'd been on her own too long to do it any other way. I picked her up at Los Cerros. She chose the restaurant, a little-old-lady hangout in the Heights called Daisy's. The parking lot was filled with big American cars. The interior was filled with potted plants. It wasn't the kind of place where I'd expect to see anyone I recognized, but I did see Sergeant Paul Deschiney, a police officer I knew slightly, having lunch with one of the old ladies. I stopped to say hello. Martha stopped too, right next to me.

"Hi, Neil," he said. "How's it going?"

"Pretty good," I replied. "How are you?" He didn't bother to introduce his companion, who could have been his mother, and I didn't introduce Martha, who definitely wasn't mine.

"Do you believe this weather?" he asked.

"Great, isn't it?"

"Fall's my favorite time of year."

"Mine, too."

"Be seein' ya."

"Bye."

That was the extent of the conversation, but short as it was and tiny as Martha Conover is, she made her disapproval felt. I could feel her tensing like a guard dog beside me. Her back got straighter, the elbow that held her purse gripped firmer, her lips pressed together tight.

The minute we reached our table, she latched onto a waitress and ordered a martini. "Do you know who that was?" she asked in a loud and irritated voice.

"Paul Deschiney," I said.

"That's one of the policemen who came to my door the night of the . . . the accident." Deschiney had suspected her of a criminal act, but that wasn't what made her really mad. "And today he didn't even recognize me." Her eyes snapped, her sprayed-in-place hairdo quivered.

I couldn't deny it. Paul Deschiney had given absolutely no sign that he'd ever laid eyes on Martha Conover before.

In fact he'd given no indication that he saw her today. I might have been standing at his table alone, for all the attention he paid her.

"As soon as your hair goes gray you become invisible to men," Martha said. "Once, I sat next to a man at a dinner party and talked to him for three hours. The next time I saw him, he didn't even remember me. Now the police are accusing me of murder, and they still don't recognize me."

She had a point. It did seem that second-degree murder or vehicular homicide ought to at least get a person some attention. When Martha's martini came, she gulped it down. I'd ordered a ginger ale myself and sipped it like a lady. To present the counterargument and also because I was curious, I said, "I understand why you're mad. On the other hand, don't you ever feel it's kind of nice to be invisible, to be able to walk into a bar or a restaurant and not have every guy in the place staring at your tits?" A few days before, that had been my dream, but like a lot of dreams, it was better in the imagining than in the reality.

"I don't go into bars, and men didn't stare at *my* breasts. Ever." She looked around the room. "Where is that waitress?"

The waitress happened to be standing within earshot, talking in Spanish to another table. "The goddamn Spanish are slower than molasses. Waitress," Martha yelled, in a shrill voice that got her attention. That's the way hostility gets spread around. A policeman insults Martha, Martha insults the waitress, who goes home and yells at her kid, the kid kicks the dog, the dog bites the mailman. The waitress gave Martha a look that said she might just dispense with the kid and kick *her*. At least it would break the chain. Instead she rolled her eyes and said "Híjole" to the other table.

"What did she say?" snapped Martha.

"Híjole."

"I can't hear you. Speak up."

"Híjole."

"What does that mean?"

"It's just an exclamation. It doesn't mean much."

"Is it a swear word?"

"No."

"I'll have another martini, young lady," Martha said to the waitress, who had arrived at our table. The waitress wrote down the order, stared at a speck on the ceiling and said nothing. I peered into Martha's angry blue eyes and for a brief minute was able to enter her world, a world where she was only five feet two, where she was getting older and weaker and more frequently ignored, where she was losing the power she'd struggled so hard to get. The world was full of pheromone secreters, and hers were all used up. She lived in a place where she was surrounded by a language she didn't understand and a culture she couldn't comprehend. On the other hand, why had she moved to a place where Anglos are in the minority? For the weather? One of nature's laws is that in any place with good weather, the locals speak a different language. Had she gone to the trouble to learn that language, it might not seem so threatening.

Martha ordered a chicken salad. I ordered the enchilada plate.

"Green chile or red?" the waitress asked.

"Green. And make it hot," I replied, even though I knew Daisy's hot green chile wouldn't rate a footnote on the menu at Arriba Tacos.

"Well, have they decided what they are going to charge me with?" Martha asked.

"Not yet."

"Then what did you want to talk to me about?"

"I've found out that Justine used the name Niki Falcón when she lived in Argentina and that the reason she left there was that she assassinated a general in Buenos Aires."

Fortunately she didn't think to ask me how I found out. "Did you know that?"

"No, but that proves I was right."

"About what?"

"That girl was a killer. Cynthia never wanted to believe me, but I knew from the day Michael met her that Justine was no good."

"The man she assassinated was a well-known pig and torturer."

"And she was a troublemaker. Michael was a bright boy with a great future ahead of him, and then she came along and ruined everything."

"It's possible Argentine hit men were after her."

"Or drug dealers."

The food arrived, and I bit into my enchilada. Daisy's hot was Arriba's lukewarm.

"I've never understood how people can eat that hot food," said Martha, picking up a fork and spearing her chicken salad.

"I like it," said I. And then we got to the issue that even more than the question of Martha's guilt or innocence was keeping me with one foot outside the door of this case.

"And I don't understand what you are doing with that man." She gave a little shiver of disapproval.

"If it's not broke, don't analyze it."

"His hands are dirty."

"He's a mechanic."

"You're a professional woman. Why don't you stick to your own kind? What's wrong with a professional man like Whit?"

"Lots," I said.

We didn't have much else to say. She picked at her lunch, I gulped down mine. When we were finished I paid the bill and drove her up the road to her town house at Los Cerros.

▽   ▽   ▽

The professional man himself showed up at my office the next morning before I did. When I got there, at a quarter of ten, the phone was ringing and Anna's computer keys were clacking. He didn't hear me open the door and come in, which gave me a chance to take a good look at him. He wore plaid pants, a navy-blue polo shirt with a mallet-swinging horseman galloping across his heart, and Top-Siders with no socks. He looked like the kind of man our former Vice-President praised for his family values. The way I saw it, that meant being tight in marriage, acquisitive in the marketplace and good at expensive sports. I was married to a man like that once (briefly, though it seemed like forever), and I know the breed. Whit was sitting, I was standing, and I could see clearly the bald spot beneath the strands of stretched and slicked-in-place hair. I could hear the breath that wheezed through his nose, see the ring he turned round and around on his little finger.

"Whit Reid," I said. "What are you doing here?"

He stood up and dropped the magazine he'd been reading onto the coffee table. The pages fluttered as they fell into place. "Can we talk?" he said.

"All right. Any messages?" I asked Anna.

"No," she replied.

I led Whit into my office and shut the door. My desk, as always, was filled to overflowing, and the potted plants were crying for water. I sent them a telepathic message. *Later*, it said. I flipped through the papers on my desk, searching for someplace to put the ashes from the cigarette I was about to light. I located an ashtray, dumped the contents into the trash, lit my butt. I don't have a big office; I don't make big money. My office had been a bedroom when Hamel and Harrison was a frame and stucco house—a small bedroom, not large enough for a king-sized bed, or a king-sized ego. I doubt if Whit felt uncomfortable very often; he was too full of his own importance and too oblivious to everyone else. It wouldn't occur to a guy who could monopolize a conversation the way he did that there were people out there who didn't like or admire or at least envy him. But he did seem ill at ease in my office. In fact he acted as though he felt the walls were closing in. He stood in front of the desk, shifting his weight from one Top-Sider to the other, twisting the ring around on his finger, casting a long shadow across my desk. Maybe he was used to bigger offices. It has been well documented that tall men are more successful in our society and they like to build themselves rooms to match their size, their success, their egos.

"Have a seat," I said. He sat, and so did I. I lit my Marlboro. "What brings you to my office?"

"I do volunteer work with minority businesses and I had to come downtown, so I decided to stop by. I'm concerned about Martha." He had reason to be; she stood a fair chance of being indicted for second-degree murder or vehicular homicide, and she would not be a model prisoner if she got sent away. "I saw her after her lunch with you yesterday. She was very upset, but she wouldn't tell me why."

"Maybe the chicken salad didn't agree with her," I said.

"Did you tell her she was going to be indicted?" He leaned forward in his chair. Every action produces a reaction, and I leaned back in mine.

"Actually, Whit, I'm not at liberty to discuss this case with you. Martha is my client, and there is the matter of client confidentiality. If you have any questions, why don't you ask her? She'll tell you whatever she wants you to know." *Exactly* what she wanted him to know.

"I don't think she understands the seriousness of the charges she's facing. She can be irrational at times."

"Martha's a woman," I said. "We're known for that." The snideness in my voice went right by him. Whit wasn't great at picking up on subtleties. He had noticed my smoke blowing by, however, and moved his chair sideways out of its path.

He leaned back and crossed his arms. "I mean big-league irrational. She changed a lot after Michael died. Before that she was quite sharp. But I don't think she's old enough to be suffering from that disease where you can't remember anything."

"You mean CRS?"

"What's that?"

"Can't remember shit." He didn't laugh. Whit's sense of humor was about as lively as a stone's.

"You know what I mean."

I did, but he was the one who'd gone to all the expensive schools; why should I have to tell him?

"Alzheimer's," he remembered. "Besides, the changes in her came on too quickly to be Alzheimer's. Her doctor says there's nothing wrong with her that a good night's sleep won't fix and just prescribes more Halcion. You've probably only seen her when she has it together. Martha can put on a good front when she has to. But Cyn and I see her when her guard is down. Sometimes she doesn't know what she's doing or even where she is. It's got to be the Halcion and the drinking, a bad combination. She used to be just a social drinker, but after Michael died she started drinking alone."

Drinking alone used to be a warning sign of alcoholism, but that had to be before everybody lived alone. Nowadays if you didn't drink alone you might never get to drink at all. At least people who drink in the privacy of their own homes don't drive while they're doing it.

Whit continued. "I was riding in her car with her one day, and she stopped at a green light. 'Why did you stop here?' I asked her. 'Because the light changed,' she said, and she got all confused and bent out of shape. But then all the other cars honked and went through the light, and she realized she'd done something dumb."

"I don't know why you're telling me all this," I said.

Both he and Cindy seemed more than eager to talk about Martha's character flaws.

"Because you're her lawyer and I'm not sure that Martha is competent to be making the right decisions about her life or is giving you the right information."

"And you are?"

"I'm more competent than she is." He shrugged.

"She seems capable enough to me." Martha was as edgy as a lapdog, the kind of dog you'd like to drop-kick across the room, but she knew where her self-interest lay.

"You can do a better job if you have all the facts," said Whit.

"Who ever has all the facts?"

"I think the Halcion defense will be her best chance, but you may have trouble getting her to agree to that."

"Really?" I picked up a rubber band, shot it at a coffee mug on my desk, missed.

"Well, I just want you to know that Cyn and I are here if you have any problems dealing with Martha. We'll be glad to talk to her if you like."

"It won't be necessary."

"If you need help, Nellie—"

"My name is Neil."

"—don't hesitate to call on us."

"Thanks a lot," I said.

"I wouldn't want you to think I don't have confidence in you. I do, and that's exactly why I recommended you to Martha."

"*You* recommended me? I thought it was Cindy."

"No, it was me."

Why me, whose office was the size of his clothes closet, I wondered, instead of some large and prestigious firm? Like lightning flashing on one dark Sandia peak and then another, my mind bolted and landed on a seemingly distant subject. "When is El Dorado going to be auctioned?" I asked him.

Whit Reid stared at me through his glasses, stretched his hands out in front of him until his knuckles cracked. "Where did you hear about that?"

"Cindy told me. I saw the picture when I was at your house. She said she thinks foreign investors are interested."

"Next week, I think," he said, giving the foreign-investor theory all the attention it deserved—none. He looked at his watch. "I have to be going. Now please don't forget you can call on us anytime if you need our help." Whit's surface politeness was as smooth as still water in whose depths sharks go efficiently about their business.

"I won't," I said.

After he left, I watered the plants. "Sorry, guys," I said. Then I got out a legal pad and drew blue circles up and down the red line, wondering why exactly Whit had come to see me and what ever had made Cindy believe the El Dorado auction would solve their financial problems. Whit was a real estate professional. He'd know what I knew: you can't get laughter out of a stone, tequila out of a turnip, or money out of a property being sold at a real estate auction, not in the current market—only he hadn't told Cindy that. Given the location—Arizona—and the times—the nineties—there was a good probability El Dorado was an S&L loan that had gone bad.

I dialed 800 information and asked for the number of Resolution Trust Corporation, the corporation that is administering the sale of the assets of the S&Ls that went belly-up. At the moment, those assets made it the largest corporation in the world, although a lot of them were really liabilities, properties that never should have gotten the loans they did in the first place. Chalk it up to bankers' optimism, stupidity, greed, or the fact that the money they were lending was savings deposits insured by the federal government. What did the S&Ls have to lose? Our money, but what the heck—we're used to seeing that go down the tubes. In the eighties, bankers looked upon Arizona the way Pizarro coveted Peru and Cortés lusted after Mexico, virgin territory to be raped and plundered, the profits to go in their pockets.

The RTC office in Washington referred me to its office in Denver, and that office referred me to Harry Chambers, the auctioneer in Phoenix who was handling the Arizona properties. I asked him if he was auctioning off El Dorado. He said he was and offered to send me a brochure.

"I'll get it in the mail today," he said. "According to RTC guidelines, that property will be sold absolute. No minimum. It goes to the highest bidder."

"Suppose there aren't any bidders?" I asked.

"Trust me. There's always somebody out there looking for a deal."

Just like the legal profession, real estate is full of bottom feeders. "Thanks," I said.

I wandered out to the reception area to see what Anna was up to and found her hard at work reading the *Journal*. "Hey, get a look at this. Women are having almost as many car accidents as men. They're driving faster and harder and wrecking their cars a lot."

"They steal and murder more too," I said.

"They also smoke," said Anna, eyeballing the lethal weapon that was slowly burning down to ashes in my hand.

"That's progress for you." Sometimes I think the women's movement tried too hard to make us more like them when what we should have done was let them be more like us. But then I remembered that what we used to be was so devalued nobody wanted it.

"Who's Whit Reid?" Anna asked. "Is he a client?"

"He's married to Cindy, Martha Conover's daughter, my old high school friend."

"He got way impatient waiting for you. He looked at his watch about a hundred times and breathed through his nose—loud—like he wanted me to be sure to notice he was around."

"Whitney James Reid III is the final flower on one branch of the civilization tree."

"Huh?"

"He was born rich, went to the best schools, was successful in business. He doesn't like to be kept waiting; he expects everybody to cater to him."

"He didn't even have an appointment, did he?"

"No."

"Why doesn't he get his nose fixed? It has to drive his wife crazy, like living with someone who snores twenty-four hours a day."

"Likes himself just the way he is, I guess."

"Does his wife like him?"

"Not as much as he does."

"Actually, he kind of reminds me of someone," Anna said.

"Who?"

"Your ex-husband, Charles."

"I was afraid of that," I said.

16

ERIC WINSTON FROM NEW WEST BANK in Phoenix called the next morning to tell me the board would reduce Sharon Amaral's mortgage payments only to the amount of the interest. "I'm really sorry about this," he said, "but there was nothing I could do."

Winston knew whether he was telling the truth about who had made the decision. I didn't know, but I had my suspicions. Who wouldn't like to have an anonymous board in his or her life to take responsibility for the tough choices? To be able to say to the Martha Conovers of this world, "Sorry, Martha, but the board says I can't represent you, and there's no arguing with the board"? Bankers get to pass the buck. Lawyers in business for themselves don't.

"Sharon was a good customer," I said. "She made all her payments on time before her husband took off. Just give her a chance to get her life straightened out."

"I can't," he said.

"You're going to be taking on an undesirable property in a declining neighborhood," I warned him.

He wasn't intimidated. Bankers know how to say no;

they get lots of practice. They get lots of practice saying what comes next too. "I'm sorry."

"Would you sign off on the note if Sharon turns the house over to you? It'll save you the time and trouble of going through foreclosure. You're not going to get any more money out of Sharon anyway."

"It's a possibility," he said. "We're going to be interviewing Albuquerque lawyers next week. Could you come over?"

"I could," I said.

"Why don't we talk about the Amaral matter then?"

"All right." My making a client out of New West Bank might help Sharon, I thought, but what would it do for me? All I'd get out of it would be the ability to pay the bills a little sooner and the aggravation of having to hound Brink. That plus a trip to Phoenix.

I called Sharon. It wasn't much, 5½ Yellow Arrow Street, but it was home, and she was going to lose it. I might be able to improve on the terms, but sooner or later she'd have to pay up or move out. I picked up the phone, dialed Sharon's number and heard an answering machine voice. It was tempting to leave a message. "Sharon, the board says you're going to lose your house, and there's nothing I can do. Sorry." I wasn't likely to get paid for my efforts in any case. "This is Neil," I said. "Call me."

Next I headed for Brink's office to tell him he could become New West's Duke City representative. He might have been burrowed somewhere under the pile of papers that was his desk, but I didn't have the heart to look. I moved on to the kitchen and found him at the Mr. Coffee machine. "Coffee?" he asked.

"No, thanks. I'm going to Phoenix next week to talk to New West."

He put a little of the powdered stuff that imitates milk in his coffee, plus a couple of pink packets of artificial sweetener. "Who gets to do the work? You or me?"

"How about whoever has the most free time?" He knew who that was.

"If I'm going to have to do the work, then I should go to Phoenix."

"You want to?" I knew I was safe; Brink liked to travel about as much as he liked to work.

"Maybe."

"Brink, there's no time for maybes. Whoever is going is going next week." I wasn't sure what a banker would make of me, but I knew what one would think of Brink. Last night's dinner was crud on his tie. His hair was uncombed, his shirt unbuttoned around his ever-expanding belly, his shoes scuffed. There are lawyers who should remain in back offices doing careful and brilliant research while their more presentable colleagues deal with the clients. Brink's research wasn't that careful or that brilliant, but his looks and personality were back office all the way.

"You go," he said. He stirred his coffee until it was the color of the Rio Grande in snowmelt.

"All right," I said.

When Sharon Amaral returned my call, "Your Good Girl's Gonna Go Bad" was playing in the background. Sometimes a woman has a wound that only Tammy Wynette can heal. "They taking my house?" she asked.

"Unless you can come up with the back payments they are."

"Fat chance."

"They're talking about foreclosing. If they do and they don't recover the amount of the mortgage by selling the house, you're liable for the difference."

"I don't have it," said Sharon.

"I know," I said, "but if you ever get any money down the road they could take it."

"Shit," said Sharon.

"I might be able to talk the bank into a better deal for you. You sign the house over to them, they sign off on the mortgage. At least you wouldn't owe them anything, and they might let you go on living in the house until they find a buyer. I'm going to Phoenix next week, and I'll talk to them about it then."

"Thanks for trying." She didn't ask me to send her a bill for my time. I didn't offer.

"It's nothing," I said.

The Kid arrived at my place that night with a big bag of tacos under his arm. "Puta madre," he said, putting the bag down on the coffee table.

He wasn't the kind of man to show up after work tired and peevish. "Qué pasa?" I asked.

"La Bailarina is gone."

"Gone?"

"Her car is not there."

"She just went out somewhere. She'll be back."

"She never goes out. Where would she go? This is her only home. Her car is always here by eight o'clock." It was true; La Bailarina was as predictable and unfortunate as the evening news. "It was the watchman, I think. He made her go. You didn't give him enough money or to drink."

"What do you mean, *I* didn't give him enough money? It's not my job to support the ballerina."

"What does it cost you to give her some money or some food? You have it."

"I don't have *that* much money."

"You have enough."

"You know, Kid, we're not talking about Mexico here. She's an adult, an American citizen; she's got a car. Why can't she take care of herself?"

"You can take care of yourself; that doesn't mean she can."

"I can take care of myself because I make the effort to take care of myself."

"If she could help herself, she would. Why you not give Truman the money?"

"How do you know I didn't give him the money? Why are you blaming me?"

"Because if you gave him the money she would be here."

"I did give him the money," I said. "That's not why she left."

"You know why?"

"Yeah, I think I do." It was the guilt we were really talking about, the guilt of good but fucked-up intentions. "I think it's because I talked to her. I left her an invitation to a party some lawyers were having. I thought she'd like the food. When I saw her at the food table I spoke to her. I told her I lived in La Vista and had given her the invitation. She said I was mistaken, and she walked away."

"You took away her dignidad, Chiquita." Pride is something a Latin American male knows all about.

"I know."

"Where will she go?"

"Somebody else's parking lot?"

"Mierda," said the Kid.

"I'm sorry. Okay?" I replied.

Harry Chambers's Resolution Trust Corporation auction brochure arrived in the Monday mail. It had a full-color cover with photos of the scenic Southwest: snow-peaked mountains, golden aspen, sixteenth-century adobes of God, orange-and-lavender-streaked sunsets, pink lightning, saguaro cacti. Inside, among the Arizona condominiums, vacant lots, four-plexes and single-family residences, I found El Dorado, a destination resort with plans for a golf course, two hundred homesites with restrictive covenants, and an uncompleted hotel that was open for inspection by potential buyers. Adobe doesn't photograph well, and imitation-adobe models photograph even worse. El Dorado looked more like an oversized mud hut than a pot of gold in its one-inch-square photo.

There are always cheap flights from Albuquerque to Phoenix, whatever the state of the economy, and they begin or end in California. You can almost count on getting bumped and getting a free ticket out of it if you go late in the day, when everyone is trying to get home. I left Tuesday morning; I didn't want to spend a night in Phoenix if I didn't have to, but I packed a bag just in case. I saw Jed White, a lawyer I knew, picking up his boarding pass at the Southwest desk and said, "Hello, Jed," which was about all I had to say to him. Southwest is one of those airlines that have no assigned seats; you board according to the number on your boarding pass. The number you're assigned depends on when you get to the airport. While I stood on line, waiting to board my flight, I listened to the mix of accents behind me: New Mex, Old Mex, New York, unaccented English that had to be from California, the one state with no discernible accent.

People dress differently when they're leaving Albuquerque than they do when they're here. You always see more cowboy hats and boots in the airport than you do anywhere else in town. One of nature's laws is, the smaller the cowboy, the bigger the hat. You also see a lot of ruffled denim skirts and silver belt buckles that are heavy enough to use for workout weights. Tourists, I wondered, or do New Mexicans dress the part only when they leave their state? The line began to move. The man taking the boarding passes had to be a native New Mexican, because he switched from

English to Spanish and back again in the same sentence. "Dame your boarding pass. Gracias." I've never heard anybody but a New Mexican do that. I handed him my pass and was walking down the ramp to the plane when I heard a man's husky voice behind me say with a distinctly Argentine *y*, "Yo no lo tengo." He was a man, apparently, who hadn't figured out the system and hadn't picked up his boarding pass. It's hard not to be obvious when you stop in a corridor to see who's behind you, but I did it anyway and found myself looking at a medium-tall guy in leotard-tight jeans and a shirt that was unbuttoned several buttons down his chest, far enough to show off his chest hair—if he'd had any. He wasn't wearing a hat, and his dark hair was slicked in place. He didn't look Southwestern or Latin American. He looked European: Italian, maybe, or Spanish, which is to say that he could easily be Argentine. When I turned around, he stopped arguing with the attendant and looked back at me with a crooked grin and an arrogant stare. Maybe he thought I was coming on to him. Maybe not. He didn't have his pass, and the attendant made him go back and get one. The crowd pulled me down the ramp. I made my way to the rear of the plane and went through the too-many-oversized-bags-in-the-overhead-compartment dance, trying to squeeze mine in. I never did see the Argentine guy get on, if he did get on. By the time I left the plane in Phoenix he was nowhere in sight.

I rented a gray subcompact at Sky Harbor Airport and negotiated my way to New West Bank. Phoenix is a grid city like Albuquerque, crisscrossed by two interstates, only they call them freeways here, the L.A. influence. It's an easy town to drive in, as long as you have air-conditioning, and no one—not even Rent A Wreck—would dare rent out a car at the Phoenix airport that didn't have air-conditioning. Phoenix couldn't exist without air-conditioning, even in November. All the escaping freon has to be doing its part to extend the hole in the ozone layer. That's one reason I live in Albuquerque. You don't need an air-conditioned car to survive, but you'd probably go out before dark a lot more if you had one.

I went up a ramp and got on a freeway that gave me a good view of the city. Palm trees lined the streets. Cone-shaped protrusions stuck up here and there, the only places in sight that hadn't been developed. A large sign beside the road said the Clean Air Police advised people to car pool and in rush hour the left lane was reserved for them. Phoenix lives in the shadow of the Tonto National Forest, where the peaks are the height of the valleys in the Land of Enchantment. The altitude of Phoenix itself is a thousand feet—four thousand feet lower than the Duke City. The air was thick and humid enough to make my hair curl. From where I sat, Phoenix looked like a green and prosperous oasis. Albuquerque from any distance—near or far—looks like a dry and dusty pit stop. Going from New Mexico to Arizona reminds me of going from Spain to Portugal, from the bare and masculine to the soft and green. I asked myself the question that those of us who come from the Duke City ask here: Is Phoenix more prosperous than Albuquerque because it's prettier, because it's lower, because it's warmer or because it's closer to California? We're closer to Texas, but Texas money doesn't flow as freely as it used to. California money may not flow as freely inside the state either, but a lot of it seems to be flowing out. That's the American way. When your own nest becomes fouled, find another.

I got off the freeway at Seventh Street and onto the surface streets that led downtown to New West. I saw a lot of anonymous gray rental cars that were exact replicas of mine. The traffic moved slowly, regularly and somnambulently. Driving here was too easy, and the persistent hum of the air-conditioning fan was the kind of white noise that could put you to sleep at the wheel. Everybody had automatic transmission, everybody was air-conditioned, everybody's windows were rolled up. When I stopped at a light I heard the whir of my fan instead of my neighbor's booming beat. I saw a lot of one-story houses, a lot of For Sale signs, and a lot of fountains on the surface streets. All over Phoenix, fountains were dripping, plopping, spurting and gushing water—water that had to be pumped in from somewhere else because it didn't flow naturally here.

New West had a fountain in the lobby, one large Indian pot that poured water into another over and over again. My fellow lawyer Jed White was waiting there, indicating that he had taken a faster route than I, indicating also that he was interviewing with New West. This time I did have something to say to him, and it was "Jed, what are you doing here?" although I'd already figured it out.

"Interviewing to be New West's representative in Albuquerque." It didn't take him long to figure it out either. We were lawyers, after all, known for our quick wits. "You, too?"

"Yeah," I said. I'd known they were going to be interviewing other people, but it seemed kind of tacky to be doing it at the same time. Were they trying to intimidate one or the other of us into working for less? Going through the motions of being an equal opportunity employer? I peeked around surreptitiously to see if there were any blacks or Hispanics in the lobby. None that appeared to be interviewing for a job. Jed looked the part of an Arizona banker's lawyer, I had to admit, casual but precise. His shirt was fresh, his suit pressed, his tie subdued, his hair short and combed, his expression eager. I could feel my own hair frizzing, my skirt wrinkling and my expression getting snarly. I considered going into the ladies' room to try to spruce myself up, but what the hell. What they saw was what they'd get. Actually, what they'd get—Brink—was worse.

If Eric Winston was embarrassed that Jed and I had arrived

at the same time, he didn't let it show. He bustled across the lobby, jacket and tie flapping and a big grin on his face. If you can fake sincerity, they say, you can fake anything. "You two know each other," he said. "Good."

Jed looked at me. I looked back. He smiled. I didn't.

"Why don't you come first, Neil?" Eric said to me.

"Okay," I said. When it comes to waiting around bank lobbies, I don't have a principle to stand on.

Eric led me to his office and sat down. He was a little short, a little plump, a little slow, a whole lot affable, the kind of guy there probably *was* a board behind. Within those limits he was pretty much what he pretended to be—nice. He was the kind of good old local boy banks like to hire and promote—up to a certain point. When they get to the executive level, they bring in someone with more polish. We went through the motions, but we both realized relatively quickly that I was not the lawyer for New West. Sitting in his office for a half hour confirmed what I already knew—I'd hate bank work, and I couldn't count on Brink to do it right. Eric said he'd talk it over with the board and call me.

"Okay," I said. I almost told him not to bother, but why give up whatever guilt leverage I had? "So what do you think about Sharon Amaral?" I asked.

He tapped his pen on his desk while five gray-haired men sat around a table behind him and conferred. "It's your call," they whispered to Eric, and then they vanished. He cleared his throat. "We could probably sign off on the mortgage if she'll turn the house over to us. We don't want to go through foreclosure if we don't have to," he said.

"Can she stay in the house until she gets her life in order?"

"How long?"

"Six months."

"All right, but we'll need to draw up a lease and charge her rent."

"How much?"

"Make me an offer."

"Seventy-five dollars a month."

"A hundred?"

"All right," I said. It was a small victory, but that's what practicing law is usually about: large losses, little wins.

I passed Jed White in the lobby on my way out. "All yours," I said.

"Huh?" replied Jed.

17

The New West interview hadn't gotten me a client, but it had brought me to Phoenix and only thirty miles from Whit Reid's golden place, El Dorado. After I left New West I got on the freeway and headed south. Following the directions in the RTC brochure, I left the freeway at Bernal Road. In my rearview mirror I saw the white car that had been behind me pull off, stop at the intersection and turn in the opposite direction, but I couldn't see who was driving it. Entering blowing dust area, the sign on one side of the road said. For sale, said the sign on the other. "Living in the Shadow of a Doubt" played on the country music station. A car passed me going eighty-five. The kid behind the wheel was wearing a scarf around his head, tied pirate style. Don't drink and drive, his bumper sticker said, you might hit a bump and spill it.

Bernal Road passed through the Sonoran Desert. Saguaro cacti stood up like thirty-foot-tall sentinels with their arms raised, providing holes for birds' nests and casting long shadows. Forget the palm trees that were imported from somewhere else—the saguaros are what make Arizona unique. They don't grow anywhere in the world but here and north-

ern Mexico and a few places in California. Saguaros have a
waiting, watching quality, which gives me the impression
that they are trying to communicate. There are people who
talk to plants. There were times when I lived in Mexico that
I came close to doing it myself. If I ever broke through the
species barrier and communicated with a plant, it would be
a saguaro, but what would it have to say anyway? You're
only passing through, but I will endure? Or: You're destroy-
ing yourselves, and you're taking me along with you?

Go west on Bernal Road for five miles and turn north, the
RTC brochure said, onto an unimproved road. That meant
dirt, and I could see it in the distance, red dust whipped to
pink vapor by the wind. At the corner was a large RTC For
Sale sign, just in case anyone hadn't been following the directions and keeping track of the odometer reading. A couple of
guys had set up shop on the corner in a pickup truck with
the tailgate flipped open. Two big saguaros wrapped in blankets stuck out of the back of the truck. I guessed what the
cacti were doing in the truck, but why the blankets? I wondered. To keep them warm in the eighty-degree heat? To protect them? To cover them up if the cops came along? The
guys were in a spot where they could see what was coming
from a long way. It's illegal to dig up and sell saguaros without a permit unless they are on your own land, but they can
bring prices in excess of ten thousand dollars, so you know
somebody's going to be doing it. If these cacti could communicate, they'd be crying "Help!" They had minuscule roots,
which made me wonder if they weren't already dead, if the
guys hadn't cut off the root systems and murdered them
when they dug them up. An elderly couple had stopped and
were negotiating with the guys. People will sell anything—
their plants, their pets, their mothers-in-law—and the reason
is, there is always someone out there ready to buy. "Don't do
it!" I sent the negotiating couple a telepathic message, but
they weren't listening.

Like the conquistadores before me, I turned north to search for El Dorado. The road was red dirt, the desert green cacti, the sky deep blue with white puffs of clouds floating across it. A large bird with a white belly and black falcon wings lifted up and flew away. A coyote ran down the road, and its white tail bobbed like a bunny's. This place was a desert paradise. If it had to have a building, it deserved at least a Frank Lloyd Wright.

What it had received was a bloated corpse rotting in the sun. I came upon it about a mile later, a sprawling unfinished hulk of a building beside a sign that labeled it El Dorado. The wooden frame stuck out like the rib cage of the corpse, where the mud-colored stucco didn't cover it up. In some places the concrete-slab foundation lay exposed, a landing pad for helicopters or extraterrestrials. A pile of plywood and pink fiberglass insulation lifted and bucked in the breeze. Wires dangled from exposed beams. The size of it was appalling; so was the ugliness, the stupidity, the greed and the waste. You don't often find water in the desert, but you do find real estate fraud. This was a Las Tramponus project, which never should have been built with depositors' money that never should have been lent. A bank had collapsed, taking El Dorado down with it, or was it the other way around? Did it matter to the taxpayers who were going to be paying for it?

El Dorado looked as though it would have a three-day-old carrion smell, and I was tempted to remain in the car, sealed in and air conditioned. "You didn't come this far just to sit in a car," I told myself, so I changed into my running shoes, got out and walked toward the building. A mourning dove cooed, a sad and lonely desert sound. The pile of warped plywood shuddered and banged. I entered the El Dorado hotel, walked across the lobby and climbed the stairs to the second floor, wondering how long it would take this monstrosity of a building to decompose and this patch of desert to return to what it had been, remote, pristine, beautiful, wild. Forever, probably. It was for sale, I remembered, and would in fact be auctioned off in a few days. Some investor would buy it and borrow more money to finish it, maybe even from New West Bank. Water would be brought in from somewhere, and before you knew it, people would be playing golf at El Dorado and building their dream houses where saguaro had stood. Whit Reid's dream would come true, but he wouldn't be part of it.

Even in running shoes my footsteps sounded loud as I walked down a corridor on unfinished plywood floors. They echoed as I passed by room after room after empty room. No one had gotten around to putting down any sound-numbing carpet, or if they had, it had been stolen. This place, derelict as it was, would be a palace to Santo and all the other homeless, but they couldn't live here; it was too far from water, too far from food. The law of supply and demand didn't work in the Arizona desert unless you had money and a car. I turned a corner and passed a small room, intended to be a bathroom. The plumbing fixtures had left holes where they'd been ripped from the wall; they probably had not been gold, as they were in some S&L rip-off buildings, but would have been expensive enough. This was, after all, supposed to be a luxury resort. I continued down the hallway and entered one of the rooms. The wall behind me had been stuccoed over, and I crossed to the far side of the building, where I could look out through a space for a sliding door that led to a terrace. The arms of the watching saguaros were raised as if they'd been held up at gunpoint. I wondered how many Whit had dug up to build this place and what he'd done with them. I heard tires approaching on gravel, then a car door shut, reminding me that I was a woman alone in a lonely place and empty-handed too. I'd locked my purse and my weapon in the car. I had nothing with me to steal, but I had nothing to protect me either.

"It's a prospective buyer," I said to myself. I crossed the

building to a window-sized hole on the parking lot side and saw a white subcompact car dusted with red Arizona dirt, but whoever had been in it had already entered the building. I heard footsteps coming slowly up the stairway. "Hello," I called, but the only answer was feet reaching the top of the stairs and turning down the hall. "Who's there?" I called again, revealing that I was a woman and probably even that I was alone, if the intruder didn't already know. The mourning dove stopped cooing. The footsteps continued. There was a hesitation in the step and a scuffing sound like one foot dragging behind the other. I looked around for some means of self-defense, found a two-by-four in the corner and whacked it hard against the wall to make my point. I made a dent in the Sheetrock; the board held solid. The footsteps kept on with their erratic beat. I thought about Justine Virga frozen in a pair of headlights, about Las Manos, about my own hands. I could live without hands if I had to, but I couldn't live without blood. This was not a good place to empty your arteries. Trying to dial a phone would be the least of your worries out here.

I heard another car approach, moving faster and less carefully than the first. The gravel spun. One door slammed and then another. "It needs a hell of a lot of work," said a man in a real estate salesman's loud and jovial voice.

"A handyman's special," said another.

The footsteps began moving rapidly away. Clutching the two-by-four, I sidled up to the doorway in time to see running shoes and a pair of jeans disappear around an unfinished corner. I looked out the window and watched two real estate men in leisure suits approach El Dorado's entrance. A man wearing a black T-shirt, jeans and running shoes ran through the doorway and burst between them. Whatever was hesitant about his gait he lost once he began to run. The interloper was quick and skinny, with curly dark hair. The real estate men were slow and fat and pale. One of them fell on his butt. The other guy helped him up. The intruder ran toward his car. If he was carrying a weapon, he had concealed it. I couldn't get a good look at his face as he jumped into the white car, but I saw enough to make me believe he spoke Spanish. He slammed the door and sped away, raising clouds of pink dust, but not before I had memorized the license number, Arizona 4FR668. I ran down the hallway and down the stairs, repeating the number to myself so I wouldn't lose it. One real estate guy was brushing the other one off.

"What happened?" they asked.

"Just a minute," I said. I went to my car and wrote down the number on a pad in my purse. Then I returned to the men. "I heard him walking down the hallway, but when you pulled up he ran away."

"Probably looking for something to steal. Happens all the time in these deserted properties," one of the men said.

"There isn't much left to take here," I said.

"Yeah, it's been pretty well cleaned out, but some of these guys are desperate."

"He has a new car."

"Probably stole that too. Those Mexicans will steal anything that's not bolted down."

"How'd you know he was a Mexican?" I asked.

"What'd he look like to you?"

"Argentine, maybe," I said.

"Yeah, well, they'll steal too." It was a snap judgment. I see it often enough—Latino men are thieves. Rapists too, but he hadn't gotten around to that yet. I hoped it wasn't a judgment I'd been making myself. If anyone knows better, it ought to be me.

"Well, what do you think, John—you want to take a look?" he asked his companion.

"Why not?" his companion answered. "We didn't drive all the way out here to play golf."

"You guys prospective buyers?" I asked.

"Yeah," he said. "Aren't you?"

"Not exactly. I'm a lawyer looking for a client of mine."

"It's not a great place for a woman alone," he said.

"What is?" I replied.

18

JUST TO REMIND MYSELF that not everything that gets built is crap, I stopped at the Arizona Biltmore for a drink when I got back to Phoenix. It's the kind of sensual luxury hotel that makes me think about midafternooners. It was four, the digital clock in the car said; not too early, not too late. Sometimes I imagine I'm the kind of woman rich men take to luxury hotels, but if I wait a few minutes the feeling goes away.

The road to the Biltmore was thick with orange trees, country-club-sized houses and For Sale signs. Palm trees strolled down the median, and the shadows of the fronds fingered the road. The flower beds were brilliant with New England colors. No xeriscaping here. This was a luxury area, and the one necessary luxury in Arizona is water. A sign beside the road said to "Drive gently."

The turrets of the Biltmore appeared over the tops of the palms. It was the ultimate desert oasis, and it probably was a true oasis when it was built, before the city grew up around it. It was a sprawling, inventive Frank Lloyd Wright building and a monument to beauty, comfort and intelligence. No detail was ignored in the Arizona Biltmore. Every surface was carved and sculpted and planned. The gardens were brilliant and perfect, the sprinklers ticked unobtrusively. Even the birds sounded happier.

I parked my car in a shady spot, nodded to the doorman and went inside to the bar, where it was cool and dark and crystal prisms hung from the ceiling, reflecting what little light there was. I felt the way I used to at the end of a day of down-and-dirty third-world traveling: hot, beat, as if I'd been on a desert expedition and had a life-threatening but mind-expanding experience, as if what I needed was a soft seat and a cold drink. In one way I felt like an outsider here—layered with desert dust, not rich enough, not cautious enough, too close to the edge. In another way I didn't; Frank Lloyd Wright knew something about the edge himself. Excellence can push at the limits, but so can failure. There are the risks you choose to take (like sex) and the risks (like poverty) that choose you.

A waitress swam out of the darkness to ask what I'd like. "A margarita up," I said. My voice came out as snappy and irritable as a commuter in a traffic jam. If I'd been behind the wheel I would have been leaning on the horn. Maybe I was closer to the edge than I thought.

"You've had a hard day, haven't you?" She smiled, and her eyes crinkled up and said: Don't worry; we'll take care of you here. I looked into those eyes and was surprised to see that she meant it, but maybe I shouldn't have been. You'd expect the Biltmore to have the best and most unobtrusive service. I don't go to places like the Biltmore in Albuquerque; we don't have places like the Biltmore in Albuquerque.

"You're right," I replied.

My margarita arrived, big and cold and encrusted with salt. In my heart I know there are no safe places, but for the moment anyway I felt coddled and secure, as though no one had been lying to me or following me, or if anyone had, he wouldn't get to me here. I licked my way through the salt, arrived at a sheltered cove of triple sec and tequila, took a sip. About halfway through my drink I felt so secure that I began peering around the bar to see if there was anyone I might be interested in exploring the long, dark corridors of the Biltmore with. There were plenty of men here, but no one who seemed the right mix, whatever that was in this dark age of disease and limited expectations. The prospects were pale and prosperous businessmen in leisure clothes, cautious in some ways, maybe, reckless in others, but they weren't my ways. I wasn't an Arizona businessman's idea of an adventure, and they weren't mine. I wasn't even sure if the idea of romantic adventure still existed.

As I finished my margarita I thought about where I'd spend the night. It wasn't going to be here, in a two-hundred-dollar-a-night room, which left me with two choices: go back to the Duke City; go someplace in Phoenix I could afford. There were questions that still needed to be asked about El Dorado and about Whit Reid, so I decided to spend my night in a Motel 9.

It was, like all Motel 9's, seedy and cheap, with a tinny stall shower and no tub, near the highway where semis roll by like waves on the interstate shore. Places like this make me feel I'm underwater. To stay in the junk-traveler mood, I'd gotten dinner to go at McDonald's. I ate my Quarter Pounder and fries, then watched Jay Leno from the bed for five minutes, until I fell asleep without even lifting a finger to zap him off. When the phone rang a few hours later, Jay had been replaced by a fuzzy blank screen. "Hello," I said before I was awake enough to remember that I shouldn't answer the phone. Nobody would be calling me; nobody knew I was here. I was as alone as a woman could be in a cheap motel in Sunbelt City.

"Your car has been in an accident," a male voice said.

I was awake enough to recognize a scam. "Bullshit," I replied.

"Your name is Neil Hamel. Right?" the voice in the darkness rasped. He had an accent, but at this hour I couldn't tell what kind. I thought about turning on the light, but who knew where the con artist was calling from and whether he was watching my room for a reaction? Wherever the voice was, he wasn't going to get me to admit my name. I didn't say anything, but that didn't stop him. "You rented a gray subcompact from Budget. Right?" He *was* right, but I didn't let him know it. "Your car ran into mine. I don't think you will want to involve the police and the insurance company, so why don't we talk about it." Still no answer from me. "I will be there in five minutes."

The object, apparently, was to get me to open the door. It wasn't a brilliant scheme, but the criminal mind is more deviant than smart. I hung up and dialed the police. "It's a scam," a bored policewoman answered. "Happens all the time. Don't open the door. They're looking to get in and rob you."

"Could you send somebody over to investigate?" I asked.

"By the time we got there, hon, the guy will be long gone. Your best bet is to call hotel security."

I called the front desk. "We'll be over in a few minutes," motel security said. "Your door has a security lock. Don't open it."

I got out of bed and went to the window. The white polyester drapes were pulled tight, and I separated them a crack to peek through. Mercury vapor lights gave the parking lot the deep shadows and the brilliant fluorescence of a combat zone. Headlights signaled from the interstate, white first, then red. A gray subcompact with a pool of shadow under it was parked out front where I remembered leaving mine. Could someone have taken my car and replaced it with its exact replica? All gray rental cars look alike to me. I couldn't remember the license number. I can't remember my own license number. If my car weren't bright yellow and loaded with bumper stickers, I'd never be able to find it in a parking lot. Raspy Voice had gotten my name and room number. How? He could have stolen the car. He could also have broken into it here and looked at the rental records. Once he had my name, it wouldn't be hard to get my room number, or would it? You'd like to think that was information the night clerk wouldn't give out.

On the other hand, he could have followed me here. I didn't want to fall into the trap of thinking that everyone who has an accent and/or looks Latin American is a criminal. I didn't want to fall into the trap of thinking that every criminal is after me. It's paranoia either way you look at it, but even paranoids get followed. I wasn't at anybody's mercy, however. I didn't have to be a victim; I had a weapon. I got dressed in the parking lot's ambient glow and took the security lock off the door. The criminal and hotel security were on their way, but I was kind of hoping the criminal would get here first. That's the kind of woman I was. Facing down trouble alone is a pattern you learn early. First you fear it, then you adjust to it, then you begin to like it. Then you find you like it so much that—like a drug—you can't live without it.

He signaled his arrival by a furtive knock at the door. I'd known he was coming; I'd heard his footsteps, and they weren't the secure and confident steps of a security guard. They were the quick and light steps of someone who was used to getting in and out fast, but they had the slight hesitation of someone who had a bad leg.

I flicked on the overhead light, yanked the door open to get a good look at him and found myself facing a black ski mask with holes for the mouth, nose and eyes, smooth and threatening as an assassin's hood. He was medium-sized, skinny and all in black: his jeans, his windbreaker, his running shoes. He moved fast. His hands were encased in black leather gloves, and in two seconds they were pushing me against the wall. Leather fingers moved from my shoulders to my collarbone and closed around my throat. "Who are you? What do you want from me?" I gagged. My voice box was jammed, my trachea squashed, and then I couldn't speak or scream or even breathe much. His knee pressed into my groin. I raised my hand with the weapon in it. He noticed, brought his knee back and kicked my arm with a fluid and powerful motion.

The weapon fell to the ground, slid across the floor and broke open against the door, releasing a sharp and pungent odor, poison in the nose and lungs, that straddled the line between smell and pain. It was the odor that will repel a man faster than any other. New Mexico's one-hundred-percent all-natural free-range skunk stunk. If smell had a color, its color would have been puke green. It had me reeling. The masked man gasped, let go of my throat and staggered out the door. I followed. Anything to get out of the fouled den my room had become.

He ran down the walkway with no trace of his limp. He seemed to possess an athlete's ability to ignore it when necessary. He'd never said a word, so I didn't know if he and Raspy Voice were one and the same. I bent over my rental car, trying to catch my breath and throw off the smell, feeling I would vomit green vapor. He was getting away from me but taking his smell with him. He'd taken a direct hit, and he didn't have any neutralizer. He'd have to burn his clothes and douse himself in tomato juice to get rid of it. He ripped off his hood, jumped into an anonymous white car at the far end of the parking lot and burned rubber getting out of there. Once again I couldn't get a good look at his face, but I did get the last two digits of his license plate number: 68.

I held my breath, went back into the room thankful I'd messed up a Motel 9 and not the Biltmore, grabbed the neutralizer and sprayed it around. It would be a long time before anyone would want to stay in here again. I sprayed my clothes too, but it would be a long time before I'd want to wear them again. While I waited for the security guard, I went out and investigated the gray rental car. It was mine; the key fit. There was no sign of breaking and entering. The rental documents were in the glove compartment, exactly as I had left them.

The security guard took his sweet time about showing up, but eventually he ambled down the walk. He was plump and bewhiskered and his nose twitched like a bunny's. From three feet away his breath had the whiskey smell. Even in my fouled clothes I caught that. Like Truman, the night watchman at La Vista, he probably spent his nights in the laundry room, rinsing his throat.

"Whew," he said. "Were you attacked by a skunk?"

"You could say that."

"Did you let him in?"

"Yeah."

"Why?"

"I wanted to see his face."

"Didn't the front desk tell you to leave the security lock on?" Already the incident bore the unmistakable imprint of becoming my fault.

"I was expecting you at any minute," I said.

"I got here as quick as I could."

"I bet," said I.

"Did he take anything?"

"No."

"Do you want to file a report?"

"All right."

I went to the police station and went through the motions. The police didn't think coming across two crooks in one day was anything out of the ordinary and didn't believe there was any relationship between the two crimes. When it came to the limp, they didn't seem to think I was a reliable witness. They did run a check on the license number and found out it belonged to a rental car that had been stolen.

19

MOTEL 9 GAVE ME ANOTHER ROOM in which to finish off the night, one that smelled more like new disinfectant than old skunk. But they weren't exactly generous about it. In fact, they made me pay another $29.95; it was my fault the room smelled as if a skunk had crawled under the foundation and croaked. By the time I left, the second room didn't smell too great either. You could spend the rest of your life smelling like road kill, I thought. Maybe some smells—like some pains—went too deep for neutralizer.

As soon as it became light enough and late enough to make phone calls, I took out the directory and looked up Harry Chambers Auctioneers. I asked Harry's secretary if I could come by and visit.

"Sure," she said. "Come on by. He's not doing anything but listening to himself talk anyway."

Harry Chambers Auctioneers was in a low-slung stucco building xeriscaped with white pebbles for a lawn and a beat-up saguaro that might have been used for target practice. It was low-water, no-maintenance landscaping, but inside, the ubiquitous fountain bubbled and gushed, white noise to hide the sounds of the city, white water to make you think the temperature is double digits when it's really one hundred and ten. The reception area was paneled in dark wood, had orange shag carpet on the floor and a Southwest painting in dubious taste on the wall, your basic pink sunset and purple mesa. I heard Harry's voice the minute I walked in the door. It was loud enough to get your attention and had the singsong rhythm of a rap artist or a Southern Baptist preacher. "Who will give me fifty, who will give me fifty? Would you give me fifty-five, would you go to sixty?" I spotted him—a talking red head about three feet by four on a color TV. "Say hello to a good buy," he said.

"Is that how it's done these days?" I asked his secretary. "By remote control on the auction channel?"

"Oh, no. Harry appears live, but he likes to watch himself practice on video. Helps him perfect his routine, he says." Her puffy blond hairdo could have been set on orange juice cans, and she wore black-framed glasses with rhinestones in the corners. She rolled her eyes as she buzzed Harry on the intercom. "What did you say your name was?" she asked me.

"Neil Hamel. I don't have an appointment."

"That's all right. He'll see you. Harry will talk to anybody anytime. Harry, Neil Hamel's here."

"Send him in," Harry growled.

"See?" the secretary asked. She pointed toward Harry's door, which was down the hall and wide open.

I stepped into the office and found myself looking at Harry Chambers and two of his exact replicas. Harry sat behind a large desk, the replicas were on either side of the room on large TV screens. All of them wore navy-blue blazers, white shirts, red and blue striped ties. Two of them were talking. "Who will give me ninety. Can you go one hundred? Yes or no, gotta go. Do I hear a hundred?" Harry's red hair was slicked back, and he had the sharp nose and glittery eyes of a fox. He was well groomed and not bad-looking, but too loud and too fast, like Robin Williams on speed. One of him was more than enough. He picked up the remote, turned to the east and zapped off Harry One, turned to the west and got rid of Harry Two. "Isn't Neil a man's name?" he asked me.

"Not when I'm wearing it," I replied in the edgy voice of someone who'd fought off an assailant and hadn't had any sleep she could remember.

"Whoa! Did you check your gun at the door?"

"Sorry," I said.

"Hey, we all have days like that. Sometimes I work up enough lather to shave the city of Phoenix." He laughed, showing a number of gold-capped teeth. "What can I do you for?"

"I'm a lawyer. I represent a woman whose husband developed a destination resort that you're going to be auctioning off for the RTC. He told her they'd get some money out of the sale." It wasn't the exact truth, but as close as I wanted to get.

"She believes that and she's either a sap or a saint. There's a woman that ought to be looking for a new husband, one with an MBA, a massive bank account."

"You could be right," I said.

He stood up and began pacing behind his desk. Like most comedians, he joked better on his feet. "I found a chain letter on my wife's bureau the other day. You know what it said? Don't send money. Put your name on the bottom of the list and send your husband to the name on the top. By the time *you* get to the top of the list you'll get sixteen thousand husbands, and one of them has gotta be better than that SOB you're living with now. But whatever you do, don't break the chain—you're likely to get your own husband back. You got a husband?"

"Nope."

"You're smart."

"Well, what do you think? Is she likely to get any money out of the sale?" I knew she wasn't, but this wasn't exactly a rhetorical question. I was fishing, although I wasn't quite sure for what. Bottom feeders, perhaps.

He laughed. I'd become the comedian now. "You know what these RTC laundromats are going for? I call 'em laundromats because S&Ls were a great place to launder money: mob money, drug money, campaign money, any kind of no-good, no-account money. They're going for pennies on the dollar. And it's not because I don't know how to talk people out of their wallets either. Hell, I've been doing it for twenty-five years. We're lucky if we get half the amount of the mortgage. Of course, most of them were overmortgaged to begin with. Bankers lent money to their developer buddies, gave the kickbacks to the politicians and spent what was left on gold faucets for their Learjets. They thought they were bulletproof, but when one went down he'd plea bargain and take all his cronies with him. It was like trees dropping in the forest. Kathump, kathump, kathump." His hand imitated the motion of falling trees.

"Do you get many bidders?"

"We get lots of lookers. Everybody's looking for a deal, and there's plenty of action up to a hundred thou. But the amount of serious bidders we get for the big properties could fit into a small room, a very small room—they could fit into the cubbyhole under my desk. The market for destination resorts in Arizona in this economy is as dead as Tucson in the summertime. You go to Red Rocks in peak season, and they aren't even half full. I keep seeing the same guys over and over again at these auctions. One takes his phone out, dials a number, the other guy, sitting across the room, answers. I'm trained to look for moving hands, you know. That's my business."

"What are they doing?"

"Divvying up the properties. One gets one, the other

184 ▽ JUDITH VAN GIESON ▽

takes the next one. They keep the prices down by not bid-
ding against each other. Real estate investors are the biggest
bunch of crooks I've ever seen. These guys would screw
their own mothers. Myself, I'd rather be auctioning estates
or Elvis Presley memorabilia—better class of people." He
paused and thought for a couple of seconds. "If your client
wants to get rid of her husband, she could try siccing the
feds on him. Where you had real estate development in this
state in the eighties, you had bank fraud, and that's a federal
crime. They'll take his money, but she might have the pleasure of seeing him do time. The feds have their own destination resort. Club Fed. I hear it's a hot place to spend the
summer."

"Well, thanks for your help," I said.

"My pleasure," he replied. He sniffed and wrinkled his
sharp nose. "What *is* that smell?"

"Road kill," I said.

He zapped the TVs on as I left the room, and the talking
Harrys started flapping their gums like ventriloquists' dum-
mies. "Do I hear one hundred? Yes or no, gotta go. That's as
cheap as I can dance."

"Is he always on like that?" I asked the secretary on my
way out.

"Always."

Harry's tone of voice and expression changed suddenly
into a scowl and a scold. He moved up close to the camera.
"I know you're on the sofa, Rex," he barked. "I can see you
up there. Get down right now, do you hear me. I said get
down!"

"His dog," the secretary said. "He leaves the tapes on at
home too."

"Atta boy," Harry said.

20

HARRY HAD A POINT, but it seemed to me that if the feds had wanted Whit Reid they would have gotten him by now. His buddy Charlie Keating had been locked up and was already rattling his bars demanding the Grey Poupon. I went next to the Federal Courthouse and scanned the microfiche, looking for the name of Whitney J. Reid III. It wasn't there. Whit had not been tried and found guilty, had not been tried and found innocent, had not been tried at all. He could have plea-bargained, however, could have been one of those trees that took the forest down. A bank fraud settlement wouldn't necessarily be a matter of public record. A man I went to UNM law school with was an assistant U.S. attorney here, I remembered. I gave him a call from the pay phone in the lobby.

"This is Neil Hamel," I said. "We were classmates at UNM. Remember?"

"You were the blonde from Texas, right? The one with great legs?" Jonathan Laswell answered.

"Wrong."

"Oh. Well, what can I do for you?"

"I stayed in Albuquerque and have my own office there.

I'm in Phoenix today, trying to get some information on Whitney J. Reid, who was a local developer before the market went bust."

"Whitney J. Reid. I believe I've heard that name."

"I think he was involved in S&L fraud, but I can't find a record of any prosecution."

"Some of the S&L settlements fell under the Bank Board's veil of secrecy and were sealed."

"You doing anything for lunch?"

"Not much. How about Romanos at twelve-thirty?"

"Okay."

"You're sure you're not the blonde from Texas."

"Positive," I said.

The Romanos in Phoenix was an exact replica of the one in Albuquerque, down to the large parking lot, the soggy pasta and the waitresses who did look like blondes from Texas and who had been trained to say Hi, I'm Cheryl, or Debbie, or Allison, and wish you a nice day. Waitresses always have names that were up-to-the-minute eighteen or twenty years ago. At least a name like Neil doesn't mark you as being of a certain age or time, not if it's worn by a woman anyway. I knew I was marked by something, however, because Jonathan Laswell picked me out immediately as being the Albuquerque lawyer who—like him—was pushing forty and who also—like him—wasn't getting rich doing it. It takes a certain kind of courage or incompetence to be a lawyer for twelve years and not make any money. Jonathan's excuse was that he was a prosecutor, and prosecutors are a special breed of lawyer, a special breed of government employee too, especially the ones that stay with it. Most prosecutors leave government service after a few years. Some go to work for large prestigious firms representing the same white-collar criminals they once prosecuted. The less accomplished or more committed go to work for themselves, defending the Mexican nationals and the child molesters they get assigned by the public defender's office. It's one way to make a living, and there is always plenty of work. Laswell, however, seemed to enjoy being a prosecutor, to be in it for life.

He'd been short and slender when I knew him, with black bangs that fell across his forehead. He was still short, but he'd added a lot of weight-lifting bulk, and his bangs had gotten streaked with gray. His muscles were bursting out of his suit. He appeared to have convicted a lot of felons; his eyes had the hyper tenacity of a bulldog, and they took in everything that went on in Romanos, especially the blond waitresses.

"You haven't changed a bit," he lied.

"Neither have you," I lied back.

Once we'd been seated and the margarita (for me) and Perrier (for him) arrived, we began playing catch-up. "So what kind of law are you doing in Albuquerque?" he asked.

"Real estate and divorce mostly, an occasional homicide. I'm representing Whit Reid's mother-in-law, who may have been involved in a traffic fatality. His wife is an old friend of mine."

"The mother-in-law didn't run into Whit, did she?"

"No."

"Pity. So what's your life like? You married?"

"No."

"Got any kids?"

"No."

"A house?"

"No."

"Pets?"

"No." He sounded like a prosecutor, and my life sounded like the desert, even to me.

"You're lucky," he said, indicating, perhaps, that he had

all of the above and that he was looking to get out of it, maybe even that he could use my help. Fortunately I lived and practiced in another state.

"So what do you know about Whitney J. Reid?" I asked.

"You mean personally or legally?"

"Both."

"Personally I know he's an arrogant asshole born with a silver racket in his mouth and he got himself in deep do-do. Ankle deep; no, knee deep. Everybody has a bucket, and Whit Reid's bucket was full."

"Then why isn't he in prison?"

"Actually, he was—for a weekend." Jonathan smiled the smile of a man who took enough pleasure in his work to keep him at it for a hundred years. "I arrested him on a Friday, held him till Monday, threw him in a holding pen with pimps and dealers. White-collar criminals hate being in jail. His cellmates were all over him like a cheap suit, and on Monday he told me everything I wanted to know. It led to some successful prosecutions. We were after Sonny Wilson, the banker, and Whit Reid was a piece of the puzzle."

"But you didn't prosecute him?" The pasta arrived. While I ate mine (green and white tortellini in a cream sauce), Jonathan talked.

"No. A: We've got too many of these S&L cases. We don't have the time or the staff or the funds to prosecute all of them, especially the million-dollar players. We go after the ones like Sonny Wilson, who stole billions. B: If we put white-collar criminals away, they go to some country-club prison and cost the taxpayers fifty thousand dollars a year. If we settle, we can get them to pay back some of what they stole without the expense of taking them to trial. We settled with Reid, and the taxpayers came out ahead. It doesn't happen very often. His former buddy Sonny Wilson went to the big house, and his mother has been complaining that her boy has to clean the latrine. Do you have any idea how much money he made? When he gets out, even after he's paid all his fines and settled his lawsuits, he'll still have hundreds of millions hidden away somewhere. Among other things, he took little old ladies' deposits and invested them in junk bonds that weren't worth the paper they were printed on. Virtually every project he lent money to has now gone belly-up. The total S&L debacle is going to cost the taxpayers two hundred billion dollars, and the amount is climbing daily. That's fifteen hundred dollars for every tax-payer." He looked at his watch. "Make that fifteen-fifty. And now Sonny Wilson will have to clean some latrines and we're supposed to feel sorry for him. But the worst part for Wilson is that he had to give up his hairpiece. He wears a baseball cap now." Laswell laughed.

I brought him back to the bit players. "So you settled with Whit Reid."

"Yeah."

"What were the terms?"

"I can't reveal them. The settlement we made comes under the Bank Board's veil of secrecy. That information is sealed. Didn't he tell his wife?"

"She says he didn't."

"How does she think he got so broke?"

"The recession."

"It's people like him that caused the recession, by glut-ting the market with useless buildings that never should have been built. Every real estate venture contains the seeds of its own destruction."

"So does every relationship. So does every life."

He smiled. "That's true. You could file under the Free-dom of Information Act if you really want to know the terms of the settlement."

"That'll take forever."

"You're right."

I looked into Jonathan Laswell's hard and bright little

eyes and saw a way to pierce the Bank Board's bureaucratic veil. He hated the arrogant rich even more than I did. "Maybe you could just tell me in general what the crimes and settlements were all about, if you can't talk specifics."

"I'd have no problem with that."

"Developers, for example. What did they do?"

"Land flips, kickbacks. They'd fraudulently flip a property to get the price and the amount of the mortgage up." He leaned across the table, dipping the corner of his sleeve into his pasta dish as he did. "I've seen them set up a row of tables in somebody's office and transfer title back and forth all day. A property could go from two million to ten million in an afternoon. Business is just a game to these guys, like moving pieces around a board."

It wasn't that big a step from moving pieces to moving people, I thought.

"The way kickbacks work is, the developer borrows more than the property is worth, then kicks back the excess to his buddy the banker, or the banker turns it over to his buddy a politician. For example, the developer borrows one hundred thousand more than he needs. He solicits checks from his employees to equal that amount. He gives the checks to the banker, who contributes them to the Republican party or the Democratic party, whoever. When it came to S&L fraud, there was only one party—the fund-raising party. The banker gets a credit with the party for future favors. The developer pays his employees back with the hundred thousand, making it look like a bonus or overtime. The developers were a part of the scam, but the people we were really after were the bankers. In most cases, the developers were more than happy to cooperate. You know Wilson's bank financed El Dorado, Reid's development. When the bank went under, the RTC foreclosed, and now they're trying to get rid of it."

"I know. I went out and took a look at it."

"It's a beaut, isn't it? It was going to be Whit's little king-dom, a planned development where he could let in whoever he wanted, keep out who he didn't. He had restrictive covenants to end all restrictive covenants. He wasn't going to allow his property owners to subscribe to *Penthouse* or *Playboy*."

"You're kidding."

"Nope. It says so right in the deed."

"So this is what it's like back in the U.S.A." We call the state I live in one of the missing fifty, because it so often gets confused with its third-world neighbor.

"That's what it's like in Arizona anyway."

"I'll say one thing about Arizona: your white-collar crooks have more imagination than ours."

"It's amazing how they discover religion and good works when they're looking at a prison sentence."

"What did you settle with the developers for?"

"As much as we could get, although it was never as much as those guys stole. They went through money like a knife through butter, and a lot of what they owned they bought at inflated prices. They believed in the boom they'd created, but when it came time to sell, the market was severely depressed. We took their cars, their houses, their polo ponies, their boats, their jewelry. Remember they were staring prison in the face, and that scared the shit out of them."

"Do you ever take it in payments?"

"We might give a guy some time to unload his assets, come up with the money he'd been hiding."

"What would happen if he missed a payment?"

"The big house. I may be talking out of school here." Laswell's eyes circled the room, either to make sure no one was listening or to keep tabs on the blond waitresses. "But Whit Reid is all paid up."

"Recently?"

"In September."

"Do you ever make community service a part of the package?"

"Often."

"Could a person perform that service in another state if he moved?"

"Could."

"I didn't think Whit Reid was noble enough to volunteer to help out minority small businesses on his own."

"Trust me, he's not," Jonathan Laswell said.

I flipped through the in-flight magazine on the way home and thought about what I would tell Cindy and Saia and Martha. Nothing, I decided. If Cindy already knew, I wouldn't be doing her any favor by revealing what she'd been trying to conceal. If she didn't know, what good would it do to tell her at this point? However, if she ever asked me to file for divorce ... As for Saia, I had no need to reveal what I'd discovered to him unless it could keep Martha from being indicted. Whit Reid was a crook and a snitch who'd turned in his banker buddy, but that didn't make him Justine Virga's killer. For one thing, he had a good alibi for the night the murder or accident or whatever it was took place. As for motive, if he was as broke as he appeared to be, why hadn't Martha been the victim? Cindy was her only heir.

What to tell Martha was more problematical. Martha Conover was not likely to go into business with a crook, and I was pretty sure she didn't know about Whit's relationship with the federal government. But what kind of friend would tell her before telling Cindy? If it had any bearing on her case, I'd be obligated to tell her, but as far as I could see now, it had none. As for its having a bearing on her life, that was a gray area. What I should do, I thought, is confront Whit and make him tell Martha and Cindy himself, but I wasn't quite ready to let him know what I knew. I decided, for the moment anyway, to keep on looking and keep my mouth shut.

I hung around the gate after I deplaned at Albuquerque, but I didn't see anybody I recognized getting off the plane. I didn't see anyone who seemed interested in getting to know me better either.

21

THE KID CAME FOR DINNER, and I cooked his favorite meal of Chile Willies. I made it the way I always did—broke the blue-corn tortillas in pieces, sautéed them until they were crisp, added the red-hot salsa, melted Monterey Jack cheese on top—but it tasted better than usual. Maybe adventure makes the taste buds grow fonder.

"This tastes good tonight, Chiquita," the Kid said.

"Thanks."

He ate fast, and when he was finished he sipped at his Tecate. When the Kid ate, he ate. When he talked, he talked. And when he made love, well, he focused on that too. "How was your trip to Arizona?"

"I didn't take the job with the bank," I said.

He nodded; that didn't surprise him. "Did you think you would?"

"Not really."

"Then why did you go?"

"To work out a better deal for Sharon Amaral." It wasn't the entire explanation. He knew it, and so did I. He waited, sipped at his beer. "I also wanted to find out what kind of trouble Whit Reid, Cindy's husband, is in. I thought he'd been lying to her about his real estate deals, and I found out he had been. I also found out he broke the law, got caught and had to pay the federal government a big fine." The Kid nodded again, indicating he knew that wasn't the whole story either. Maybe I was getting too predictable; maybe he was starting to know me too well. Maybe he'd noticed the red finger-shaped welts on my neck, which weren't quite hidden by makeup or a scarf. I'm not the kind of woman who wears scarves or makeup, and the Kid knew that too. "Somebody was chasing me. I went into the desert to look at Whit Reid's resort, and I thought I saw a white car follow me off the freeway. But it turned in the opposite direction. Later, when I was alone at the property, I heard somebody drive in and walk down the hallway toward me. I asked who was there. He didn't answer, but he kept on coming. When somebody else drove up, he ran away."

"Why you go there alone, Chiquita?"

"Because I didn't have anybody to go with. Besides, what's the point in living, Kid, if you can't go anyplace alone?"

It was a rhetorical question, and he didn't answer it. "Did you see the guy?"

"Not very well, but I got his license number. Last night I stayed in a Motel 9, and in the middle of the night somebody called with a bullshit story about my rental car being in an accident. He said he wanted to come by and talk to me."

"Did you let him in?" he asked, but he already knew the answer. As he'd told me once before, I never know when to quit. The Kid had warned me, but he'd never tried to stop me. Maybe he knew it wouldn't work; maybe he didn't really want me to stop. If I were the kind of woman who took no risks, he wouldn't be interested in me. If I were more cautious, I wouldn't be interested in him.

"Yeah, I let him in; I had a weapon."

The Kid raised his eyebrows. We'd had an argument before about my carrying a gun, his theory being that when you have a gun it's just as likely to be used against you as by you.

"It was a skunk gun," I said. "It's full of skunk juice, and the smell drives an assailant away."

He shook his head. The things people did in this country remained incomprehensible to him, but it was his country now, whether he liked to admit it or not. "Was it the same guy?"

"Probably, but he wore a ski mask and I never got a good look at his face. Both guys were the same size and shape, and they drove the same car. They acted like they'd had a slight leg injury. Both walked with a limp and ran without it. I had to fight him off, Kid. He had his hands around my neck."

"I can see that," he said, looking at the marks on my neck, which had gotten more vivid as the day went on.

"When I pulled out the skunk gun he kicked it out of my hand, but it went off anyway. He had a powerful kick. I never heard him speak, but I did hear someone behind me in the airport when I was going over there talking Argentine."

"He could be a soccer player. Some soccer players can forget they are hurt when they are playing, and Argentinos are good at soccer."

"I know," I said. And I knew they could be connected to the guys at Mighty, but I didn't think Ramón Ortiz was the one to ask.

"But what they do best is polo. They are the best polo players in the world. Everybody wants to have an Argentino on their team. It's one way to get out of Argentina."

"Do you think he could have been one of Las Manos?"

"Why would they be after you?"

"Because I am the only one who is investigating Niki Falcón's death. If the police are doing anything, no one's telling me about it."

"I don't know, Chiquita. I think if Las Manos wanted to kill you, you would be dead."

"What I don't understand, Kid, is if Niki Falcón was killed by hit men, why didn't they just go back to Argentina and disappear afterwards? It wouldn't make any difference then if I found them out."

"Maybe they don't want to go back to Argentina. Maybe they like it here. Maybe business is better in this country."

"But why follow me to Arizona? Why not go after me here?"

"You don't go out in the desert and stay in motels alone here, do you?"

"No," I said.

We took off our clothes later and got into bed. The parking lot's light filtered in through the curtains, giving the bedroom the ambience of a Motel 9. A car in the lot squawked as a remote unlocked it and then yelled "Break in" in an automaton's loud voice. There was another squeal, and the remote zapped the voice off. The sounds of high-tech progress at La Vista could make you long for the days before cars found their voice. It got quiet again in the bedroom; I could hear the Kid's steady and regular breathing. He curled up next to me, sniffed my hair and my skin.

"You have the smell of . . . "

"Road kill?"

"La hedionda." Literally that means the foul-smelling one or the skunk, but it also means death, and in New Mexico folklore, death is an old woman. Enough light came in through the curtains so the Kid could see the finger marks on my neck. "People in South America have hard lives, Chiquita," he said.

"I know."

"The killers there are cruel and brutal."

"They are not exactly nice guys here."

"Believe me, Chiquita, they are worse there."

"Felons are felons. You just think they are worse because you were a boy when you lived there and everything looks bigger when you're a child."

"Why don't you bring your gun home with you?"

"You're the one who complained about guns in the house, Kid."

"This is an exception." He touched the marks on my neck. "Cuidado con la hedionda," he said. Watch out for la hedionda.

I stopped by Martha Conover's in the morning to tell her what had happened since the last time I saw her, as much as I thought was advisable anyway. I didn't feel especially guilty about withholding certain facts at this point, because she hadn't always told me the whole truth. Martha measured out the truth the way she measured out her love—using the bottom line of the measuring cup. I looked around me as I drove up the Los Cerros road. She maintained her property a lot better than the absentee owners of La Vista did. The grounds were manicured, the sprinklers ticked, there were no pets, there was no litter, the children and the handicapped were confined to a limited area. In my hallway the paint cracked and peeled, the indoor/outdoor carpeting was stained, the night watchman got drunk. As I parked the Nissan in a space marked for visitors, I remembered what Jonathan Laswell had said about every real estate venture containing the seeds of its own destruction, and I thought about who would look after this place if Martha went to prison. She'd have to give someone power of attorney; she wouldn't be able to collect her rents, pay her bills and harangue her staff from a prison cell. There were people who could manage Los Cerros, but was there anybody who would do it as carefully as she had?

As I walked toward her town house I saw Martha standing in front of her door, clutching her keys in one hand and her purse in the other. In front of her was a locked door and behind her a view that went into the next county. The getting old resemble the very young: they change so quickly that the person you see today is not necessarily the one you saw a week ago. Martha stared at me as if she didn't know who I was. A window opened up in her eyes, and I was able—briefly—to peer into her interior world. It looked as though an intruder had disconnected the wires, broken in and ransacked her brain. The hand that held her keys trembled like a frightened bird. She was talking, but she didn't know whom she was talking to. "I can't remember whether I was coming in or going out," she said in a dazed voice.

"Let's go in." I reached to take the keys from her hand, but she wouldn't release them. She clutched them tight in her fingers and stared at me as if she was thinking: I know you, I know you and I don't approve of you. Then she snapped out of it, the wires reconnected, the juice came back on and she was her old self again.

"I can open my own door," she said. The change from Martha's confused, vulnerable self to her bossy, in-control self was rapid and extreme. Every way-out form of behavior contains the seed of its own opposite, but swinging from one extreme to another is no way to create a balance. I couldn't blame her for overreacting, however; I wouldn't want to be old and infirm and depending on me for help.

She opened the door to let us in, and a pink Post-it fluttered to the floor. She put her purse down on the table and walked toward the kitchen. "Can I get you a drink?" she asked.

"No."

Life sucks, and then you lose your body or your mind, I thought as I listened to her open the freezer door, take out the vodka and pour herself a large one with no ice. She might have just had a slight stroke. She might also have had one the night that Justine died. The part of her brain that stored the events of that night, that had or had not registered Justine in the headlights, could be a burned-out microchip inaccessible to her or anyone else. Someone should tell her she needed medical help, but the someone was her daughter, not me.

She sat down on her chintz sofa, crossed her legs at the ankles, straightened her back, swallowed some vodka.

"We can talk some other time if you're . . . sick," I said.

"There's nothing wrong with me. Nothing," she said. "What did you want?"

"I took a trip to Arizona to talk to some bankers, and I think someone followed me over there. Whoever it was attacked me in my motel room. I fought him off."

"What did he look like?"

"Young . . . skinny."

"Spanish?"

"Latin American. Look, I've asked you this before, but I have to do it again. Is there anyone you think could have set you up? Anyone with anything to gain by putting you in prison?"

"I've told you before that Mina Alarid hates me and would do anything to destroy me."

"But she didn't hate Justine, did she? Why would she destroy her?"

"Emilio Velásquez had a disturbed relationship with that girl. He's probably the one who turned her on to drugs. Maybe she knew too much and he had to get rid of her. He hates me too, and by blaming it on me he could get rid of both of us at once."

If you accepted the premise that Emilio was a scumbag, it had a certain kind of logic.

"I'm not a fool," Martha continued. "I know he was living here and seeing Cynthia and Michael. I know he went on seeing Justine after Michael died, but I wouldn't make a martyr out of him by kicking him out."

"If you know Emilio is living here, you should tell Cindy that."

"I'll tell Cynthia what I want to tell Cynthia."

This family was a raw onion. Peel off one tear-inducing layer of deception, and you found another. Real estate and divorce were looking better all the time. "I have to go," I said.

Martha walked me to the door, carrying her half-finished vodka. Maybe she didn't use ice because she didn't want to hear it rattle in her trembling hand.

When I got back to the office I called Cindy. "I think Martha might have had a slight stroke," I said.

"My mother?"

"I just came from her place. When I got there she was standing in front of her door extremely confused. She said she couldn't remember whether she was going in or out."

"She gets absentminded sometimes. It happens to everybody."

"This was more serious than that."

"Maybe she'd had a Halcion or a drink . . . or both."

"Maybe, but it wouldn't hurt to have a doctor look at her."

"She wouldn't go. I know my mother."

"That could be what happened the night Justine died, you know. It's kind of hard for me to figure out what took place if Martha doesn't know herself." But what happened happened whether there was anyone home to register it or not.

"My mother couldn't have had a stroke. She's too strong." Cindy was hiding in the dark den of denial, and she didn't want to come out. She was living with her mother's substance abuse; she was used to that. The effects of the vodka and Halcion were self-induced and, presumably, reversible, but physical deterioration was something else. Once the aging body and mind start to go, there are good days and bad days, but there's no turning back. Watching an all-powerful mother change into a frail and dependent mother can't be easy. For one thing, it means you've got to do a lot of adjusting yourself.

"I'd have her checked if I were you."

"I'll try. You never really think your mother's going to get old and sick. You always think she's going to live for-ever. I mean a mother like mine anyway, one of the tough ones."

I knew my mother wouldn't live forever, that she might live only as long as I remembered her, but if she lived only as I remembered her she'd never get old. As for how tough she was, I didn't know.

"Well, thanks for calling, Neil. I'll see what I can do."

"Okay," I said. There were more questions that needed to be asked, but Cindy wasn't the one to answer them.

I called Emilio. "Hey, Neil," he said. "How's it going?"

"Pretty good. There are some things I want to talk to you about."

"Can you come over?"

"How about this afternoon?"

"Okay. I'm going to Arroyo del Oso to watch the soccer game. Could you meet me there at four?"

"Yeah," I said.

My next call was to Anthony Saia, to tell him about the Ari-zona trip. Either his back was to the wall or his bucket was full. He was in a bad mood and didn't want to listen to what I had to say. Present an opposing point of view to a man who's down and he's liable to attack, and the way a man attacks a woman (if he doesn't punch her out) is to tell her, in one way or another, that she's stupid. Maybe they do that to each other too. Who am I to say?

"You're imagining things, Neil," Saia said. "Why would some guys kill Justine Virga and then try to do you?"

"Justine Virga because she is Niki Falcón and she assassinated a general in Buenos Aires. Me because I'm doing the APD's job for them."

"Hearsay. You heard Justine Virga was Niki Falcón. There's no evidence to support that theory."

"There is evidence that someone attacked me, if you want to see it. Big red welts on my neck."

"So some douchebag was trying to rob you or get into your pants, and you're making a big-deal conspiracy out of it."

If that kind of talk made him feel like a superior man, what did it make me? A paranoid bimbo? "Fuck you, Saia," I said.

"You, too," he replied and hung up.

Anthony Saia was the friend I counted on to chase away the legal blues and raise the level of any old boring day, the professional associate who would laugh, flirt and do what was necessary to maintain the feeling that life doesn't suck before you die. We'd had the bond of You jolly me up, I'll do it for you. No more than that, but it was a bond, and he had violated it. A grouchy man can ruin your day faster than a flat tire in a rainstorm—if you let him. I picked up a rubber band, shot it at the coffee cup on my desk, lit a cigarette.

When the phone rang, I let Anna answer it. "It's Saia," she yelled. "For you."

I picked up my end. "Yeah." I didn't think he would go so far as to actually apologize, and I was right.

What he said was, "I've had a bad day."

"No shit."

"C'mon, Neil, cut me a little slack, will you? Dorman's been on my case." It was about as much as you could expect and more than you usually got. "I do have some interesting news for you."

"What's that?"

"The APD checked out the headlight glass at Atalaya and found it didn't come from Conover's car. As for the tinted glass, Martha's car doesn't have tinted glass. None of her windows were broken anyway."

"Thanks," I said.

"Glad to do it," he replied.

22

∧∧∧∧∧∧

THE ARROYO DEL OSO or Bear Creek soccer fields have a wide-angle view toward the west, big enough to show several storm systems at once. It could be raining in gray sheets in the South Valley, sunny in the North, and you'd see it all from up there. When you see that far, you have the feeling that if you took a giant step you'd end up in the sky, and you can easily forget you're in a city. Emilio had parked his van beneath the trees. He wasn't supposed to park there, but his license plate had wheels on it and his bumper wore a sticker that said Vietnam Vet, so he knew no one was going to bother him. He had rolled his wheelchair into the shade. It was a trimmed-down racing model, nothing but seat and wheels canted out for balance and speed. He wore black leather fingerless gloves, and his legs were strapped in with a black belt. It was a clear, crisp fall day, a relief after the heat of summer that presses you into the pavement. The match had started. Teenage boys ran down the field in their shorts, bouncing the ball off their thighs and their heads.

"Hey, Nellie," Emilio said when he saw me.

"Hola." I bent down and gave him a kiss.

"Miguel loved to play soccer. Did I ever tell you that?"

"No." Emiliano had been a good soccer player himself. I remembered games he'd organized on the playing fields of Ithaca, New York.

"He had hot feet. I saw him score four goals once right here. That's one reason I don't leave Los Cerros. I like to come here." Emiliano was connected to another life that had screeched to a stop in midflight and kept him from going forward. "I'm glad I've gotten to the point where I *can* come here again," he said. "The old lady hardly ever watched Miguel play, only she came the day he scored all the goals. She's too dignified to yell, but you should have seen her shake her little fists. It was something. I was parked in my van on the other side of the field, and I had to try real hard not to let on that I was Miguel's dad."

"You weren't as subtle as you thought."

"She knows?"

"Yeah."

"No shit? And she never let on?"

"I guess not."

"She's tough."

"Maybe, but nobody comes in tough, and nobody goes out that way, either," I said.

"Some do. I've seen some go out that were real tough." He shook his head. "You have to give the old lady credit. She doesn't miss much."

Not when all her circuits were connecting anyway. "She says she didn't want to make a martyr out of you by kicking you out of your apartment."

"Maybe she just wanted to keep an eye on me."

"Maybe."

I hated standing over Emilio and looking down at him, so I sat on the grass, which happened to be damp from a watering system or dog piss. I felt around for a dry spot, but I couldn't find one in the shade. "You haven't seen any dogs go by here, have you?"

He laughed. "Not recently."

"Good," I said.

He stared at me with his whiskey-colored eyes. "What's on your mind, Nellie?"

"Martha thinks Michael and Justine were into drugs," I said. I'd already tried this approach with Cindy, and it hadn't worked. I was hoping Emilio either knew more or would be more objective.

"She's wrong. I would have known if they were. I know a lot more about drugs than the old lady does."

"About some kinds of drugs."

"That's true, but those are the kinds of drugs Miguel and Justy would have been into—if they were into drugs."

I tore off a couple of blades of grass and squeezed them between my fingers like the whistles I made as a kid. I was getting to the hard part. "When did Michael buy the Porsche?" I asked him.

"About a month before he died."

"You're sure Martha didn't give it to him?" It was a diversionary tactic. I knew that Martha didn't give Michael the Porsche and Emilio knew that I knew, but I wanted to take his mind off the previous question, a question that, if I'd believed Emilio, I wouldn't have had to ask. He stared at me with his Jack Daniel's eyes, and once again I had the feeling the color was about to bleed out.

"I'm positive," he said. "Can't you ever forget that you're a lawyer, Nellie?"

"Yeah, but not when I'm working. There's one more thing. I was wondering if you could give me Mina Alarid's address and phone number. I tried information, and she's not listed."

"Why do you want to talk to her?"

"I was hoping she could confirm that Niki Falcón assassinated Jaime Córdova and that hit men were after her. The deputy DA doesn't want to believe me."

"Nobody believes anybody in this case, do they?"

"No," I said.

A player in a blue jersey broke away from the pack and ran down the field. He had long muscular legs and kicked the ball with a perfect sideways kick. The goalie lunged at it, fell on his face, the ball went in. Emilio was running in place, sliding his leather gloves up and down the edges of the wheels. "All right," he yelled. "Did you see that kick?"

"Yeah."

"I bet your boyfriend can play soccer."

"You're right."

"Would you love him if he ended up like me?"

Would I? Would the Kid love me if I ended up a paraplegic? Did we love each other now?

"Cindy loves me. She'll always love me, and there hasn't been a damn thing we could do about it," he said.

The next morning my Bic pen drew circles up and down the lines on my yellow legal pad while I thought about Michael Velásquez. If Emilio had told the truth, his son bought the Porsche a month before he died. If he paid five hundred dollars for it, he'd had a lucky break one day that turned out to be fatally unlucky a month later. If Emilio was wrong and Michael had paid what the Porsche was worth, where did he get the money? The obvious answer was drugs, the backbeat of the American economy. A lot of the money that got laundered and squandered in S&Ls came from drugs. It's convenient and tempting to blame drugs for everything that goes wrong, but it's a path I don't like to take; it's too easy.

I left work in the middle of the morning and walked over to the library. Before I did, I loaded my pockets with change. Nobody walks in Albuquerque, but it was only a few blocks, and for the duration I pretended I lived in a city where people did walk. I kind of like the renovation of downtown and the new tall buildings. Now it looks like anywhere, U.S.A., when it used to look like nowhere. The skyscrapers make deep shadows, pockets of cool in the middle of the day. I walked past the parking lot where three pastel smokestacks vent air against a brick wall. It had the look of another decade, and so did the guys in camouflage gear sitting in front of the library with their hands out. I didn't begrudge them the change, but I hate the process of fumbling through my purse, looking for it. I reached deep in my pockets and put quarters in some grubby palms, but not all of them; I hadn't brought enough.

I entered the library, climbed the stairs to the second floor and went to the microfilm file for the *Journal*, which was organized in drawers of six years and rolls of three months. I opened the most recent drawer and found the roll for July, August, September, three years back. To give myself leeway, I started in mid-September and cranked my way through the Sunday classifieds: lost and found, auctions, money wanted, garage sales and flea markets, until I came to automobiles. I didn't find any Porsches for sale on September 14 or 21, but on September 28 I did. There it was, exactly as Emilio had said, used Porsche for sale $500, 55,000 miles, with a phone number in an exchange I knew to be on the fringes of Porsche country. "All right," I said, loud enough to wake the man at a nearby table from his morning nap. I copied down the phone number, put the microfilm back, ran a couple of dollars through the copier change machine, and dropped the quarters in the palms of the guys I'd missed on my way in.

"Where have you been?" Anna asked when I got back to the office. I was the boss. I was the one who was supposed to ask suspicious questions.

"The library," I said. If she wondered what I had been reading, she didn't ask.

The number I had copied was three years old. It could have been reassigned many times in three years, but I dialed it anyway. "Hello," growled the voice of an angry woman.

"Hello," I said. "My name is Neil Hamel. I'm a lawyer and—"

"You're not representing my ex-husband are you? 'Cause if you are, I'm gonna hang up right now."

"No. I don't even know who your ex-husband is. I'm investigating a Porsche that was supposedly sold by someone at this number three years ago."

"Some Porsche has been in an accident, and you think you're gonna sue me for it? I got news for you: somebody already died in that car when it got totaled."

"Thanks. That's what I wanted to know. Just one more thing: did you really sell it for five hundred dollars?" If she had, I'd have to eat my cynicism.

"I didn't. My ex-husband did. That son of a bitch sold off everything he could get his hands on. This is a community property state. I got half of what was left, and you know what that amounted to? Three thousand dollars. That's what I got, plus a house that was mortgaged up the ying-yang."

"Why didn't you put the car title in both your names?"

"Because he bought it with our joint savings while I was in Oklahoma visiting my mother and he registered it in his name. Any more questions?"

"No. But I have a suggestion. If you ever get divorced again, get yourself a good lawyer."

"I'm never gonna get divorced again, and you know why? I'm never gonna get married again. I don't even talk to the sons of bitches anymore if I can help it."

23

I LEFT WORK EARLY THAT AFTERNOON and went to see Mina Alarid. She lived off Tramway in a subdivision that was tucked into the crotch of the Sandias where the view on one side is boulders and cacti and on the other the endless sky, where you don't dare let your pets out because they're coyote fodder, where the diversion channels turn to class-ten rapids in the rainy season. A powder-blue Ford was parked in the driveway. Her house was vanilla stucco in substance and California modern in style; it had a lot of glass and five or six different roof angles, combining the roundness of a dome with the sharpness of an A-frame.

Her bell had a musical chime loud enough to set dishes rattling in the depths of the house. Mina Alarid came to a window beside the front door with her glasses dangling from a ribbon around her neck. She picked up the glasses, balanced them on her nose and looked over my shoulder into the driveway, where my car was parked. She seemed to relax when she saw I was driving a yellow Nissan, enough to open her inner door anyway. She dropped the glasses to inspect me, one of those people, apparently, who can see up close but need glasses to get the long view. Obviously I wasn't selling Girl Scout cookies. So what are you doing here? her wary eyes said. The outer door, a combination storm/screen, remained closed. Most people don't bother with storm doors in New Mexico. Since this was fall, you'd expect to find glass in the door, not screens, but I would have been willing to bet my Nissan that the glass stayed in this door year round and that it was locked too. The puffy clouds drifting across the horizon behind me reflected in the glass and obscured Mina Alarid's face.

"I'm Neil Hamel," I said. "I'm a lawyer representing Martha Conover."

Mina Alarid stiffened right up when she heard Martha's name, and she started to close the inner door. "I can't help you," she said.

"Wait," I replied. "I think whoever killed Justine has been trying to kill me."

"Martha Conover killed Justine."

"I went to Arizona a few days ago, and I was followed and attacked by a man who spoke Argentine Spanish."

"What do you know about Argentine Spanish?" Her English was crisp and precise and had no noticeable accent.

"I have a friend from Argentina."

My hand was still on the inner door; her face drifted in and out of the clouds. She sighed and unlocked the storm door. "All right. Come in."

She was a slim, elegant, erect woman. Her black hair was pulled straight back in a tight bun, and a few gray wisps curled loose around her face. She wore a white silk blouse with a scalloped collar and a gray skirt. I followed her into her living room, which was as soft and cluttered as the view outside (if she ever opened the curtains) was spare and empty. The knee-jerk femininity of the house probably came from the same impulse that made pioneer women plant flowers and attempt to civilize the windy prairie. I was reminded of a house I saw once in Santa Fe, where the owner was watering limp petunias and trying to keep them alive when across the road wildflowers grew in abundance. My own personal style is about as stark inside as it is out, but then I hadn't been through what Mina had.

She wasn't a woman who opened her windows in rainstorms to let the ozone blow in. The air in the living room was sealed-tight stale. The long white curtains dripped like candle wax onto the off-white rug. The chairs were in the ornate style of some French despot, white upholstery with gold arms and legs. A large mirror with a gilt frame hung over the sofa, also white, with sleeves across the arms to keep them clean. The lamps on the end tables were painted with pictures of plump maidens sitting in a swing. A vase of pink silk flowers sat on the coffee table. If this room were a pet, it would be a clipped white poodle. It was a city room, but that of a closed-in European city, not the Duke's wild West. The softness and fussiness might have been an attempt to keep bitter reality at bay, but it made me feel I'd eaten too much and was wearing tight underwear. The only harsh notes in this room were me and a picture of Justine with her wild gypsy eyes. Justine was wearing a pink dress in this picture, and her long hair swung loose. She was smiling and looked younger and softer than in any of the other pictures, but the eyes were the same. I looked into those eyes and wondered what she had thought of her aunt, of this room, and how confined a woman reckless enough to have blown up Jaime Córdova must have felt in a house like this. All I knew of Justine came from the picture and from other people. It wasn't enough.

Mina sat down in a straight-backed chair. I sat on the sofa and picked up the picture. "Justine . . . did you call her Justine?" I asked.

"Yes."

"She looks like a gypsy."

"She was a very pretty girl." Mina obviously preferred to

have the picture in place on the table, so I put it back. "And Miguel was a handsome boy. They were a lovely couple. Romeo and Juliet, I called them. They're buried next to each other in Heavenly Gate Cemetery. Martha Conover can't keep them apart now." I was beginning to understand the decor. Mina was a romantic. Romance causes frustration, frustration leads to violence, violence leads to litigation and litigation leads to people like Saia and me.

"I understand Justine came from Argentina and her real name was Niki Falcón."

"So?"

"And she killed Jaime Córdova, a general in Buenos Aires."

"Who told you that?"

"Emilio Velásquez. I'm an old friend of his and Cindy's. My friend from Argentina confirmed it." Mina Alarid said nothing. "You know the Argentines could have set Martha up."

"How would they have done that?"

"They could have taken her car while she was at the AWC meeting or after she got home, killed Justine with it somewhere else and planted the body at Los Cerros. Argentines run the Mighty, where Martha had her car serviced, and had access to her key. Do you know them?"

"No. I avoid my countrymen whenever possible."

"You told the *Journal* you saw someone driving up and down your street the weekend before Justine died. You thought it was Martha Conover." Mina folded her hands in her lap and didn't confirm or deny that that was what she had said. "Could you describe the vehicle for me?"

"It was a large gray American car."

"Did you notice the make or model?"

"No."

"Did you actually see who was driving?"

"No, but I know it was Martha. She hates us. She always

thought she was better than we are. We're from South America. That means we're drug addicts and thieves, who have no culture."

"You said you could see the car clearly but you couldn't see who was driving?"

"Yes."

"Why not?"

"It had tinted glass."

"That's it," I said, showing more enthusiasm than a lawyer ought to. "Martha's car doesn't have tinted glass. That sounds like the car that I saw when I was inspecting the Atalaya lot, where I thought Justine might have been killed."

Mina got up, went to the window, balanced her glasses on her nose, parted the drapes a crack and looked nervously out. She saw nothing, apparently, came back, sat down, dropped the glasses and gripped the arms of her Louis-something chair. "If they're after you they will get you, you know. They will stop at nothing. Nothing. I never wanted to take in Justine in the first place, but she was my sister's daughter. What else could I do?"

There was one more thing I needed to know. "Was there a price on her head?"

"Yes. A very high price, and every year she remained free the price got higher. The man she killed came from a wealthy, proud and powerful family, who will never forget what she did. They wanted Justine to pay. I told her she shouldn't come back here anymore; it was too dangerous; but she insisted on visiting Miguel's grave every year. That was more important to her than whether she lived or died."

"Did she know she was being followed?"

"Yes."

"Do you know about the note that was found with her: 'I knew this was going to happen, but I couldn't prevent it?'"

"Yes."

"Emilio thinks Justine wrote the note herself. That her death was a sort of suicide. That she jumped in front of Martha's car."

"Emilio is wrong. I wrote it. After Emilio took Cindy home, Justine and I were alone in his apartment. I told her not to go to the cemetery. We argued about it. I pleaded with her, but she insisted on going there and going alone. Maybe she didn't want to believe she was in danger. Maybe she'd stopped caring whether or not she got caught."

"She had a gun. Maybe she thought that would protect her."

"Justine was a very reckless and headstrong girl. The more you told her not to do something, the more she insisted on doing it. It was a terrible responsibility to try to look after her. I couldn't keep her under lock and key, but I wanted my sister to know I hadn't been a fool, that I had foreseen the danger and had tried to protect her daughter. My sister thinks like a mother, that there is always something you can do to protect your children. Sometimes there isn't, not if they don't want to be protected. I was very angry when I gave Justine the note. It was a childish gesture, I suppose, like what is it that children in this country say? I told you so?"

"Adults say it too."

She threw up her hands. "Well, I was right, wasn't I? One thing I have learned in life is that destiny cannot be stopped." She dropped her hands to her lap. "I can't say it gives me any pleasure to be vindicated."

"You're willing to let Martha be indicted for Justine's death?" I asked her.

Mina held her head high, as if she was balancing something fragile and worth preserving. "Nobody has proven to me that Martha didn't kill my niece. The fact that my countrymen were looking for her doesn't rule out the possibility that Martha got there first. I doubt the Córdova family would have had Justine killed anyway. They'd want her taken alive for the pleasure of torturing her themselves."

"If the Argentines didn't kill Justine, then why are they pursuing me?"

"When they catch up to you—and they will: you can count on it—why don't you ask them?"

That was the kind of question that made me think of getting a refill of skunk juice or stopping by Ron Peterson's gun store for ammunition.

"And now I want you to leave my house and not come back," Mina said. "I don't want those assassins following you here. I'm tired of living in fear; tired of my family, tired of Martha Conover's family; tired of violence; dead tired, bone tired, tired to death of Argentina."

On my way home I stopped at Heavenly Gate Cemetery and located the graves of Michael Velásquez and Justine Virga. In the villages along the high road, cemeteries are the gayest spot in town, decorated with plastic flowers that never fade or wilt—the Chicano influence, perhaps. In Mexico they have a different attitude toward death. They celebrate it, they look at it, they joke about it, they deal with it. We block it out of our real lives, which may be why we are so obsessed with it in our entertainment. Mexicans eat candy shaped like skeletons and mummies. On El Día de los Muertos they camp out on the graves of their loved ones, eating, drinking, dancing, calling up the spirits.

I didn't expect to find any plastic flowers on Michael Velásquez's grave, and I was right. His life and death were marked by a simple brass plaque in the ground. Next to his grave was a new one, as yet unmarked—Verónica Falcón's. I wondered who was responsible for putting Falcón here—

Cindy Reid, Mina Alarid, Emilio Velásquez, or the three of them together? And I wondered what Martha thought about it, if she knew. She ought to know, but it was hard to figure what got entered and erased from the hard drive of her brain.

I stood at Justine Virga/Verónica Falcón's grave and thought about what had happened on Halloween night—what was fact, what was speculation. She had come here (probable fact), fired a bullet somewhere (also a probable fact), fired it that night (speculation). Someone had put the gun in the glove compartment of her car. It was Halloween night, the cemetery was isolated, no one would have heard the shot—if there was a shot—or whoever did hear it might have thought it was part of the Halloween noise. "Were you here that night?" I asked Justine's grave. "Did you fire the gun? At whom? Did you go to see Martha, or did someone get to you first? Has anybody collected the price on your head? Has anybody paid?" The wind lifted a piece of paper and spun it around in a gyre, but Justine did not answer.

She was a big question mark, a person who had committed an irrevocable act. There were three of those that came to mind: creating someone, killing someone, abandoning someone. Things that once done can't be undone. As Emilio said, doing the forbidden doesn't make you inhuman, but it does take you over a border, and you're going to be living by different rules afterwards. Still you'd also be living by some of the same rules, and I wondered if regret was one.

You're representing Martha Conover, not Justine Virga, I reminded myself. It doesn't really matter who Justine was or what she thought or felt; Martha Conover is paying your fee. Your job is to keep the DA's office from indicting her and, if that doesn't work, to keep them from getting a conviction.

I leaned over, touched Justine's grave, then Michael's, the star-crossed lovers who'd ended up together in the dirt. "Vaya con Dios," I said.

▽   ▽   ▽

It was the Kid's night to play the accordion at El Lobo. Since he wasn't going to be around to warn any intruders away, I'd taken his advice, loaded my LadySmith and brought it home. I dead-bolted myself in, got into bed, turned out the light and began drifting down the lonesome highway, when I heard the sound of a cricket chirp. It can't be a cricket in November, I thought, until he chirped again. The crickets we have in New Mexico are giant, Texas-sized athletes, and they have a sound to match their size. You have to put up with them all summer when they sneak into the bedroom, their favorite place, but by now they should have gone south or underground or wherever it is that crickets go when summer is over. This one sounded way loud, even for New Mexico, as if he was singing into an amplifier. It's the males that make the noise, I knew, by rubbing their legs together. Maybe his was the last cry of summer, maybe he was looking for a mate and was getting desperate, maybe he was trapped somewhere and screaming to get out. Whatever, he was making me long for a hard frost.

I'd been through the dance of the cricket-in-the-bedroom before, and I knew where it led—to sleeplessness and swearing. Crickets are the ventriloquists of the insect world, and their sound is never where it appears to be coming from. I'd ripped my bedroom apart before, looking for them. I also knew that as soon as the light goes out they start to rub their legs together, and they don't stop until you turn on the light or you catch them and flush them down the toilet. Maybe this cricket was worn out from a long summer of chirping, I thought optimistically, and would wind down and shut up. He didn't. He chirped and chirped, louder and louder. "Go away. Leave me alone," I said. Chirp.

I turned on the light, prepared to hunt him down if it took all night. As soon as the light went on, the cricket shut up. I got out of bed and turned the light off. There was enough light from the parking lot to find my way around.

The cricket began to chirp again, in excitement or joy or fear or whatever it was that motivated him. The sound seemed to be emanating from the southeast corner of the room, behind the television set. I walked over there and pulled the TV stand away from the wall. No intruder jumped out at me or crouched silhouetted against the baseboard. He continued to sing, but now from the opposite corner, in my clothes closet. I went into the closet, turned on the overhead light. He wasn't behind my shoes or in the laundry basket. The sound, in fact, now seemed to be coming from behind the bed. This guy was a trickster, the Houdini of the insect world, and he was making a fool of me. I yanked the bed away from the wall and found three used Kleenex, a safety pin and a Bic pen. I pulled out the dresser and exposed its dust balls next. He wasn't hiding there either, but he was somewhere in this room, his mating song throbbing, as predictable as summer, as elusive as the truth, right under your nose when you think it's out there somewhere. I turned southeast, northwest, stopped in the middle, under the ceiling fixture. "Where the hell are you?" I asked. "Here," came the answer, loud and clear.

The sound hadn't been coming from the north, south, east or west. It was directly overhead, in the ceiling fixture, but how had the cricket gotten up there? I turned on the bedside lamp, climbed up on the bed. True to form, as soon as the light went on, the cricket shut up. I saw him, a black lump about an inch long behind the plastic in the ceiling fixture, eight feet off the ground and six feet off the bed. Either someone had put him there to torment me or he'd taken a monumental leap, but why had he bothered? Did he think true love was waiting in the ceiling fixture? Someone else might have taken the .38 and blasted him to bits, but I'm a lawyer, after all, reasonable and precise. I unscrewed the knob that held the plastic and the cricket in place. We were face-to-face. He was a big, fat, lusty specimen. I was tired and irritable myself. I put my hand over him, jumped off the bed and flipped the plastic shade over on the floor before he had a chance to leap out. Now that he was trapped and at my mercy, what was I going to do with him? On the assumption that any cricket stupid enough or brave enough to jump into a ceiling fixture deserves better than the toilet bowl, I opened the window and threw him out. I noticed as I did that the parking space next to the Dumpster was filled. La Bailarina had come home.

24

When I woke up alone the next day, Saturday, thinking about means and motive, I decided to take a trip to Santa Fe. I didn't tell the Kid I was going; he had to work, and I knew what he'd say anyway: Cuidado con la hedionda. I wanted to know if the price on Justine's head had been paid and who had collected. My questions could best be answered by an Argentine, and there were two places in New Mexico where I knew they hung out. One was Mighty, but I wouldn't go there without a police escort. The other was a polo field. As the Kid said, Argentines play polo better than anyone else. There was a field in La Cienega, just south of Santa Fe, that being the one place in New Mexico rich enough to play polo. It was open space, in danger of being turned into a Las Tramponus development but tied up in litigation at the moment. Polo was played there on weekends, I knew. "How dangerous could a polo field be in the middle of the afternoon?" I asked myself. "Not very," I replied, but I took my gun anyway and put it in my purse. It's illegal to carry a concealed weapon in New Mexico, but it's only a misdemeanor, the equivalent of a traffic violation.

It's been said that the highway is the best—if not the

only—place to think, and the Big I between Albuquerque and Santa Fe used to be a thinking person's road. It still is, late at night or early in the morning. In the old days you could get on the interstate in Albuquerque at any time, day or night, turn your mind loose and get off in Santa Fe with the answer to your question. Now there's traffic to think about and road construction and exits leading nowhere. The construction on I-25 was supposed to have been completed by fall; it hadn't been. From Placitas to Algodones it was one lane in each direction, with a concrete divider down the middle to separate the outgoing from the incoming. Threading my way between a hard place and the orange barrels of construction, I watched a tall crane beside the road lift a large weight and drop it to the ground. The purpose was either to test the soil or to flatten the ground for the new road. Some people got so engrossed in watching it that they drove off the interstate and into the orange barrels, but not me. I kept my mind on what I was doing. The highway opened up again after Algodones, and the traffic went from single file to double and picked up speed. At La Bajada it expanded to three lanes and herd formation. La Bajada is the ultimate test of a car's age and power and ability to function at higher elevations. The Nissan got a B minus, but still I had enough horsepower to pass a pickup truck with three cowboy hats balanced like sitting ducks in the cab and a junker with a stupidly smiling Garfield stuck to the window. I had my moment in the fast lane until a turquoise Honda got on my tail and forced me to pull over. On my right, in the climbing lane, was a long red horse trailer in immaculate condition, pulled by an equally red and immaculate truck. Coming down the other side of La Bajada, the Honda was long gone and the horse trailer picked up speed and passed me. The trouble with a subcompact is that you can pass them going up but they catch up to you going down. You can never get up enough speed to get rid of them forever. You could play interstate truck tag like that from one end of the country to the other. The trucker you were playing it with would think you'd fallen in love, when all you wanted was to go at your own chosen speed. As the trailer passed me I counted the faces of the horses in the windows—twelve, more than enough for a polo team. The rig was going a lot faster than I would have with twelve horses behind me. I watched it pull off at the La Cienega exit.

It was lunchtime, so I continued on to Santa Fe and stopped at the Indian restaurant on Cerrillos. I wanted to see what their hot food was like. Not as hot as ours, but hot enough and subtly spiced. The vegetable samosas came with a tamarind sauce to leave home for. The Indian waiter hovered over me with a politeness that bordered on obsequiousness and invaded my space. While I ate I willed him to back off and thought about India and colonialism and what I knew about polo, which wasn't much except that it was a rich man's sport and they played it in India and in Santa Fe, two places with an explosive colonial past. I'd heard somewhere that the pieces of turf that the horses kick up are called divots and the periods are chukkers. It's the kind of useless information you file in the recesses of your brain, only to surface at those moments when you can't remember your best friend's name.

I finished my lunch and got back on Cerrillos, the motel and junk food strip that could be anywhere U.S.A. Tourists don't go there because it's too much like home. The natives go there because the tourists don't. I turned right on Airport Road and looked for the polo field. After I passed the airport turnoff, I could see it in the west, hovering between dust-colored foreground and purple mountains. One of nature's laws in Santa Fe is that the better the neighborhood, the worse the roads. Dirt roads are a status symbol here, along with horses and Mercedes-Benz jeeps. I turned down this one, rattled by ruts and pursued by my own personal dust devil.

As I approached the polo field I saw the lineup of trailers and trucks facing it. The red trailer I'd seen on the interstate was stuck between a shiny black rig and a dusty brown one. There were enough trailers to make me believe a tournament was in progress. There happened to be a lull in the proceedings, and horses were being walked around to dry off their sweat. People strolled the field, kicking the divots back in place. I parked the Nissan inconspicuously at the far edge of the field beyond the horse trailers, where a lot of people might think it belonged. On the edge of this crowd was where I preferred to be anyway. Someone honked a horn, indicating that a new chukker was ready to begin. The divot kickers walked off the field and leaned on their cars or sat in folding chairs with cervezas in their hands. I hung my purse over my shoulder, got out of the Nissan and sat on the hood.

The horses and riders came back onto the field, eight of each, four on a team. The men on one team wore white pants, red T-shirts and helmets. The men on the other wore white pants, navy-blue T-shirts and helmets. The horses had wraps on their legs to match the players' shirts. Both teams were all male and the same mix of two overweight middle-aged white guys and two skinny young dark guys, the money and the skill, nobody I recognized. The white guys had chin bars on their helmets. The other guys didn't.

The horses and riders thundered down to my end of the field, sounding like hard rain on a tight drum. Mallets were lifted and swung, and occasionally they connected. When they didn't, there was a lot of swearing in English and Spanish: shit, mierda; fuck, boludo; asshole, maricón. The horses turned and galloped back. Someone whacked the ball hard, and a goal got scored at the far goalpost. It was a long field, and all I could see from where I stood were rumps and mallets. I couldn't tell whether the person who scored was a dark guy or a white guy. Whoever, score one for the blues. The fans honked their horns and cheered.

The players lined up. A referee placed the ball in the middle of the field and started the game again. Horseflesh and humans pressed against one another, jockeying for position. A dark guy in a red shirt broke loose and whacked the ball toward my end of the field. He and his horse caught up to it with a clear shot at the goal. He seemed to have a centaur's communication with his horse—each end knowing exactly what the other end was doing. It was an exhibition of power, skill, animal coordination and high-speed maneuvering that could be exciting or threatening, depending upon your point of view. Superior physical specimens tend to be one or the other. I jumped off the Nissan and stood beside it to watch better. The player brought his mallet back, poised to even the score. "Leave it," a voice behind him yelled. The first rider spun around, brought his horse to a stop and lowered his mallet when he saw where the voice was coming from. Mr. Leave It galloped up. He was wearing the red T-shirt of his teammate, and beneath it the folds on his belly bounced. He looked like a fat white colonial on a quick brown horse, a horse that seemed way too small for him. Even I could see that he didn't have the strength and coordination of the other guy. He raised his mallet, swung, hit the ball sideways with a dull thud. A red shirt blocked a blue shirt, and there was still no one between him and the goal. The ball dribbled across the grass and rolled in. The rider who had (technically) scored rode up the field, proud as a conquistador, waving his mallet triumphantly while the horns honked. He was the one who had the money to pay someone younger, fitter and poorer to win his games; he got to claim the victory.

The rider who gave up the goal galloped by me. Veins bulged like barbed wire in his bare arms. The expression on his face was a snarl; he'd been hired to play a game he loved but hadn't been allowed to do it right. He looked as if he wished the other guy a lifetime of quick stops in a western saddle. He leaned across his horse and spat a wad at the field. "Mierda," he swore.

The players got into position; the referee put the ball in play again. A foul was called, and the rumps lined up to give the fouled player a fair shot. Everyone's eyes were on the far end of the field, except for two that were focused on the small of my back, watching the pistol that jabbed into me.

"Movete," a man's voice ordered in Argentine Spanish. Move it. He grabbed the shoulder strap of my purse and yanked it from my arm.

"Where?" I replied.

"Allá." He directed me away from my car, toward a horse trailer. As he turned me around, I got a good look at him. He was medium tall and skinny, with wiry black hair. I'd seen him before, but only at a distance or behind a mask. Up close I could see he had an assassin's cold, unblinking, milky green eyes and the lizard skin of Manuel Noriega. He also had a limp.

"What do you want from me anyway?" I asked, although I suspected I already knew.

"Callate," he said, pushing me toward the rig, which would block us from view. No one was looking this way; they were either watching the match or playing in it. Another goal got scored. Horns blew and people yelled, but the spectators might as well have been in Tucumcari for all the good they were doing me. My options were to wait for the cheering to stop and scream or to keep my mouth shut and keep on walking. If I screamed, there was the remote possibility he'd take his gun, run away and disappear from my life forever. There was also the possibility he'd shoot to stop, and once he did it wouldn't make a lot of difference to me whether he disappeared or not. He didn't strike me as a person who cared much about my health or had a lot to lose. I walked.

The rig was long, dusty and black. When we passed the cab, he threw my purse in through an open window. Then he nudged me toward the far end and prodded me up the ramp. The door was open; I felt a blast of hot air and smelled the ripe odor of horse sweat and manure. The trailer had been sitting too long in the sun. I balked. This was not a place where I wanted to spend the rest of the afternoon or the rest of my life, which could be the same thing. He pushed me forward. I stuck my leg out and kicked his shin, knocking him off balance, but instead of falling sideways off the ramp, as I'd hoped, he fell forward, pushing us both face-down into the trailer. My face landed in a mound of hay, but underneath I felt the hard metal floor. He landed on top of me. I tried to push him off, but he had the leverage, and he used it to press me down. Stuck between him and a hard place, I bucked and kicked. He grabbed my left arm and twisted it behind me until I thought he would yank it loose. To stop myself from crying out I bit my lip, drawing blood. The pain of my lip diverted me from the pain in my shoulder. He got to his knees and hit me on the side of the head with his handgun for good measure. Stars spun, and I saw whirling moons and pink lightning.

He climbed off me, crossed the trailer, which was about as wide as a horse is long, and sat down with his knees up and the gun pointing at me. He happened to be sitting on a pile of hay, but that didn't stop him from lighting a cigarette. I wanted that cigarette almost as much as I wanted my free-dom, but I didn't ask. He had too much power over me already; I wasn't going to let my nicotine need give him any more. I sat up and for a moment saw two heads, four knees, two guns and a whole lot of lizards, but then my vision cleared and I saw it was just him and his 9-mm semiautomatic, capa-ble of blowing a hole through me, a couple of horses and the trailer too. "What do you want?" I asked. "Money?" I rubbed my fingers together in the universal gesture of greed.

His conversation was limited. "Callate," he said.

And that's how we spent the rest of the polo match. My head throbbed, and I got hotter and thirstier by the minute. Just to break the monotony I tried periodically to make conversation.

"Who are we waiting for?"

"When am I going to get out of here?"

"What do you want anyway?"

"Can I take a leak?"

All of it met with silence. He didn't say a word, just stared at me with eyes as still and clouded as stagnant water. Either he didn't speak my language or he'd already shot his conversational wad. My instinct was to speak only English to him. Although my Spanish isn't perfect, I can usually make myself understood and get the point of what is being said, but I preferred that he didn't know that. We seemed to be waiting for someone. Chances were that person was a native Spanish speaker, and it would be better if the two of them thought I didn't understand them. The polo match continued without us. Eventually I heard the sounds of victory, then the sounds of cars driving away, and finally hooves approaching the trailer and clomping up the ramp. The door burst open, and I was temporarily blinded by the daylight that flooded in through the opening. The hay dust filled the light with the luminescence of the finger of God in a Renaissance painting. The person and horse standing in the doorway were a chiaroscuro of black silhouette against golden light, but the beauty of the picture was wasted on me. He stepped into the trailer, pulling his horse behind him. "Hola, Manolo," he said to my captor.

"Qué tal, Jorge?" the captor replied.

"So you got her," he said in English for my benefit. His English was clear, but his voice was raspy. "Qué bueno!"

Now that Jorge had stepped out of the sun and I got a good look at him, I realized that I'd seen *him* before too—at Albuquerque International, waiting on line behind me. He was holding a short, sharp whip in his hand. His hair was slicked back and his clothes were skin-tight. His white polo pants and red T-shirt were too clean to have seen much action. He hadn't played while I was watching anyway; I'd have noticed. I ranked him somewhere between the player who should have scored the goal and Manolo in the pecking order. He didn't have the player's aristocratic good looks and powerful build, but he was fitter and better-looking than Manolo. Maybe he hired Manolo to do his dirty work—but when he flashed a malevolent white smile at me, I saw this was a guy who'd be happy to do his own dirty work.

"What do you want from me?" I asked.

He handed the horse over to Manolo. The animal had already been dried off and had his saddle removed. Rope was hanging in loops beneath the tiny windows the horses got to peek out through. Manolo tied the horse to a loop with the rope attached to his bridle. "What do *you* want?" Jorge asked, tapping the whip against his riding boot.

"To get out of here."

Manolo had finished tying up the horse, and Jorge told him in Spanish to get the rest of them. "So sorry," he said to me, "but I can't do that. You want to know what happened to Niki Falcón, right?" He flicked the whip by me with a quick, casting motion. "I am going to help you find out." The good news was that meant he didn't intend to kill me immediately.

Manolo brought another horse to the door. "Put Cinco next to Arturo," Jorge ordered in Spanish.

"They don't like each other," Manolo said. "They will fight."

"Exactamente," replied Jorge.

Manolo brought more horses in and tied them up where he was told. The horses weren't happy with their trailer mates, and they bit and kicked at each other. Jorge ordered Manolo to muzzle the rowdier ones so they wouldn't take chunks out of each other's hide. They were too valuable to be marked with bite marks, he said. As the trailer filled up with horses, there was less and less room for me, and I slid down into the corner near the door to get away from the kicking hooves.

"Where are you taking me?" I asked.

"You have too many questions," Jorge said. "I think we will have to keep you quiet. You hold her," he told Manolo in Spanish. His sentences were punctuated by the thumps of hooves hitting the aluminum walls of the trailer.

I tried to squirm away from Manolo, but there was no place to go, with a metal wall behind me, kicking horses on one side, a flicking whip on the other. The whip struck like a small, nasty viper, taking a nick out of my cheek and driving me toward Manolo. He was skinny but strong, and my arm hurt from being yanked nearly out of its socket. He pulled my arms behind me and held them there while Jorge used some horse rope to tie my hands together tight. Jorge picked a black rag off the floor, a rag that had probably been used to wipe sweat from horses, and while Manolo held me in place and I squirmed, he stuffed the rag into my mouth and tied it behind my head.

"You talk too much," he said.

They brought in two more horses and tied them in place. The van was full to capacity now, and there was no place for me but pressed into the corner next to a horse they called Ernesto, one of the gentler ones that didn't get muzzled. "Adiós," Jorge said, slamming the door shut behind himself and his minion.

One of them started up the truck and drove away from

the polo field with a heavy foot. This wasn't the first time I'd cursed Santa Fe's bumpy dirt roads, but I swear better when I'm not chewing on a filthy rag. It *was* the first time taking the bumps felt like a matter of life and death. I've ridden in cars with no shocks before, but this ride entered another dimension. The trailer took the bumps like a porpoise. One end went down, the other end went up, and we hit another bump and started a new cycle before we'd even finished the first one. The trailer swung from side to side too. I lurched and looked for something to grab onto. The only grip handy was the rope looped around the bale of hay that Ernesto was chewing on. I edged toward it. Ernesto snorted and whinnied, showing big yellow teeth, but he let me approach. To reach the bale with my hands tied behind me I had to bend forward and grab it from behind. It would have been uncomfortable even if my left arm weren't an adventure in pain.

Maybe the horses had been on the losing team; they were not in a good mood when they entered the trailer. Being tied up next to their rivals and getting flung around didn't improve their dispositions any. Their tails swished at flies. Cinco nipped at Arturo, Arturo kicked back. They lunged at each other and tried to bite, but they couldn't because their heads were tied and muzzled. That frustrated them even more, and they whinnied inside the muzzles and kicked out. Their kicks hit the side of the trailer with a sharp thwang. If this pissed-off horsepower had been harnessed, we wouldn't have needed gasoline to get us to wherever we were going. There was a certain amount of methane gas being emitted that could have been useful too.

On the downhill side of the bumps I got pulled forward, going uphill I got yanked back. I wedged my fingers under the baling rope and held on. With one part of my brain I listened to Ernesto chew. With another I tried to keep track of where we were going. Sooner or later we would reach the interstate, and I wanted to observe which direction we turned when we did. We went up an incline that I thought I recognized as the access to the bridge across the river in La Cienega. That was good because it pressed me into my corner, but when we went back down and took a curve the trailer swung wide; I fell forward, clutched at the rope but lost my grip. I rolled onto my side when I landed and slid across the floor like grease on a hot pan. I didn't like horses much before this experience; I like them less now. I was running a gauntlet of hooves and shit. Arturo dropped a load of steaming manure. Cinco let loose with an angry kick. I saw his hoof coming at my face with slow-motion clarity, the way things move when you're in deep trouble. I could see the shoe on the hoof, the nails in the shoe. I also saw my head bursting open like a watermelon and my thoughts falling out in black seeds. I screamed, but it didn't do any good. My scream hit a wall—the rag—and doubled back on me the way rotten food does. I continued my headfirst slide. Cinco's hoof flew over my head, missing my brain by half an inch, and slammed into the wall with the sharp sound of metal hitting metal. I hit the far end of the trailer with a thunk of my own. For the moment I was safe. There was another bale of hay at this side of the trailer, which no one was chewing on. I was able to grab it and hold myself in place.

The road leveled off and smoothed out, meaning we were approaching the interstate. The trailer climbed an incline. We turned onto I-25 heading south toward Albuquerque or Socorro or Argentina. The smoother ride of the interstate quieted the horses. Maybe they'd realized they couldn't do any harm to their rivals with their muzzles on. I put my energy into figuring out where we were going. It was difficult to keep track of time when every second felt like a minute and every minute an hour and a bale of hay was my mooring. I observed the labored climb up La Bajada, the free-fall going down, and I noticed later when the trailer slowed down. The concrete divider at Algodones, I figured. I noticed the lane changes of increasing traffic when we passed the divider and approached the Duke City. Then the van jerked to a stop, turned right and headed west.

25

ONCE WE LEFT THE INTERSTATE, the horses got restless again, more so with every turn in the road or change in its surface from pavement to dirt. They swatted their tails, jerked their heads and danced in place. Their desire to be on the move reminded me of the way rental horses take off when you turn back to the stable or a dog heads for the door when he notices you're packing your bags. It seems you're crossing a species barrier of communication, but all it really means is that the animals are watching and listening and picking up on the clues that matter to them. The horses knew they were going home. The turns we'd made were taking us in the direction of Corrales or the North Valley. Was it our final destination, I wondered, or just a place to drop off the horses? A lot of people in the valley kept horses—they kept llamas and chickens and potbellied pigs too—but nobody I knew.

The trailer jerked to a stop. I heard footsteps on the ramp; the door opened. I was hoping to see a new face, the owner of the trailer, maybe, the power behind the crime, but all I got was Manolo and Jorge, two guys who cared a lot about the horses and not a bit about me.

"Where are you?" Jorge called out in singsong English, feigning surprise, as if he were playing hide-and-seek. He knew I was inside: there was no way out; what he didn't know was whether I was dead or alive or had been kicked somewhere in between. It didn't make much difference to him. "Did you kick her, Ernesto?" he asked. He bent down, peered between the horses' legs and saw me scrunched up in the far corner. "She is still alive. She must be very smart or very lucky. Being smart, that's good, but luck—luck runs out. Still curious?" he asked me.

"Um," I mumbled into the rag.

"Well, hold your horses." He laughed, and his teeth flashed quick and bright as a knife blade. It was a stupid joke, and he had a stupid sense of humor, although you have to have a fairly good command of a language to be able to joke in it. I gave him credit for that.

"So full of curiosity," he said. He clucked his tongue as though he were talking to a horse. "You asked too many questions, and now you will have to keep your mouth shut."

They began unloading the horses one by one. Cinco, the biggest and meanest, the king of the machos, snorted, flicked his head and took a last lunge at Arturo before he went out. I waited my turn. There was no guarantee the next place would be any better than this one, but at least it would be a change.

After the last horse clomped down the ramp, Jorge shut the door and padlocked it. "Adiós," he said. I heard the lock close with the terminal click of a cell door slamming on a lifer. "Hey," I yelled into my gag. "Let me out of here." I kicked the door and got a dull thud in reply. A running shoe doesn't make the same kind of statement as a hoof with a thousand pounds of horseflesh behind it.

"Why are you always so impatient? We will be back when we are ready," Jorge said.

They weren't ready for several hours. The sky changed

from late-afternoon blue to midnight black while I waited. We were in a bosque somewhere. I could see cottonwood trees and the corner of a barn through the horses' tiny windows. I watched the bare arms of the cottonwoods scratch the sky and then disappear into it. I spent the time pacing the trailer, kicking the walls and wishing I had a cigarette. By the time it got dark I'd memorized the confines of the trailer and knew where all the manure piles were. I didn't need light to find my way around, but I still craved it. One of the worst things about being stuck here was the darkness. Like my need for cigarettes, I promised myself that my desire for light was something I wouldn't reveal to my captors; it would give them more power over me. One reason people smoke is that focusing all the intensity of your desire on one reasonably satisfiable craving takes your mind off the other things you need. Thinking about cigarettes (opening the pack, lighting the match, sucking in the smoke, exhaling it) kept me from thinking about life, death, food, water and going to the bathroom. I know cigarettes are death too, but it's a ways down the road and there was a good chance something else was going to get me first. What form would it take? I wondered: a knife, a gun, a kick in the head, the loss of my hands?

I can't sit still for long thinking thoughts like that, with or without cigarettes. I paced from one end of my cell to the other like an animal in a cage, a lion the circus left behind in a boxcar on a siding. I pulled against the rope until my wrists were rubbed raw, but I couldn't loosen the knots, and I couldn't get my gag untied either. The day got darker and colder, and I couldn't even sing or scream to keep myself company. The deepening darkness became an empty canvas like the black velvet people paint pictures of tigers and Elvis Presley on. I had nothing better to do, so I filled up the canvas, and the face I created had the outlaw eyes of Niki Falcón. What had made her kill Jaime Córdova and precipitate this sequence of events? It was an act a lot of women might have considered but few would have committed, even if Jaime Córdova had deserved it. Maybe Niki's bucket had been full of love or hate or recklessness. I imagined what her life would have been like if she'd gotten caught. This trailer was a mountain resort compared to the inner-city hell she'd have gone through. She'd have been confined to a cold, dank cell or a stinking hot one, lucky if she had a hole to piss in or a mattress to sleep on or edible food, waiting to be raped or tortured by the machine. Compared to that, Martha Conover and a big American car could seem like a blessing.

As time went by I also got a sense of the ambiguity a prisoner feels about her jailer. You hate the guy, but his is the only face you see all day, the only hands that can release or feed you or let in light, and you do begin to feel something like relief when he comes back. When I heard the footsteps on the ramp, the key in the lock, I was almost looking forward to Jorge's smile.

It was in place and as malevolent as I remembered, but I didn't get to see it for long. Lights blazed briefly, long enough for me to see Jorge in the doorway and Manolo with a bandanna in his hand, though not long enough for my pupils to adjust to the change. The men grabbed me, tied the bandanna tight around my eyes, dragged me out of the trailer, pushed me forward, dumped me on the floor of a car and threw a blanket over me. One of them sat down and put his feet on the blanket to keep it and me in place. It was an abduction in the best Argentine thugs' manner. I couldn't speak or see any evil, but I could hear Manolo giving directions, an indication those were his feet on my back and he was the one who knew where we were going—east and uphill all the way.

When we reached our destination, Manolo lifted his feet

and the blanket, pulled me out of the car and pushed me forward. "Tenés las llaves?" asked Jorge. Do you have the keys?

"Sí," said Manolo.

I heard one of them try several keys in a lock. When he found the right one, he opened the door. They pushed me forward. I stumbled on a hardwood floor and tripped on a rug. My shoulder landed hard against a banister, and I heard the sound of metal rattling against wood. "Silencio," Manolo whispered, jabbing me in the back with his gun. It was a very quiet place and dark too. Only a sliver of light came in under my blindfold.

"¿Ádónde vamos?" asked Jorge.

"Allá," said Manolo.

They pushed me forward stumbling through a large house. We walked down hallways, crossed rooms. A door opened, a light came on, my feet stepped on a thick carpet.

"Shit," a voice I recognized said. "How in the hell did you get in?" It was a question I might have answered myself if my mouth hadn't been tied shut. They had a key, taken most likely from Martha Conover's key ring by their buddies at Mighty. The house we were in belonged to her, although she didn't live in it. "What are you doing here?"

"We heard you wanted to talk to us," Jorge, the spokesman, said.

"To you, yes, but what did you bring Hamel here for?" I could have answered that one, too, if I hadn't been gagged.

Someone untied my blindfold but left my gag in place. I blinked back the light. We were in a house I knew but a room I hadn't seen yet, a large study with wall-to-wall carpeting, bookshelves and shabby but valuable furniture. It had the look of old money gone threadbare or broke. A brass lamp with a green shade sat on a large mahogany desk. The light switch on the wall beside me was flipped up, indicating, possibly, that it controlled the green lamp, the only light in the room. It illuminated the apoplectic face of Whitney J. Reid III, who was standing behind the desk, wheezing and drumming his thick fingers on the polished wood.

"She made the connection," Jorge said. "She went to Mighty and was asking questions about Argentina and the car keys. She told the courtesy van to take her here. We got curious and we started to follow her. She went to Atalaya. She went to your building in Arizona. She came to the polo field. She knows about you and us."

"You guys are really brilliant. Hamel didn't know a thing until you brought her here," Whit said. "She's a two-bit divorce lawyer with no credentials or experience, whom my mother-in-law hired to represent her. If you'd left things alone she would have fucked the case up and my mother-in-law would have gone to prison for sure."

And he would have gained control of her business and her bank account and gotten a head start on life after foreclosure. The reason, apparently, Whit Reid had recommended me was that he thought I wasn't up to the job, that my incompetence would get Martha a prison term and out of his way. I *had* made the right connection. Whit needed money. He played polo. He knew Niki Falcón came to Albuquerque and visited Michael Velásquez's grave every Halloween night. He'd found out there was a price on her head, and he knew Argentine polo players who wanted to help him collect it. Whit Reid had turned his stepson's girlfriend over to assassins for blood money, as if she were another piece of real estate to be bought and sold. As a side benefit he appeared to have set up Martha Conover.

"You were supposed to have gone to Argentina and come back with the money before now," he said. "Did you bring it?"

"The Córdovas want evidence that the girl that died is Verónica Falcón," Jorge said. "She shot Manolo in the leg and got away from us at the cemetery before we got proof."

Whit looked at Manolo and shook his head. "You guys are real screw-ups. You let a girl shoot you and get away."

"You didn't tell us she would have a gun."

"She was a known assassin. Did you think she'd just give up?"

Jorge shrugged. They hadn't, apparently, expected to encounter a woman as competent or as tough as Niki Falcón. If the Argentines hadn't killed her, it put a new slant on this case that turned me back toward where all roads had been leading but where I hadn't wanted to follow—square one, Los Cerros, with the headlights on.

"She didn't trust you," Jorge said to Whit. "She asked if you were the one who sent us. She wanted to know what we were going to do with her next."

"Did you tell her?"

"Claro. Why not? She had the gun."

"Brilliant," Whit said. "Well, she's dead now. What difference does it make what she knew? It was a lucky break for you guys that the way things happened she died anyway."

"Yes, but we cannot get the second payment without proof that the girl who died was Verónica Falcón."

I could see conflict and anger ripple across Whit's face. He was pissed, and he didn't trust his associates any longer, if he ever had. Criminals usually know better than to trust each other, and these criminals were also separated by a canyon of language and culture. If Whit had the proof and he gave it to them, he would lose whatever leverage he had, but if he didn't produce it, he wouldn't get his second payment. "You can take it from me she was Justine Virga *and* Verónica Falcón."

"Your word is not enough. The Córdovas looked for Niki Falcón for a long time. They have already paid you very well and they will pay more, but they must have proof. If we had gotten the girl we would have taken something for identification." He smiled his knife-blade smile. "Her hands, maybe, for the prints. Do you have proof?"

Greed won Whit's battle. He reached into his desk drawer, opened a box and pulled a piece of jewelry out of a bed of cotton, a heart-shaped locket on a chain that looked precarious as a butterfly in his thick fingers. He tossed the locket to Jorge, edged his hand back into the drawer and breathed heavily through his flattened nose. "Falcón's aunt gave this to my wife. She was wearing it when she died."

"You traitor," I squawked into the muffler of my gag.

"Shut up, Nellie," Whit said.

Jorge inspected the locket. "Bueno." Inside was the photograph of Justine and Michael smiling like newlyweds for the camera. The back was engraved with the initials VF. "The Córdovas will be very happy with this, very happy." He smiled and put the locket in his pocket. "Muchas gracias, señor. And now it looks like our business is finished."

"Our business will be finished when I get the final payment," said Whit, drumming the fingers of his left hand on his desk.

"Verdad?" Jorge laughed. Manolo watched them intently, his stagnant-water eyes moving back and forth from Jorge to Whit, his hand reaching into his pocket. "It has been a pleasure doing business with you, señor."

Their business deal was breaking up in Whit Reid's study. A contract to commit an illegal act is not legally enforceable, but there are always extralegal means, and people who enter into illegal contracts don't hesitate to use them. The Argentines had what they wanted; Whit was of no more use to them. He was, in fact, an unnecessary expense. Whit was used to having high-priced lawyers fight his battles, but they weren't any good to him now. It was his businessman's cunning against the Argentines' street smarts. We were on Whit's territory, which gave him one advantage, but it looked to me as if the winner of this contest would be the one with the fastest draw and the biggest weapon. Whit's right hand inched deeper into the drawer. "Self-defense," he would say, if the last word was his. "They were robbers who broke into my house. It wasn't my fault."

My future was looking dimmer than the green desk lamp's bulb. Whoever won the draw, I'd witness it. Since I'd be the only one left to incriminate the survivor, the next bullet would have my name on it. I visualized the scene if Manolo won. Their horses hadn't kicked me to death, but the Argentines would get another opportunity to finish me off—here. Manolo's gun would end up in my hand, with no prints on it but mine. Whit and I would be found dead together in this study. I'd hate to have anyone think it had been a lovers' quarrel. I didn't know how Whit would explain my body on his floor if he won, but he was enterprising enough to think of something. "Which one do you want to be killed by?" I asked myself. "Neither," myself replied. There was another woman in the house. Whose side was she on? Where was she? The men glared at each other. It took only a fraction of a second for them to act, but it felt like a slow-motion tango. The hands came up, the guns appeared. I threw myself against the light switch, hoping the green desk lamp would answer. The light went off, the guns fired, one right after the other. I rolled to the floor, taking an end table with me. Someone swore in Spanish. Someone else screamed, but I couldn't tell who. Pain speaks a universal language.

The study door opened a crack, and light filtered in. "Neil," I heard my old friend Cindy whisper. "Over here." I slid through the door. Cindy pulled it shut and began to shove a large and ugly corner cupboard against it. I helped her by backing against the cupboard and pushing with my butt. "What should we do now?" she asked.

I squawked and pointed toward my gagged mouth. Cindy untied the gag by the light from the street lamp. I grimaced and tried to work up enough saliva to speak again.

"Did Whit get shot?" she asked.

"I don't know." They were the first words I'd spoken all evening, and they stuck to my tongue.

"Whit," Cindy called, "are you all right?" There was no answer. Only two bullets had been fired. At least one person was alive in that den, and dangerous as a cornered cobra. It's a female fantasy that furniture against a door will keep the killers away; it could only be considered a temporary solution.

"Can you get the rope off my hands?" I croaked.

Cindy struggled with the knots, but they had worked themselves into a deep snarl. "Have you got a knife, clippers, scissors?" I said.

"Let's go into the kitchen," she replied. We ran through the living room, with Whit's mother watching us from her perch on the wall. Cindy flicked on the light in the kitchen, pulled a knife out of a drawer, put my hands behind me on the butcher block and cut through the rope. "The arguing woke me up," she said with a shiver. She was in her nightgown. Her eyes were dazed and her hair hung loose around her face. "I don't get it. Those men paid Whit to find Justine?"

"They paid him to tell them where she'd be and when she'd be there."

"Why would Whit do that?"

"He needed the money. He owed it to the federal government for S&L fraud. It was that or prison."

"He told me when we sold everything that would pay his fine."

"He was lying."

She pressed her hands down on the counter. "I was the one who told him Justine was Niki Falcón. I told him she went to the cemetery. It's my fault."

This was no time to be indulging in guilt. We could hear the sounds of the door being pushed and the cupboard scraping slowly across the floor. The rope dropped off, and my hands broke free. I was ready to use them.

I remembered the guns in the gun rack that I'd heard rattling when I came in. "The guns in the hallway," I asked. "Are they loaded? Do they work?"

"I don't know," Cindy answered.

"Call 911 and get out of the house."

"Where will I go?"

"Anywhere, but get out of here."

"What about you?"

"I'll get a gun."

I ran through the living room, dodging the overstuffed furniture, and crossed the dining room beneath the crystal chandelier that glittered in the light from the street. I reached the hallway, where the stuffed bear loomed, casting a long shadow even in the dim light. I heard the cupboard slide, then fall to the floor with a crash that had to echo from here to the valley. Dishes fell out and shattered. Wood snapped as someone pushed open a door and stepped on the back of the cupboard. I'd reached the gun rack, and I ran my hand quickly across the butts, feeling for one that had my name on it. None did. I grabbed one, any one, hoping I'd found the weapon that would save my skin.

Footsteps creaked on the living room's hardwood floors. All was quiet in the rest of the house. I inched behind the dusty bear, tucked myself into its shadow, the gun in my hand.

"Marco," a voice called out with a maniacal laugh. Of the three killers in the den, I'd gotten the one with the raspy voice, the sense of humor and the malevolent smile, the guy who could be the most deadly, one on one. I drew further into the bear's shadow and held my breath. "Marco," the voice called again, laughing and sending the lizard crawling up my spine. It was the child's game played in swimming pools in summer. I said not a word. I didn't even breathe.

But the voice and the footsteps proceeded in my direction across the living room, into the dining room, circled the table. "Marco," he called. "Marco."

He seemed to know exactly where I was, but how? Did he have a sixth sense? Was he smelling la hedionda?

The footsteps entered the hallway. "Marco," he called once again and laughed. He walked across the floor, put his hand on the bear. "Qué tal, oso?" he said. I came out from behind the bear and pulled the trigger on the antique rifle. It didn't go off, but I was close enough to jam the barrel into his gut. His 9 mm handgun got off a round, but he had doubled over by the time it did, and the bullet went into the floor. His head was down around his knees by then, and I took the butt end of the rifle and smashed it. "Puta madre," he mumbled.

A light came on. Cindy stood in the doorway armed for combat, with the kitchen knife in one hand and a frying pan in the other.

Jorge appeared to be out, but I hit him once more for good measure. "Polo," I said.

26

MANOLO GUTIÉRREZ DIED in Whit Reid's study. Whit didn't die, but he had been wounded badly enough to make Jorge Fuentes believe he was dead. Whit had been either a luckier man that night or a better shot. The killing of Manolo Gutiérrez could have been self-defense, or it could have been murder. It was a close call. The DA agreed not to press charges for the Gutiérrez killing if Whit pleaded guilty to conspiracy to murder Justine Virga, an easier crime to prosecute because Jorge Fuentes had confessed and turned state's evidence in exchange for a reduced sentence for his part in the conspiracy. Whit might have gotten himself a better deal if he'd been able to hire a first-rate defense lawyer, but he was way broke. He had to sell his mother's antiques to pay the lawyer he did get. Compared to an Argentine torture cell, the state pen could feel like the Biltmore to Jorge Fuentes, but it would be a hellhole for Whit Reid. No polo matches or tennis games to amuse him there, and the special treatment the other inmates thought his background entitled him to would not be Whit Reid's idea of entitlement. He would have been better off if he hadn't paid his fine and had gone to Club Fed with all the other S&L

crooks. At least he would have been among his own kind.

When the DA made his decision about how he intended to charge Martha, Anthony Saia invited me over to his office to talk about it. He had that shorn look men get right after they've been to the barber.

We sat down in our respective places in his office. "You had your hair cut," I said. He ran his fingers through it and waited as if my appraisal would make or break his morning.

"You like it?"

"It is a little short for winter," I told him.

"It doesn't get that cold in Albuquerque," he replied.

"Cold enough." I bit the bullet. "Well, what's it going to be for Martha Conover?"

He picked up a rubber band, stretched it between his index fingers and began moving the fingers back and forth in opposition, like a sideways seesaw. We were back where we'd started from, facing each other across the desk and hoping to see justice served or at least to reach a settlement on what happened Halloween night when two women, an old one and a young one, apparently faced each other across the headlights of a Buick.

"Like I said before, it's a tough call. There's no legal precedent for this case in New Mexico, and there are circumstances that make prosecution difficult. There weren't any witnesses. Although Jorge Fuentes and Whit Reid's version of events implicates your client, theirs is a self-serving account."

They'd had no reason to lie when I heard their version in Whit's study, I thought.

"Your client is an old lady."

She wasn't *that* old.

"It could be difficult to convince a jury that she belongs in prison with a bunch of hookers and drug dealers."

They did it to Leona Helmsley.

"Justine Virga/Niki Falcón was a known assassin."

Yeah, but the guy she assassinated was a pig.

"It would be hard to work up any sympathy for Justine in a courtroom."

I'd like to give it a try, only I had been hired to defend Martha Conover, not Justine Virga, and Justine Virga had paid for her crime.

"Your client might have felt threatened . . . "

She might. She might also have been suffering from Halcion-induced paranoia. Justine's gun was locked in her glove compartment. She was unarmed.

". . . and acted in the heat of passion. On the other hand, there may have been premeditation. When you get right down to it, there's no way of proving or even knowing what went on in those ladies' minds that night."

Maybe, but there were no brake marks in the road; Martha hadn't even slowed down.

"Still there's no doubt that Conover's car hit her and that she was driving it. We do have the evidence to prove that. Dorman wants to file charges of second-degree murder and vehicular homicide alternatively and let the judge decide which one to try."

Saia had been verbally presenting my arguments to me; I'd been mentally presenting his arguments to me. I knew why I'd been countering, but what had he been up to? He appeared to be telling me that he didn't want to prosecute this case and that he was looking to plea-bargain. "Suppose Martha agrees to plead no contest to involuntary manslaughter?" I asked. "I think she might go for that because she wouldn't be admitting to hitting Justine with intent." Involuntary manslaughter is a fourth-degree felony with a maximum of eighteen months in jail and a five-thousand-dollar fine, a minimum of one year probation.

"How about she also agrees never to drive again?"

"I'll see what I can do."

"All right. You talk to Conover. I'll run it by Dorman."

"Okay."

Saia ran his fingers through his hair once more, trying, maybe, to make it look longer. "You really think it's too short?"

"It'll grow."

He stood up and put his hand out; I took it. "Pleasure as always working with you."

"You, too, Anthony," I said.

Prison got Whit out of Cindy Reid's life, but even before he was sentenced she moved to her own apartment at Los Cerros. She and Emilio began spending a lot of time together. Their high school dream had come true but, as happens with dreams that come true, not exactly in the way they'd intended. Martha put up with Cindy's seeing Emilio, or maybe she didn't notice. Learning that her ideal son-in-law had plotted to incapacitate her and take over her business was a blow, and she was fading. The vaguer she got, the more Cindy took charge. They went through that dance where the child becomes the mother and the mother the child. Martha wasn't going gracefully into old age, however, which wouldn't make mothering any easier for Cindy. I wondered if she'd be any better at it than her mother had been. Cindy had reached that point where you have to decide whether you'll be there for the mother who wasn't there for you, be tolerant of the mother who didn't know tolerance. Be good, be kind, be mature and—if you're not careful—be manipulated. Sometimes it's a fine line.

The day after I saw Saia, I went by Martha's to tell her what had been said. Cindy was there, rattling glasses in the kitchen, and Mozart was playing on the CD. It was the kind of music that makes you want to move but not to dance. When I was in college I used to get stoned and play my roommate's Mozart tapes when I had papers to type. Mozart has a certain kind of regular rhythm that's good for typing. It wasn't bad for mixing drinks either.

Martha came to the door immaculately groomed, as if she were going to court, and in a way she was. "I'll get you a drink," she said to me. "What is it you like? Gin and tonic?"

"I'll have a vodka," I answered. This was a business meeting, but what the hell. Whatever help was available today, I felt entitled to it. "Hold the ice," I said.

"You got it," Cindy responded, opening the kitchen cabinet, taking out a glass and banging it against the counter.

"I'm capable of getting my guest a drink." Martha moved toward the kitchen.

"No one said you weren't capable, Mother, but I happened to be in the kitchen, and I know how Neil likes her drinks."

"So do I. No ice." And only a few minutes before, Martha had been offering me a gin and tonic. "Why are you using that glass?" she snapped at Cindy in her best disapproving-mother voice. "That glass has dishwasher spots all over it."

"So what?" Cindy answered back.

"How many times have I told you not to put those glasses in the dishwasher?"

"About a thousand, Mother, if you really want to know, or maybe it's two thousand. I'd say you've told me at least two thousand times not to put those glasses in the dishwasher."

"Then why do you insist on doing it?"

"I hardly ever wash the glasses, Mother. You do. You're the one who puts the goddamn glasses in the goddamn fucking dishwasher." I'd be willing to bet that was the first time Cindy had ever said the *f* word in this household. Was that empowerment? The Mozart symphony or concerto or whatever it was built to a crescendo, brass answering brass. Maybe it was music to fight by. If Mozart, the supreme genius of music, was the one who understood the power of harmony, then he'd know what you have to go through sometimes to get there.

"You don't have to shout at me. I'm not deaf, you know," said Martha.

"Who's shouting?" said Cindy.

"You are."

"I am not."

The surge passed. The music leveled off. The strings came forward. "I forget sometimes," Martha said in a small voice.

Cindy bent close to hear her. "What?" she asked.

"I forget."

"I know." Cindy put her arm around her mother. The time when the child becomes the mother and the mother the child doesn't happen all at once. A powerful mother can turn frail and weak and then turn unexpectedly strong again. It's a dance to the death. Till then, Cindy would probably go on loving her one minute, resenting her the next.

"What happened to my drink?" I asked.

Cindy opened the freezer, took out the smoking-cold bottle, poured a shot. "Here it is."

"Thanks," I said. "And now, Cindy, if you'll excuse us, I need to talk to your mother alone."

"Okay," Cindy said. She left, and the music ended on a harmonious note that made me wish life were as orderly as Mozart. Martha turned off the CD, and we sat down on the chintz sofa. She placed her glass squarely in the middle of a coaster. I took one large sip from mine, put it down on an end table and left it alone; sooner or later I'd be driving home.

"The DA wants to file charges of second-degree murder and vehicular homicide and let the judge decide which charge to try," I said.

Martha pressed her hands together tight. "What are the penalties?"

I had already told her, but I went over it once again. "The maximum for second-degree murder is nine years and a ten-thousand-dollar fine. Vehicular homicide is a third-degree felony, with a maximum of three years and a fine of five thousand dollars. If he had charged you with first-degree murder, the penalty would be life."

She winced at that. "But it wasn't my fault."

"I think we could work out a plea bargain if you plead no contest to involuntary manslaughter, a fourth-degree felony. You'd be admitting to being in a fatal accident but not to intent to hit Justine."

"What's the penalty for that?"

"A maximum of eighteen months and a five-thousand-dollar fine. A minimum of one year on probation. I think there's a good chance you'll get probation. You're an upstanding citizen with no record, and they don't really want to put you in prison. They would like you to agree never to drive again as part of the bargain."

"But I can't do that," she objected.

"Why not? Losing your license is a small price to pay for staying out of prison." Besides, I thought, we'll all be safer if you just stay home.

"But that will mean I'll be dependent on Cindy or someone to take me everywhere."

Those are the breaks, I thought, but what I said was, "We know more or less what happened now." The only thing we didn't know was what had gone on in the participants' heads. "Your son-in-law tried to set you up, but it didn't work; Justine got away from Jorge Fuentes and Manolo Gutiérrez. The Argentines intended to hit Justine with your car and frame you. They screwed up, but you did it yourself." It was one of those bends in the highway, one of those strange events that once set in motion seem to take on a destiny all their own. "Justine came to see you, and you ran her down." In cold blood, too, was one possibility.

"She stepped out in front of the car in the middle of the night. I didn't know what she wanted. She killed Michael, my grandson. For all I knew, she had a weapon. I had no time to react." The truth we'd been dancing around had surfaced now, sitting like a lump of mud on Martha's coffee table.

"You could have stepped on the brake," I said.

"My foot slipped off."

"And you could have told me the truth in the very beginning."

"I was under the influence of Halcion; I didn't know what I was doing. It seemed so unreal to me, like a bad dream. Like it had happened to someone else."

It might have been a substance-induced fog, but it hadn't been a bad dream. "For you, maybe; for Justine Virga it was the end of her life."

"Maybe she wanted to end it."

Maybe.

"I'm not the kind of person who murders people. I always fulfilled my responsibilities. I kept my family together, and I raised Cynthia all by myself, you know."

I knew.

"I don't belong in prison. It was an accident, a bad accident."

One woman's accident is another's subconscious wish. "Did it ever occur to you that Justine wasn't a threat, that she found out Whit had plotted to set you up and she'd come to tell you?"

"Not until recently."

"Well, what's it going to be? The prosecution has a strong case. Your car hit and killed Justine—there's no denying that or that you were driving it. I can't stand up in a courtroom and say it didn't happen. You can take the risk and the expense of a trial, or you can plead no contest to involuntary manslaughter and give up your license. The judge will be more lenient if you plead."

"What do you recommend?"

"That you plead no contest." There was one more option if she chose to pursue it. "But you might find another lawyer who sees it differently."

She thought it over, twisting her ring around on her finger, wondering, maybe, if there was a man out there who would take her case and make it all right again. Does anyone ever get old enough or powerful enough to stop thinking that? She took a big sip of her drink. "All right," she said. "I'll plead."

Before I left I went to her bathroom, opened the medicine chest and put back all that were left of the Halcion I had removed. I gave the container a shake, watching the pills while they settled in place. It looked to me as if her stash hadn't diminished much since the last time I was here.

When the sentencing hearing came up, I advised Martha to show remorse. Maybe she did, maybe she didn't; maybe her idea of remorse was different from mine. She had her own excuse for what she'd done. As every New Mexican knows, our criminal justice system takes a tolerant view of substance abuse. "It was the Halcion, Your Honor," Martha said. "My doctor didn't warn me that drug causes confusion in combination with alcohol. I wasn't myself that night. I couldn't react quickly enough. I've stopped taking the Halcion now, and I am not a danger to society." Her performance satisfied the judge; she got the minimum sentence—one year probation—and the maximum fine: five thousand dollars. I drove her home afterwards and parked the Nissan in her space at Los Cerros, right at the edge of the hundred-mile view. She sat in my passenger seat with her purse placed square in her lap.

"You will be sending me your bill?" she asked.

"Yes."

"Thank you very much for your help." She reached for the handle on the door.

I had another question, but it was one I hadn't wanted to ask until now. "Tell me one thing," I said. "Were you really under the influence when you hit Justine that night?"

She straightened her back and looked at me with her ice-blue eyes. "Only as much as I had to be," she replied.

I let Martha out, drove down the road and went to Emilio's apartment, where he and Cindy were waiting. Emilio put three Tecates, a plate of sliced limes and a shaker of salt on the coffee table. Cindy and I sat on the sofa. He sat in his wheelchair. We were like three teenagers conspiring to do the forbidden again, except that Emilio had lost his legs, Cindy had lost her child and I was a lawyer. Cindy reached across the coffee table and held Emilio's hand while I told them that Martha, blaming Halcion, had received the minimum sentence and the maximum fine.

"The old lady joins the killers club"—Emilio shook his head—"and *she* gets a fine. That won't hurt." He squeezed some lime juice on top of his Tecate can. "You know what the penalty would have been if I'd been driving that car?"

It wouldn't have been probation and a fine. I knew that.

He sipped at the beer. "You did a good job for her, Nellie."

"I guess," I said. Martha, who'd played the part of a woman addled by Halcion, had had enough rattled moments herself to be convincing. She'd won the legal game, and one part of me—the lawyer part—had to admire her for it. "What do you think?" I asked them. "Is it worse to kill somebody when you're under the influence or sober?" It's a question I've never been able to answer.

"Sober," said Emilio. "It's worse when you know what you're doing. I always thought I was sober when I pulled the trigger in Vietnam, but I could have been wrong."

"Under the influence," said Cindy. "It's so irresponsible.

You could kill anybody at all when you're loaded." She sighed. "I should go to Mother; she'll need me now."

"Why?" asked Emilio. "She got off, didn't she?"

"Yeah," said Cindy. "But she won't see it that way. She'd think any penalty was unjust. Life is so much easier when you get along with her, but no matter how you slice it, your mother is your mother. When she suffers, so do you. When she gets older, so do you. When she dies, some of you gets buried too. You have to hope you get a good one, because right or wrong, good or bad, there's a part of you that needs to love your mother. You're connected to her by a cord you'll never be able to sever."

Cindy knew what was at the end of her cord, but what was at the other end of mine? A woman at the wheel of a convertible? A grasping tentacle? A black hole? Even Los Desaparecidos make themselves felt, sending signals like the ones amputees receive from their phantom limbs.

Cindy stood up and put her hand on Emilio's shoulder. "Mother was terrible to you, Emiliano, and she lied to you, Neil. I know that, but I have to go."

He put his hand on top of hers. "Don't worry about it."

"Do what you have to, Cindy," I said.

After she left, Emilio and I sipped at our beer. "Have a smoke if you want," he said. "It doesn't bother me."

"Okay." I lit up. For lack of an ashtray, I dropped the match in the empty lime dish. "Cindy is pretty forgiving."

Emilio shrugged. "Considering that none of us is perfect and every one of us is gonna die, what else is there to be?"

There wasn't much to say after that, so I put my cigarette out, finished my Tecate and went home to La Vista.

The Kid came for dinner, stopping by the parking lot on his way in to leave a couple of tacos for La Bailarina. After she came back, they had picked up where they left off. He gave her the food; she kept her pride and her distance. Martha's sentence was a victory of sorts, but I wasn't feeling any pheromones or power. The Kid and I argued about nothing at all and everything. The tacos were not hot enough, the beer was not cold enough, someone had promised to buy limes and forgotten. When we'd finished eating and I cleaned up by throwing the wrappers away, we got into bed and tried to resolve the tension.

Something woke me later—the wind, maybe, rattling a leaf or a branch against the window. Winter was in the wind, and snow would be falling in the higher elevations. It was the hour the infomercials come on TV, when the secure and the steady are fast asleep, when the man in dark glasses plugs God and the fat boy dances in the street, when even the homeless have found a den somewhere and burrowed into it for the night. I got out of bed, pulled on a pair of jeans, a sweater and running shoes, went to my purse, took out all I had, five twenties, put them in an envelope, went outside and shut the door behind me. The moon sat on the horizon like a half-full cup. The air smelled of piñon burning, and I could see the shape of my breath. In the medium distance eighteen-wheelers crisscrossed the Big I. In the near distance, La Vista's parking lot, La Bailarina's van was in place.

I walked across the lot and looked in through a space where the curtains didn't meet. There was enough light to see her curled up in the back like a sack of old clothes. There's no pride or pretense or bravado in sleep, and she looked like what she was—vulnerable and sad. She might be a woman who found herself somehow without a job or a man in midlife. She might also be one of those reckless women who'd cut the cord and committed herself to the lonesome highway. If she had, did she ever wish she could find the way back? Was she too ashamed or too weak or too sad or too proud? I took the envelope from my pocket, folded it and stuck it under the windshield wiper. "Don't blow it all in one place," I said. I rapped on the window so she'd know it was there and get it before someone else did.

I went back inside, took off my clothes, got into bed, closed my eyes and turned the headlights on my own life. I saw a bend in the highway. The high beams made a long arc that landed on a woman in midflight. I put my foot on the brake, slowed down and took a good look. It was one of those nights when people reveal just what they are capable of. The woman stopped running, turned to face the light, and her hair fell down around her shoulders. Her eyes glittered, red and blank like the eyes of animals you come across in the road at night. She was no longer laughing or at the peak of her power. Her hair had turned gray, and her chin and breasts were showing the sag of gravity's pull. Like everyone else who lives long enough, she was growing old. She began to shrivel under the high beams' glare. Her shoulders hunched over, her knees bent. She put up a hand to protect herself from the light, but she got small as a child anyway. What should have happened over thirty long years was taking place in a flash. She was losing her desire, her youth, her power to hurt or to nourish. "You have to make peace with what can't be resolved. I did what I had to. I'm sorry," she said. There was nothing left in the highway, and the headlights went out.

I made a noise in my sleep or touched the Kid with my cold feet. He woke up, turned over and put his arm around me. "You have that dream again, Chiquita?" he asked.

"Not exactly," I said.